# False Start

ALICE DUKE

*A Romantic Comedy*

Alice Duke
Copyright 2022

# Chapter One

TESSA

YOU WOULD THINK that it would be impossible to have a moment while a car alarm is going off beside you. You'd be *totally* wrong.

I'm having one right now.

It's that glimmer in his eye. I've always been a sucker for glimmers and this one glints with the glintiest. Is that a word? I'm not sure I care.

He's twinkling at me as we share this moment — two strangers caught up in a scene of sheer ridiculousness as we look over the hood of a car at each other. The owner of the car is oblivious, of course, caught up in the frustration of seeing his day totally ruined. Understandable. He's turning the air blue as the Pacific Ocean and I can only make out the odd word or two with his alarm screaming in the background. He's fortyish, a bit soft and bearded, and his hands look like they don't even know what a wrench is, so this is all beyond him.

"It's the security feature," I try to call over the noise.

It doesn't help that my mouth is full of the best taco in the world but that's not really my fault since we're literally parked in front of Patrick's Tacos. Which, I will grant you, is the worst possible name for a taco food truck. I grabbed a taco right before Forty-ish asked me to help boost his ride.

"I don't know what's happening!" he yells, reaching to tug at the booster cables linking our batteries together. I see one drifting toward the black cable like he's going to remove that one first. My mouth is just forming an "O" of warning.

To my relief, Twinkle-eyes bats his hand away, makes eye contact with me again, and laughs. It's like he's talking to me without talking. He's saying "What have we two stumbled upon here and is someone going to end up dead and chronicled in a book about strange accidents?"

"It won't start because the security features think it's being stolen," the man with the twinkle in his eyes tries to tell Forty-ish.

He's not listening. That's panic in his eyes now, the look of a man who is so far out of his depth that he'd take refuge on the Titanic if it sailed by.

Look, I'd be irritated, too, under any normal circumstances. I really would. Car alarms aren't my idea of a good time.

But the young man with the twinkling eyes is about my age and he has a dimple. Did I mention that? There's grease in the fingerprints of the hands that are adjusting those booster cables and the best grin I've ever seen. I'm not normally one for blonds, but that tousled hair is working for me and so is the day-old beard and the rippling biceps. And that tan. Maybe the sun worships him instead of the other way around. I could see it. Push over sun, I've got this now.

His T-shirt is so well-worn that the edges of the sleeves are ragged. It's thin enough that I can basically see his abs — hard — and chest — very nicely shaped — through the thin cotton. Call me shallow all you want, but it's working just fine for me. I could easily sit here and eat the rest of this taco and watch him and I wouldn't care if the car alarm turned into a tornado warning or a nuclear strike alert. I'd just be living in a moment of pure bliss.

Which I am.

I'm a happy person. I don't look gift horses in their mouths, or shoot messengers, or do any of the things cranky, cynical people do. I drink sweet drinks that barely resemble coffee with too much whipped cream on top, and eat marshmallows without even toasting them first — although I'm also first in line if someone says "bonfire" — and I pet every dog I see, and make goofy faces at babies, and you'd better damn well believe I bask in the sight of a gorgeous man trying to be a good Samaritan.

It's like rainbows and sunflowers — they're specifically created to bring a smile to the lips and a lightness to the heart and who am I to say no to that?

I wouldn't dare.

I wink at Twinkle-eyes as Forty-ish hops in his car and tries to start it again, only to scream another curse. And I lick my fingers clean. How is that taco gone already? I might need another one.

Carefully, I unhook the booster cables from my battery while the pretty man whose name I really think I need to know unhooks them from the other battery.

My SUV and the one belonging to Forty-ish are the only ones in the lot. It's a long-haul bus stop and people don't really hang out here between buses. They're usually coming or going. I'm here early on purpose because seriously who can say no to a chance to grab tacos from Patrick's? And I don't know why Forty-ish is here because he accosted me while I was still ordering and begged me to boost his ride and I've been listening to the car alarm ever since.

It dies so suddenly that my ears aren't sure if they've been tricked.

"I guess I'm walking," Forty-ish says as he exits his vehicle head bowed down.

"I can give you a lift," I offer.

It's a beautiful sunny day. And I love to drive.

"It's only four blocks," he says, dejected.

"You just need to fully charge the battery," I tell him. "It's not getting enough juice from the boost."

"Or replace it," Tousled-Hair says tossing a knowing look at me. "With one that holds a charge better."

I'm definitely going to need his name.

"Sure," the guy says with a wave, but he's already walking away without even a thank you.

Oh well, no skin off my nose. I start to bundle up the booster cables — yeah, I carry them around with me ever since the first time my own battery died somewhere and my dad fussed over it — and Tousled-Hair closes the hood of Forty-ish's SUV.

"You're in an awfully good mood for a girl who was just serenaded by Toyota's best security system," he says, a laugh dancing around his mouth.

I grin back. I love that smile. It's to die for.

"It's hard to be miserable when there are tacos," I say, throwing the cables in the back and slamming my rear door and hood shut.

I'm already eyeing up the taco stand again to try to pretend it's what's on my mind and not this delicious man standing beside me. It's not entirely a ruse. I have twenty whole minutes to stuff my face with more of them and I know for a fact that Patrick deep fries churros, too. For a pasty white Canadian, he sure can cook Mexican food.

"He didn't even thank you," Tousled-Hair says, frowning at the man shuffling away down the road.

The bus station is right along a river, and there are ducks quacking, and puffy white clouds. It's impossible for any sane human to look as glum as the man who abandoned his vehicle with the hood still up.

I can't help the laugh that slips out of me. "No, he didn't. Maybe he'll thank me by selling that 4Runner to me when he decides he's too cheap for a new battery. You know that look in his eyes said he's never ever upgrading it."

His eyes twinkle at my words and I wish I could bottle up that twinkle to save for later. I have to look away so that he doesn't see my scary eyes or my bright, happy cheeks. I don't want him to know that I want to keep bits of him when we've only just met.

My eyes fall on my ride. My vehicle is a 4Runner, too, and I adore it. It's my third one. Yeah, I'm hard on vehicles, even ones I love. I like to drive fast and turn quick, and while that's super attractive in a guy, it's apparently "crazy" in a woman so I try not to mention it to people I don't know.

"Well, maybe I can buy you a taco as a thank you."

I look back at him as he runs his hand through his hair, messing it up even more and I'm dead. Men shouldn't look so pretty. Especially men with faint accents. What is that? New Zealand? South Africa?

"Why would you be thanking me when he's the one with the car?"

I'm walking to the taco truck, though. We're buying tacos no matter who is paying.

"Maybe I just want to eat one with you," he says. And there's something in his eyes that I can't quite parse. A kind of darkening, a serious look like I'm an engine with a funny tick he's trying to diagnose — and not just any engine, a fancy race engine he wishes he owns instead of just working on.

"Maybe you can do that for free," I reply, leaning over to wipe a smear of dirt from his face. Fortyish has not cleaned his engine compartment in basically forever.

"Maybe I will," he says, his lips staying parted even after he's done speaking.

His eyes have widened and that glint in them is brighter like he just found something he lost and thought was gone forever, and oh damn is my heart kicking up a gear because this is ridiculous. Girls like me don't meet adorable guys over the open hood of another guy's car and actually attract them. That only happens in car-themed comics, and only when the girl is dressed like Jessica Rabbit.

We order our food from Patrick who seems very unconcerned about either the car alarm that was blaring just minutes ago or the full-on love story unfolding over his tacos, but maybe that's why he's the best. Single-minded. I could learn from him.

My mind is not single. It's everywhere. And my eyes are huge, and I can't stop smiling and laughing at everything like someone just gave me a million dollars or something stupid. But why wouldn't I enjoy this? It's not every day I eat the gods' own food on a worn-out picnic table with someone who knows that you sit on the top not on those cramped little benches — they're for your feet, people.

I toss my long black ponytail over my shoulder and take a bite. My appreciative sound is echoed by the gorgeous man in the ass-hugging jeans beside me. Yeah, I checked him out. He's as great below the belt as he is above it. Seriously, ladies, you are all missing out here.

"You seem to know a lot about cars," he says through a bite of tacos. That dimple is back, harmonizing with the twinkle in his eyes, lulling me into a kind of taco and hot guy trance. "Not many people would know that the security system was triggered by his drained battery or that he needs to fully charge it because that same system is draining it when you try to boost it."

"I thought you were going to say 'not many women' and then I'd have to make you pay for the churros," I say playfully.

I'm teasing but I'm not teasing. A ridiculous number of

people get surprised when they find out I know about cars and it's not because I'm a successful vlogger. Nope. It's because I'm tiny and curvy and very, very much a girl even if I like to wear car-themed T-shirts to everything.

He laughs, "Oh, I think I'm paying for the churros no matter what. And I am not so much of a fool as to think that girls don't know about cars. What do you do for work?"

"Oh you know," I say breezily, tossing my ponytail again. "Car stuff. You?"

He laughs like I'm the best joke and I like how husky his laugh is paired with the dark look in his eyes. I can imagine that laugh gusting out directly on my skin.

"Car stuff."

"Golly," I widen my eyes to really play it up. "We're like...the same."

He looks me up and down, appreciation in his eyes, and then he bites his lower lip, sliding it between his teeth before he says. "Nope."

I laugh again. He's adorable. My cheeks hurt just being around him. He looks up at me through a fringe of lashes too dark for that light-colored hair and my breath tumbles for a moment.

"Why don't I know you?" I ask him, finishing my second taco. I need to slow down or I will have no room at all for the big family dinner tonight and mom will pitch a fit. Actually, I probably should slow down with more than just the tacos. I'm walking a fine line here. "I know basically everyone around here who's into cars."

"I'm not from anywhere near here," he says, smirking. "Or at least I haven't been for a long time."

"Home town boy returns?" I ask, reaching for my drink. When he's silent for too long I look up and see him watching me suck on the straw with big eyes. Seriously? What is this even? I've drunk pop a thousand times and no one took it as a sexual thing before this exact moment.

He's looking at me with that twinkle again but it's all mixed up in that dark look in his eyes and mingled with a suppressed grin like he's some kind of bomb of playfulness and sexuality that's about to go off. Wow, that metaphor might be too much for me to handle. Just thinking it is making me sweat a bit.

I swear I've never had this type of thing with someone before *ever*. It's like we both keep catching each other on fire and it's addictive, and hilarious, and totally unbelievable, and the hottest fucking thing ever, all rolled into one.

"Look," I say, "In a few minutes I'm going to have to go. And what a shame it would be if I never spoke to you again."

"A crime," he says a little breathily and his eyes are caught on my lips like he wants to kiss me.

"Precisely. I mean what if I need to totally fail to boost someone's ride in the future and I don't have your number? What will I even do?"

"Succeed?" His dimple is the worst. Or the best. I don't know. I'm not thinking with my brain right now, ladies. You know how that is.

"Probably. And where would the fun be in that?"

"There wouldn't be any fun," he agrees very seriously, sliding across the rough wooden picnic table until his hip bumps mine.

Which means that when my eyes fall naturally downward they snag on the truly epic bulge in those jeans. Good lord. How much spice did Patrick put in this taco? I feel like I need to drink five more sodas.

Slowly.

Through the straw.

Or something.

"So," I say and my voice is just a bit strangled. "I think you should give me your number."

"Yeah," he agrees, and his voice sounds thick.

His Adam's apple bobs as he swallows and I reach for my phone, but I don't get that far because my gaze lands on his, and the smolder in his eye is making that twinkle into a roaring flame and I can't help it, I lick my lips and he gasps, his heavy gaze falling to my mouth.

His voice is a growl when he speaks. "I think I'm going to kiss you now."

"No one's stopping you," I gasp, and then he hops off the picnic table and his hands find my hips.

He spins me so that my butt hits the edge of the table and I can lean against it as he steps forward and pulls me snugly against that marvelous bulge in his jeans. Yep. It's big. And his lips find mine and my hands tangle up into that tousled hair and I swear I'm not usually this girl, but nothing like this has *ever* happened to me and it would be just the worst waste to miss out on it now that it has and ...

Clarity of thought has left me. It's okay. I didn't need it.

I'm way too caught up in the rough feel of his unshaven face on mine and the crush of his lips as they slide over mine.

He opens my mouth with a slip of his tongue, and I taste the cinnamon from the churros as his tongue dips inside and finds mine. I'm pretty sure I make a hungry sound in his mouth — justified, obviously — and I kiss him back fiercely because this is amazing. I want just as much of it as he'll give me. Every taste, every touch. He's ... perfect for me. The perfect fit, the perfect humor, the perfect twinkle, and I absolutely refuse to be the idiot who lets it slip away when it's literally right here making out with me as if sex on a picnic table outside a taco truck might be a possibility.

He pulls back, gasping and laughing, and I laugh too as he swipes my phone and puts his number in, and then blinks.

"I'm already in your phone?" he says and he sounds like he doesn't know what to think of this. I mean, neither do I. This is not a man I would forget.

"No," I say, "That's your phone."

He lifts it and wiggles it and yes that's my distinctive phone case that looks like wood and has a carved outline of Lake Superior on the back. Yes, it's cheesy, I know, but even this girl has hometown spirit sometimes.

"My name in your phone is 'My brother's friend Brent.'" He stumbles backward a step and his face is suddenly pale just like mine. His words are wooden and precise. "You're Tessa. You're here to pick me up from the bus."

I shake my head, but honestly, it's really more wishful thinking than confusion. "Your bus doesn't get in for ten more minutes."

I mean he was here when I arrived. Sitting on this damn picnic table. Which I'm realizing has a duffle bag under it.

Oops.

He throws my phone at me like it scalded him. Cool trick, phone.

"I caught an earlier bus," he says and we look at each other in horror.

And you know what? I think the twinkle might be gone. And the dark sexy eyes. And all the possibilities I'd been thinking of when his tongue was in my mouth.

# Chapter Two

BRENT

OH, shit.

I run my hands through my hair and draw in a long breath. Ian is going to kill me. Literally, take me out behind his house and ... I don't know, whatever it is brothers do to best friends who just kissed their sister.

Actually, he won't do anything and I already know that. Which makes me pause for its own stomach-twisting reasons.

I hadn't done anything to him when he kissed *my* sister a month after meeting us. Or when he'd eloped with her a month after that. Or when he convinced us both to join him in Canada four months after that. To meet his family.

My eyes shoot up and catch hers. This family right here who I was just kissing.

Shit.

Look, I'm not that kind of guy. Not normally. But she made me laugh, and girls never make me laugh. They make me feel stupid, yes. Or they irritate me. Double yes. They definitely don't make me laugh or want to sit and eat tacos with them, and

I thought, *Why not? Why not follow my gut this one time instead of gaming out all the possibilities first? What's the worst that can happen?*

This.

This is the worst that can happen.

Because Ian has been talking about his sister to me for months now, building her up as this sweet, chaste, nearly holy saint whose feet I am not worthy to kiss, but who he definitely wants to set me up with because wouldn't it be amazing if I married his sister just like he married mine?

Every single time he says anything about it, I feel more and more trapped, like an animal in a wire noose. The more I struggle the tighter it gets. And all of Olivia's sly smiles and little hints tell me she's just waiting to maneuver me into place for this setup, too. There's nothing she would love more than to see us enmeshed together for all of time. And there will go my freedom to travel and to race, to spend my money, or while away my time as I please. I won't stand a chance.

If someone was listening to this rant inside my head, they'd be asking how the hell I didn't recognize her if I knew I was going to meet her, and they'd be shaking their heads at the answer because the fact of the matter is that I've been shown her picture about a thousand times probably — I just never really looked because I didn't really care. There was no fucking way I was going near Ian's sister no matter what she looked like. I remember nothing more than a human-shaped blur. They'd even tried to make me watch her vlog — which I hear is fairly popular even if it doesn't get the views ours does — and I'm pretty sure I remember hearing her voice talking about engines in the background, but I really just nodded and smiled to Ian without watching it. I didn't think I needed to watch it.

And now I'm living with the consequences of that choice. A huge, massive fuck-up on my part.

Her hazel eyes are watching me and shit, she doesn't look

any different than she did a few minutes ago. Then, she was turning that impish grin on me with the corners of her eyes all crinkled up when she laughed — exactly what I like in a girl. Then, it was all dark dusky looks and little flickering smirks.

She's still smoking hot in tight black jeans and a muffler T-shirt that hugs all her curves. Still has that long black ponytail. But now her eyes aren't dancing with laughter and sex like they were before. Now they're wide and she looks a little green around the jaw like she might be sick.

She kissed me and now she feels sick about it. I did that to a woman. Made her feel regret at being close to me. Put her in an awkward situation. Shit.

And that settles it. This was the world's hugest mistake.

If she was pushing for this after she learned who I was, then I really would be trapped. Especially after that very enthusiastic greeting. Instead, she looks like she's going to puke because she just kissed her brother's best friend. Clearly, we're on the same page here. Neither of us wants this.

So why does it hurt to see that look in her eyes? Like I wanted her to want me?

I feel ... dirty somehow. I don't know how to apologize and I hate it. I grab my bag roughly from under the picnic table.

"I guess you're my ride." I don't look at her again. I don't think I can. I feel like I just lost something I didn't know I wanted.

If my voice is harsh, then that's what it is. What do you expect from me? I've just been kicked in the balls and I'm still reeling from it.

"Well, you know which one it is," she says brightly like she hasn't just gutted me with one look.

I pretty much run to the SUV. It's embarrassing. If anyone other than her or Patrick saw it, I'd have to leave the country immediately. Patrick. What kind of stupid name is that for someone who sells tacos anyway? He should get a better name.

She hops in the vehicle and starts it with a cheery wave goodbye for Patrick and why is this SUV so tiny inside? I feel like I'm in a little box with her and it's getting smaller by the kilometer. We're in Canada, so it's kilometers, not miles. It makes it look like we're trying to set a speed record instead of just rolling down the highway a little faster than the cops would like.

"So, how was the bus trip?" she asks me breezily, as if we've just met. "I bet it was a doozy. Thirty hours. Oof-dah."

"I thought only Minnesotans said 'Oof-dah.'" I say, scowling now because it's a cute thing to say and she's not allowed to be cute. Not anymore.

She pouts for a moment and she's a really good pouter. It makes her look instantly kissable. I feel my lips tingling already thinking about taking the wheel, pulling us over, and catching that pout in my lips to pick up where we left off.

Dammit.

"Oh," she says with mock innocence. "Was that word trademarked? Crap. I guess I'm in big trouble now. What will I do?"

Did she just roll her eyes?

I stare out the passenger window so I don't have to look at her. It's the height of summer and everything is insultingly green as if it's trying to convince us it's not even real.

"You must have seen pictures of *me* before," I say, accusing her of what I feel guilty about. "I've spent the last year with your brother. We filmed online videos. He told me you watched every one on our channel."

"And where were you in all this time you spent with my brother?" I feel as though she's mocking me. "Was it possibly behind the camera?"

Okay fine. I feel my face grow hot. I do operate the camera.

"My voice, then. You've heard my voice." Seriously, this can't be happening.

"Yes, and it's so sexy that after hearing it ask my brother

questions, I just close my eyes every time I meet a stranger and I think, 'Wow is that ... could that be ... *him?*'"

Okay, she's definitely mocking me.

"They had to have shown you wedding pictures. I was there when they eloped. I know there were pictures of the two of them at the courthouse."

"I've seen about a hundred," she agrees before meeting my eyes with her lips pressed tightly together like she's holding back a laugh. "And they're really good, Brent. You're a great photographer."

Shit. She's right. I took all the pictures. I'm not in any of them.

This is a disaster. Not the green landscape. The girl. The hell but I'm muddled up. It is not helping that she smells like something amazing. Apples? Can girls smell like apples?

It makes my mouth water and it's not supposed to do that for her now that I know who she is.

"Look," she says and when I peek at her, her mouth is twisted into an ironic smirk. She's still laughing. I feel like someone shoved me naked onto a stage somewhere but not her. No embarrassment for her. She thinks this is hilarious. "We could act like we just sucked face with a stranger and then got caught out, or we can pretend that you just got off the bus and I picked you up exactly like I promised Ian, and wow, how nice is that? So nice. It's amazing to meet you. You, too! How was the ride? Aw shucks, it was great. And then life can go on as if nothing happened. What's it gonna be, Bub?"

"Bub?"

She oughta be ashamed of herself talking like she's eighty.

She just looks at me, blinking.

"Sucked face? That was not sucking face. That was kissing at its sexiest."

"It's not at its sexiest if my feet are still on the ground," she says, pulling the hair tie out of her ponytail and shaking out her long hair before glancing in the rearview mirror to fluff it with her fingers. It hangs in perfectly straight sheets with a part down the middle. I don't like the Cher look. Or rather, I *didn't* like it before this exact moment. Suddenly it seems no one told my body it's not our thing because it is urgently telling me that it likes it very much.

"What are you doing?" I ask in horror.

"I'm getting ready for an afternoon of family fun and laughter. What are you doing?"

"Freaking out."

She laughs. "Yeah, I see that. Do you think you could stop?"

"No. And your feet *were* off the ground."

"Only because I'm short. They were metaphorically on the ground."

"Is the tick I hear in your engine metaphorical, too?"

There *is* a tick in her engine. Maybe I can distract her with it.

She laughs again. "You're too much, Brent. Are you always this cranky, or only when you've been cock-blocked by reality? It's an exhaust leak. I know about it. I have a gasket on order."

I stare at her. She just said "cock-blocked" and "exhaust leak" in the same sentence which basically makes her my dream girl and my stomach is doing flips like crazy, and I'm trying to forcefully remind it that she is *not an option*.

"You had to know it was me there at the bus stop. You came to pick me up." I'm clinging to the last thing I have.

"You weren't supposed to be there for twenty more minutes and it's a busy stop. I have never picked anyone up there before, but I had tacos at that exact table last Saturday and six different people sat down and ate with me and then left. Four were men close in age to me."

"Exactly how many tacos did you eat?"

"Not so many that I wasn't attractive to four men, so go ahead and mock."

"Wow," I say. "Just wow."

I take a breath. I regroup.

She grabs a mascara from the console and applies it in the rearview mirror while going twenty kilometers an hour over the speed limit. I feel ill, but mostly just because I'm apparently driving with Miss Irresponsible and I think we might die.

"Ian never said what you do for work," I say, snatching desperately at politeness to try to pull out of this tailspin.

"Oh, I doubt that. When he pitched me to you for the arranged marriage he and your sister are dead set on, I bet it was the first thing he said," she says, giving me side-eye as she finishes applying her makeup.

I feel my cheeks heat. And I bet she sees that, too.

"Shit," I mutter.

"I'll do you a favor and pretend you don't already know so we can make small talk," she says brightly. And thank goodness she's done and has put her mascara away before we died in a fiery crash.

Instead of focusing on how we shared interests and she was "quite pretty in a disheveled way" maybe Ian should have led with the fact that she's whip-quick and about twice as smart as he is. That might have sucked me in before I realized what an astronomically bad idea it is to date his sister.

She continues on blithely. "I work for myself as a vlogger. My channel is "Stock Metal" and I mostly focus on stock car builds but I span all kinds of car-related events, shows, and projects. I was traveling for it before I decided to build my own car. People like the 'young woman exploring motorsports' vibe. I hope to keep making a career out of it — especially now that I'll be racing, too — but it's not quite there yet so for now I live in my parent's attic, like the truly classy dame I am. How about you?"

"Dame?" That makes me crack a smile.

"Look, it's a classier word than the one you just spat out, so I can see why it's tripping you up. It's like the female equivalent to a knight — which I definitely am — or an elderly woman — which I definitely am not. But go ahead and take your pick."

"I race stock cars. For prize money," I say and I think I'm blushing even further because now we're on familiar territory — the kind where I look like an idiot to women. "And I share an online channel with your brother where I film the ins and outs of it with him as the star. But you know that."

"Mmhmm," she says, still smiling brightly. I wonder what it takes to get her down. Probably not much. I'd kind of like to push things to find out, but that might seem like flirting, and I'm not up for that. "So now I know two things about you. One, you like cars. Two, you like sex."

And just like that, she takes me from calm to jumpy with a single comment.

"Woah there. Where did two come from?"

She looks at me wide-eyed. "The kissing of course. You told me with your body."

"I didn't."

She laughs. "Okay, tell me what you love about cars."

"I love that they're all rumbly and powerful."

"Me, too," she purrs, wiggling her eyebrows.

"I love that I feel free when I'm driving like nothing else in the world matters."

"Me, too." She's laughing but I don't get the joke.

"I like that they're mine, okay? I can do what I want with them. Be as creative or daring as I want to be."

Now she's laughing so hard that I'm worried about her driving. She pulls suddenly into a long driveway framed by vine-covered stone pillars. That sounds classy, but no one has bothered to weed around them in ages and the vines have gone wild so mostly it just looks "country."

As we wind up the long driveway between the trees, she shoots me a devilish glance and says, "Cars only make sense when you realize they're a metaphor for sex."

And I don't know what to make of that. But I'm replaying my answers in my head and groaning deep inside. Uhh.

"You can tell almost everything about a person by how they drive. I bet you're very intentional, aren't you? You're skilled, but you're just a teeny tiny bit insecure."

I feel like someone has frozen me and it's only her coy look that breaks me from my horrified rigor.

"I bet you're more enthusiastic than skilled," I shoot back. "A bit wild and likely to crash."

"Yeah," she says in a smoky voice. "Isn't that perfect?"

And I'm still groaning and running a frustrated hand over my face when she parks her SUV outside a three-bay garage and announces, "We made it! Now you can tell everyone ... you came."

And just then her brother and my sister practically burst out the door of the nearby house, smiles wide and eyes bright as if they don't know what kind of a hellion they sent to pick me up.

# Chapter Three

*TESSA*

Okay, well maybe this is a *bit* fun after all. Brent is hilariously easy to wind up and his blushes are adorable. Like seriously, I want to collect the whole set and keep them in a lit display case.

I hop out of the SUV because if I don't, I'll just be mobbed anyway. Ian and Olivia have been gushing about Brent and telling us about him constantly for the entire four days since they got here. Which is honestly why no one should blame me for not realizing that was him at the bus station. According to them, he's basically a superhero-slash-ninja-slash-navy-seal-slash-racing-legend. I expected someone eight feet tall with a tidy haircut, steely blue eyes, and possibly a flack jacket.

I did not expect a rumpled, laughing mess of a man who kissed me almost immediately, tasted of mint gum and tacos, and smelled like soap and musk all mixed together.

Seriously. If anything, this is Ian's fault. Like always.

"Brent!" Olivia screams, throwing herself into her brother's arms. He hugs her tightly with very realistic affection, like he's not a complete bastard who can just turn it off and on like he did with me. And why am I even upset about this?

I've spent four days swearing to myself that no matter how perfect he is I won't look twice at him. Only now, I find out he's not perfect in the ways they described, but maybe just a little perfect in the ways I like. Because OMG that kiss. It was incredibly snackable right up until it was ripped away from me. I can still taste his lips and feel the outline of them between mine. I can still breathe in and feel his hands on my waist, fingers splayed as if he was trying to touch all of me at once. And the hunger he stirred up is still there. I still want him more than Patrick's Tacos. I want to keep tasting, and tasting, until I've tasted all of him. Even his grumpy car self didn't change that.

But I'm not upset. Why would I be upset? I have a whole day with my family today. I'm happy as a puppy with two bones.

"I told you he was amazing," Ian murmurs to me.

Sneak attack. Somehow he found his way to my shoulder in the middle of all this sibling affection.

"Every time you say that I wonder if you married the wrong sibling," I say with a sweet smile. "Are you sure it shouldn't be Brent and Ian forever?"

I love having Ian back. He understands all the little things about living here, and he's easy company, and he takes some of the pressure off me where the parents are concerned. They don't love having their twenty-three-year-old daughter living in the attic. It ignites all kinds of parental angst about what they did wrong that I'm such a disaster. I swear it will be okay. It really will. I just need to keep my nose to the grindstone and get the content I need and my big break will come eventually. And they just need to be patient for a little while longer.

Ian rolls his eyes at me as Mom and Dad hurry out of the house for their own greetings. They're glued at the hip, those two.

My mom is a retired nurse, and if you don't have one in your family then maybe you don't know that they love managing the minutia of people's lives so much that they take it up as a hobby with their families. I've had a lecture on fiber twice this week, though I will say the motherly concern is a bit heartwarming. My bestie — Kati — has a college professor for a mom and she does not get the fiber lectures but she also doesn't get apple pie at dinner and a scoop of vanilla ice cream along with a heavy dose of extreme motherly affection, so it all evens out.

Dad was in construction and he's a walking advertisement for why that's a bad idea, with the trick knee, and the bad back, and the sloping shoulders of a man who worked too hard for too long. Fortunately, he has his own nurse on call day or night to manage all that for him.

"We were thinking about a quad ride into the back," my dad is saying with a huge grin. I can tell he's already taken to Brent. Of course, he'd take to him. He adores Olivia after only four days. I saw him tipping her off to where he keeps his "secret" candy stash away from my mom. Hint, it's no secret. And he lights up for her like he's the sun and she's the beautiful bright green and blue globe.

I'm not jealous, okay? I know I'm loved and I love my family, too. What you're hearing here are nerves. Why, you might ask. And hey, that's fair. But if you'd been here the past four days you wouldn't have to ask because it's pretty obvious that everyone related to me and also standing on this big front porch wants the same thing. They want a second wedding and they want it as soon as possible.

And they want it for good, wholesome, family reasons like fidelity and loyalty and mutual support, not for the reasons that are running around like madmen with flamethrowers in the back of my head screaming, "Sex! Hotness! Fun!" and lighting everything on fire.

The Brent and Tessa train started almost the moment that Ian swept into the house with his new bride.

"So *you're* Tessa," she'd said as I hugged her awkwardly and gave her my congratulations.

Olivia, for the record, is basically perfect and not in the way where you're required to hate her, in the way where she's one hundred percent likely to end up like my mom, just one huge soft-centered ball of kindness and generosity. It's literally impossible to hate her. And she has perfect hair.

Olivia and Mom cried when they hugged the first time and Dad watched them with misty eyes before looking at me and saying, "I guess you're next, kiddo."

And when I tried to laugh it off by changing the subject, they'd all stopped and looked at me and Olivia had clasped her delicate hands — shining with my brother's huge-ass diamond, by the way — and said, "Oh Tessa, we have just the perfect man for you. You're going to love my brother Brent. And then we can all be one big happy family together and do traditional holidays, and go on tropical vacations, and raise our little kids together." She glanced at my mom. "Did you want grandkids, Diane?"

And my mom basically died right there. I had to go into the kitchen to find a spatula to scrape her up off the floor. I've added too much butter to cookies that were less melty than Mom. Also, her cookies were over-baked because she couldn't tear herself away from Olivia and the only other time my mom ever over-baked her cookies was when she got the call that Grandpa had a heart attack.

"Seriously," Ian had said, following me into the kitchen. "Brent is just the best guy. A genius with motors. The best driver I've ever met. And he was great in Australia. He shared everything with me. He did all the filming for the channel. I seriously wouldn't have all the success I do without him."

Had I been just a touch envious of that? Yes, yes I had.

Because Ian caught the eye of Big Daddy BOOM — the billionaire motorsports mogul who started as a social media star and then built his own platform (yes, I'm a fan) — and now Ian has a sweet job waiting for him with BOOM Motorsports. Lucky duck.

That was the first time I asked Ian if he'd married the wrong sibling.

"I saved him for you. You know, orange tax," he'd said with a big melty grin.

When we were kids I adored mandarin oranges and whenever we found one anywhere, I insisted that Ian save a section of his for me and I called it the "orange tax" and Ian, sweet boy that he was, would bring me home a section of mandarin orange from all over the place — school, a restaurant, a Christmas pageant, anywhere. And now he was bringing me Brent. The — doubtless — perfect brother of his perfect wife.

"I'm really happy for you and Olivia," I'd said brightly. And I was happy. Brent and Olivia are orphans. They were raised by a single mom who died of a brain aneurysm two years ago. And getting my family along with Ian is part of the deal for Olivia, and that seems pretty fair to me.

But I was not happy about Brent.

And I became progressively less happy over the next four days as my mom and Olivia slipped further and further into Family Dreamland — building in their minds this incredibly blush-and-sunshine future where Olivia and Ian, and me and the looming Brent, bore many fat babies and raised them with my mom right there for every second of it. I couldn't break their hearts by directly saying no, but I was starting to feel like I was drowning in cotton candy and champagne.

I spent a lot more time in my shop, busting knuckles and my butt as I filmed more and more content, but that only made it worse.

"She's the perfect match for him," I heard Olivia whispering to my mom as they planted annuals together. "He's always in the shop, too."

And then later when Dad was complaining that I'm too strong-willed because I won't just film his buddy Ron's hotrod for my channel — it doesn't fit the vibe, okay? He didn't even build it. He just bought it and drives it to shows — and Olivia said, "She'll be perfect for Brent. He needs a strong woman in his life."

And now here he is, being hugged by Olivia and Mom and even Dad.

Dad. Hugging someone. That's basically against the construction worker's code unless they are blood-related, which I guess Dad has decided Brent is.

My dad still has his hand clapped on Brent's shoulder. I can't tear my eyes off it. It's like watching a knife held to someone's throat. One slip and a life might be over.

"We thought a nice quad bike adventure would get things rolling and then we'll come home for a family dinner. You like adventure, right Brent?"

"Sure, Mr. Harstone." I don't like Brent's voice. It has this harmonic thing that's resonating in my spine somehow and it's annoying as hell. Get it out! He has no right to have a resonant voice. That's practically a war crime.

I look sharply around the group. Has anyone else noticed that his voice has a sexy bur? Like he's doing that on purpose?

"It's Steve, not Mr. Harstone!" Dad says, grinning ear to ear. He's almost a head shorter than Brent, but he seems to steer him as he walks toward the shop. "Let me show you your ride."

"Shouldn't we let him get settled in first?" I ask brightly, but no one is listening. They're all so thrilled for the adventure that Olivia and Mom are packing picnic lunches in the two-up seats of the quads before Ian even has the garage doors all the way open.

"Oh! What's this?" Brent asks with delight in his voice as he hurries over to Ian's stock car.

"I told you that you didn't need to ship yours here," Ian says proudly. "The old Hurricane is perfect for your race tour."

Race tour? My eyes are wide with that little revelation. Ian never lets anyone drive the Hurricane — his name for the bright yellow stock car he built before his Australia tour. I'd called and begged to take it racing more than once. He'd brushed me off every time, and now he's going to hand it over to Brent?

I mean, I don't need it now. I built my own. And my first race with it is supposed to be tomorrow night. So, it's not like I need Ian's hand-me-downs, but maybe it smarts a bit that he'd let Brent drive it when he could have shaved a year off my time waiting to drive if he'd let me drive it while he was gone.

I'm feeling just a tad bit punch drunk when he says, "I already have six sponsors lined up for you, buddy! She'll be ready by go time, trust me. And I've got a great truck and trailer combo I'm borrowing off a friend. You'll love it."

Six sponsors? I have four. And I've been begging people to sponsor me for six months. I take a step backward and step right into the quad. Ow. Who even parked these like this?

Me. I parked them. For Dad this morning when he asked me to prepare for a family quad ride.

"You're a good friend, Ian." Brent's eyes are glowing almost exactly the way they were when I first met him and I have to swallow down a lump in my throat and look away. Great. There *is* something that excites him as much as I did. It's racing. Which should totally attract me to him if he wasn't currently snatching up everything that should kind of belong to me. There's no way I'm going to let him snatch up my heart with the rest. He'd probably stick it to the body of the Hurricane along with his six sponsorship stickers.

And then suddenly Ian is telling Brent how he's landed him a huge deal with BOOM Motorsports for Brent to film the whole circuit as he races and BOOM Motorsports will stream it on their subscription platform. I feel like my stomach might drop right through the floor. Is it hot in here or is it just me?

"I told you my new job with them would help you out, Brent, my man!"

And I'm just staring open-mouthed as Mom squeals and hugs my brother. "You got the job? In Utah? Oh, Ian, that's amazing!"

I forgot that he hadn't told them yet. It's going to be hard on Mom and Dad to see him go again so soon.

"But we'll be back all the time, Diane!" Olivia is assuring her. "And eventually we'll settle down here. It's just for a little while."

"Of course it is, honey." Olivia is getting a patented Mom Hug, too.

It's so damn heartwarming that I want to be sick.

Or maybe it's the intense jealousy that's making me feel that way. Because I have a stock car building and racing channel, too. And I've been grinding hard getting content out, just hoping for a big break while Ian was in Australia living it up without me, and now, when he has an in with someone and a chance to make someone a huge name ... he picks Brent. Not his sister. Brent. With the blond hair and slight Australian accent. That Brent.

"That's so huge, man," Brent is saying with a dimpled grin on his face, as if he didn't already know the news, though I'm sure he did. "This will make my career. Seriously. It's my big break and I owe it all to you."

Yes, the opportunity will make his career. And dammit, it should have been mine. I'm so upset that I don't have words. Just roaring emotions I can't put labels on. They feel like a 747 is trying to land inside my chest. Is that a named emotion? No? Follow me for more totally new feelings no one has ever had to endure.

"Well," my dad says, grinning hugely. "This will just make

the day more fun. How long do you have before you have to go, son?"

"Two weeks," Ian says with a huge grin. "And that's when Brent needs to get on the circuit, too. We're going to have to work hard. Seriously, Dad. This chance to work for BOOM is so huge. And it has a salary with benefits."

"I'm proud of you, son." Dad's all choked up but he hides it by motioning to the quads. "We have one hundred and twenty acres, Brent, and I want you and Olivia to see all of it! Diane and I will take the red quad. It has the fancy passenger seat for her injury. And of course, the lovebirds, Ian and Olivia, will take his quad. Brent you can drive Tessa on the spare."

I force a smile. "Actually, I'm really busy this afternoon. I'll just join you for dinner."

"Nonsense!" Dad gives me the eye as everyone else climbs aboard their assigned rides. You know, the one parents hide behind a false smile for guests but it says clearly, 'You'd better do this or else.' "I'm sure your brother and Brent have things to do, too, but they're taking the day off. And so can you."

And he doesn't wait to hear my answer, he just starts his quad and takes off with Mom.

"Follow us!" Ian calls as he and Olivia leave with spinning tires and a delighted shriek from Olivia, and now it's just me and Brent and the damn quad, and this one doesn't even have a two-up seat so whoever is the passenger is going to have to full-on cling to the driver like a terrified starfish.

"I'll drive," I say with a big friendly smile so Brent won't be able to say no. But he calls my bluff, snatching the keys from my hand.

"Your dad invited me to drive."

He jumps on and starts it up and looks at me and now I can choose. Stay at home and pout like a child, or get on the quad and continue my humiliation. I guess I can eat crow. But I'll need a lot of tacos to disguise the taste of it.

I force a bright smile and hop on the back of the quad. I don't have to touch him if I grab the rack behind my seat. But before I'm even settled he takes off — too quickly — and I'm compelled to grab his waist or be left in the dust and I swear I hear him snort a laugh over it.

Chapter Four

BRENT

HONESTLY, I'm kind of on top of the world. This is amazing.

The wind is in my face. The heady summer scent of long grass, warm earth, and growing pine needles fill my nose. The quad bike under me responds nicely to every desire I have and right now that desire is *faster! Further!*

Joy at seeing Olivia and Ian again puts a permanent smile on my face. I'm still a bit choked up at how well Olivia is fitting in with Ian's family. It's been hard on her to be without Mom. Even more than on me. But now she's going to have a home with them. She can come here on holidays or when things aren't going well, and these people will open their arms to her. It makes me feel all warm inside, just like I did the day Ian married my sister and I felt the massive relief of knowing I wasn't her only person anymore.

It's good. It's really good.

And that's what I need to focus on.

This place is beautiful. It's a spruce forest mostly with poplars and pines and the occasional birch scattered in. Ferns as high as my waist line the trail. Dragonflies flit over glassy, pollen-skimmed ponds. It's almost ridiculously pretty, like it can't be real.

None of this feels real.

I mean, Ian has a race car, a trailer, a job, and a plan for me. It's all lined up.

Seriously. This guy is the best friend I could have.

And all I have to do is keep pretending his sister isn't clinging to my back right now. Which is tough since she's cursing as every bump and jostle presses her sexy body against me. But it will be just fine.

I can pretend I can't feel every inch of her like a luxurious new sweater with a fluffy inside. I can deny that I'm not reliving that kiss over and over again smelling her apple and cinnamon scent, feeling the curve of her body under my hands, the power of her reaction to me as her eyes darken and her shoulders relax and her whole body melts into my arms like it was made to mold to me. I can forget it.

Maybe.

Honestly, it's like a recurring nightmare only the opposite. I keep getting little flashes of soft lips in my mind, little memories of her bold tongue pressing into my mouth, of her small, grasping hands holding me tight as if she wanted to keep me.

It'll be fine. Totally fine.

"Damn. You. Brent."

That's just the most recent in a long line of curses featuring me, but this time I laugh. As long as she's cursing me she can't be kissing me, right?

"Too much for you?" I call over my shoulder before I hit the throttle again. I'm not sure why I have to go so fast — but I do. It's a gut feeling I'm following since I can't follow all the other instincts trying to drive me.

Pressing the throttle makes her thighs wrap around mine

and her torso press into me and ... is she squeezing me like a horse she's riding?

I've lost Ian and his parents, but I can't seem to focus on that as I race over a wooden bridge that spans a creek. Reeds wave and toss in the wind and we kick up a flurry of flies as we cross.

"Do you have any idea how rough it is back here?"

She's going to be hard to ignore if she keeps holding my hips like that. I know it's for a purpose — to stay on — but it's still driving me crazy. I want her hands all over me, gripping me just like that, like they're claiming me as hers.

I force out an answer. "You don't like it rough. Noted."

I try to keep the burr out of my voice. The last thing she needs to know is that I still find her attractive. It's the one thing that could ruin this whole great setup.

I shouldn't be wishing for it. I certainly shouldn't do anything to promote it.

Her breath is hot on my neck and her voice jars with every bump and it *does things* to me that I probably don't have to elaborate, right? I mean, there's usually only one reason a woman's voice is breathy and hitched, and this quad ride is making a very decent facsimile of that.

"Actually, I like it long, and slow, and gentle, but it's plain to see that I'll have to find that elsewhere."

The quiet snarl that tears out of me is my only outlet for all the frustration building up. I'm thinking about her getting it how she likes it and it's making me all tingly and making it hard to care about quad biking when we're in the middle of nowhere and I could just pull over and ...

"Look, I wouldn't have kissed you if I knew who you were, so maybe take it down a notch," she says literally right into my ear so I can feel her breath tickling the shell of my ear. "We don't have to be all tense and angsty. We can just play happy family for a few days and then part ways."

That makes something in my belly clench and I don't know

why. Maybe because as much as I want to be a family with my sister and her new in-laws, I *don't* want to be family with this bright sparkling girl behind me. I can literally feel her breasts pressed against my back and trust me, the way that makes me feel is not familial. Maybe the turn up ahead would be the right place to stop for a moment.

"You didn't kiss me, I kissed you," I growl and she laughs.

"And now you're going to be cranky about it? It was a good kiss. You should just be glad I gave it to you instead of all twisted up now that you know I'm your beloved Ian's little sister. Take a left here."

I get that she knows the trails, but I see fresh tracks going straight, not to the left, so I stay straight, too.

"I'm not twisted up," I say. I need to stop thinking about pulling over and get my head straight. Tessa is not an option. She is a sexy, dangerous, laughing little temptation who is *absolutely not an option.*

She drawls when she answers me. "Sure, you aren't. Look, maybe I should drive. I know the trails."

"Not a chance." I grit my teeth. "We're right on their tail."

The feeling of her shifting against me, trying to move forward on the seat, makes me feel hot. If I rode *behind* her, it would be even worse.

"Okay, then *please* take your next left or we'll never meet up with everyone else again, and they'll all be so smug when we get back that I won't make it through dinner."

"Smug?"

"They'll think we wanted to get away on our own and that all their plans to throw us together are finally working."

"We are *not* getting together," I grind out. God have mercy. I need to build up mental walls in every direction because my defenses aren't just down, they're smoking rubble. They're radioactive. They won't be rebuildable for up to two hundred years — until they cool off.

"Exactly," she says breezily. "So let's spare ourselves the annoyance of being teased about it."

"Don't worry," I say grimly. "I can handle myself."

"I'm sure you can," she says in a teasing tone as the quad races up a hill and over a rise.

My best bet at getting through this ride without combusting is to catch up with the others. The sooner the better.

Below us is a pond held in place by a beaver dam and through the tall grass, I can see the trail goes right over the dam. I lean forward and let the quad pick up speed.

"In fact, the way you are with the ladies, I'm pretty sure it's *only* you doing the handling ... wait ... slow down."

Her voice gets louder, creeping up an octave, but *hello*, I think I can handle crossing one little beaver dam. We're on the dam already. See? I didn't need to slow down. Besides, I don't want to hear more from her. I want her focused on the ride.

"Stop!"

And just as I hear her, the front left tire hits a hole that came out of nowhere, plunging the front of the quad down and kicking us both into the air.

I'm in the pond so suddenly that I don't even realize what has happened until I surface, sputtering and shocked. The air smells like dead plants and mud sucks at my feet. I stare, stunned, at the quad that's so much farther away than I would have guessed.

I never crash.

Never.

Shit.

Where's Tessa? I spin around me, gasping, searching for her, and find her crawling out of the pond on the other side. She's soaking wet. It makes her muffler t-shirt cling to all her curves and — wow — she's got a great body. But that great body is giving me a stormy look that could incinerate anyone not currently chest-deep in water and sludge.

"Brent. Bolt." She's shaking and flushed. Her eyes are like plasma cutters. "I swear to the depths of this pond that you are the biggest dumbass I have ever met. Why do you think I was telling you to stop?"

"So you could drive?" I suggest.

At least the cold pond water has worked its magic. All that sizzling popping feeling I get around her is soggy and breaking apart. And suddenly I can think clearly again and I'm coming to the conclusion that I may have just made a mistake.

"So that you wouldn't hit the hidden holes," she says, slowly and with a false calm that's frankly kind of hilarious — especially when combined with her soaking hair and mud-streaked face — but even I know that laughing right now will make things a thousand times worse.

I wade out of the pond and catch her watching me without even pretending not to be checking out every single inch of my body revealed by my wet white T-shirt and clinging jeans. Whatever. It's not like we haven't had our bodies pressed together twice in the past hour.

I did screw up. I was so distracted that I ignored her twice and now here I am soaking wet and looking like a fool. I bite my lower lip and taste dirt. Awesome.

"Look," I say, taking a few steps forward so that we're close enough we could kiss. Which isn't going to happen, Brent. "I'm really sorry. I should have listened to you."

"You're sorry," she says, pausing before widening her eyes more. "You are. *You.*"

Like it's unbelievable that I could be sorry about something. I move to reach for her but stop. Wow, my neck feels all turned around. I must have twisted funny when I fell.

"Well yeah, obviously, I'm sorry," I say, and now I'm irritated because I don't throw apologies everywhere like parade candy. I'm not a fucking Canadian. I'm an American who has lived in

Australia for the past two years. What does she expect of me? Also, my neck hurts. Quite a bit.

She crosses her arms over her chest in a way that seems to just push her breasts more to the forefront and pops a hip which only makes it hotter. I stop, staring.

I can't help but blush. Wow, but she's stunning. I look quickly away when she catches me staring and smirks, her bright eyes lighting right up.

"Come on." She's already moving. "Let's haul the quad out of the hole. And then, if it still runs, I'm driving."

We fight the bike out of the hole together and she leaps on as if she drives it every day, nodding at me to take the seat behind her, and I want to be grumpy, but it's hard to do it when I have a curvy woman tucked into the notch of my thighs where I can press right up against her. I go ahead and put both hands on her waist.

It's not helping. But remember how I said there were no more walls? Now even the guards at the gates are dropping their weapons and running away.

"What?" I say innocently when she looks back at me. "I don't want to fall off."

She shoots me a wry look.

"It can happen," I say, deadpanning. "In fact, a friend of mine actually hit this hole in a beaver dam and flew right into a pond."

I don't think she planned to laugh at my joke, but even though she tries to suppress it, it comes out through her nose in a snort.

Which is good, right? Because I like making her laugh and also because even if I have to avoid starting a romantic relationship with my best friend's sister, it's probably good for us to be friends.

Friends. Ha. I guess I can try.

I find a smile playing around the edges of my mouth.

"See?" I whisper in her ear. "You still find me hilarious."

"I have a dark sense of humor," she counters.

"We could be friends," I suggest, trying my best to be charming.

"Could we?" She asks me, seeming to be as skeptical as I am. She turns so she can look at me with wide eyes and I swear that when she does it, she's completely intentional with how she twists her nicely shaped ass so it rubs right into my crotch. I have to bite my lip in concentration to keep from responding to that. "Wouldn't that be nice?"

And then she offers me the sweetest, most innocent smile — yeah, right — and without warning, she starts the quad — looks like it didn't get enough water in it to damage it — and then she guns it, and this time I have to cling to her as we fly down the trail, our wet clothes sticking to each other like we're mating salamanders.

# Chapter Five



I ... should probably be mad at Brent. Right? A normal person would be.

Look, he's really attractive. And it's not just his looks. He drives like the quad is part of his body with easy grace that would have gone a lot easier if he'd listened for even one moment to the voice of reason — which is me, hello. But yes, he's also attractive physically in a kind of primal, animal way. I think he might have shaken some of that water off like a mastiff. It didn't work. I could still see right through that white shirt.

Worst of all is when he presses his dripping wet body against mine. It's warm and sensual even if he does smell like pond scum. It draws me in like a powerful winch with two really good anchor points. Maybe he's not Olivia's brother at all. Maybe Ian grew him in a lab and has now unleashed him on me as a custom-made kryptonite.

Focus, Tessa, focus.

I have no idea how I get us to where my mom has a snack spread out on a picnic blanket. Muscle memory, I guess.

Instincts. All those things I have that everyone is discounting in me all the time.

I needed it this time because our previous kiss and now the soaking wet, big portable heater of his body are occupying every extra sliver of thought I have.

The looks on my family's faces when they see us are unreal. I think my dad doesn't know if he's going to swallow his own tongue. He settles for coughing, and then choking, until Mom pounds him hard on the back with a manic smile on her face as if her only daughter shows up every day dripping wet with a hot man plastered to her back.

"What happened?" Ian asks, his hand — holding one of Mom's classic chocolate chip cookies — frozen halfway to his mouth.

Olivia is the only one who looks totally calm. Her smile is serene and her hair is seriously perfect. Honestly, some shampoo company should sponsor her life. And if they did, they'd just die for this scene right here. My mom set this on the top of a hill that used to be farm fields and from here you can see the winding creek and fields and fields of wildflowers rolling out to the east. In the distance are blue hills and a bluer sky — like an ad for living in Northwestern Ontario.

"Is everyone okay?" Olivia glides over the wildflower field. "We heard some shouting."

"We're fine," I say with a bright smile. "Tiny mishap is all. Brent here just loves the scenery so much that he wanted to make out with it."

"Then why are you wet, too?" Ian asks, raising an eyebrow.

"Here, try a cookie, Brent," Olivia says smoothly. "They're Diane's family recipe and they're amazing."

"So amazing," Brent says sincerely around his first mouthful. I shoot him a look. He's spreading it on rather thick.

He jams the cookie into his mouth so quickly that I'm worried Mom is going to have to pound his back, too. I think he has this idea that if everyone is staring at his mouth, then they won't notice the rest of him super-glued to me. He hasn't moved even a fraction of an inch away from my back. The caught-in-the-act look in his eyes is making it hard for me to keep the grin off my face. Maybe he thinks this is a Regency Romance and when everyone sees we've been compromised they'll hustle us off to the altar.

"Well, that's the danger of riding two to a quad. If one person falls, the other isn't far behind. I think we're going to need to shower," I say.

"Together?" Ian asks in a small voice before Olivia jams him hard in the ribs. My father is choking again, his eyes wheeling wildly to my face as if he's trying to decide if I'm as innocent as I'm pretending to be, or if I've arranged this somehow.

"Oh! Oh, yes," Mom agrees, bustling over and handing Brent another cookie. "I need to get back to check the roast anyway." She kisses my cheek, which I swear is so sweet that it's impossible to be annoyed at her. "You'll feel better after a hot shower, honey bunny."

I risk a glance at Brent as she kisses his cheek, too, and I expect him to be smirking at "honey bunny" but instead, the look on his face makes me pause. He's stunned by my mom's kindness. Touched and hungry all at once. His eyes are misty and one of his arms rises up to wrap around her. And for a breath, I don't see the attractive man in the transparent shirt, just the motherless boy being cosseted by my sweet Mom.

I have to swallow and look away.

Look, I'm a sucker for heartwarming, okay? And heartwarming is just one step away from empathy, and if I take those steps, I'll be trapped in the "Tessa-Lurves-Brent" plan everyone is sure will work out — especially now that they've seen us dripping wet together.

"I'll meet you all back at home, okay?" I say quickly and the nods around are unanimous.

Ian's eyes look so huge he could double as an owl. Olivia is trying to tell Brent something with the look in *her* eyes, but I can't tell what it is. Hopefully, it's not "We've arranged a marriage for you two after dinner."

I wave and smile brightly. The only way to counter this is with complete obliviousness. You think we make a great couple? No. Not us. You must be joking, you!

And then I take off at the top manageable speed down the trail we *should* have taken and straight back home. It will be bumpy for Brent. Serves him right for doing the same thing to me.

It's a pretty ride home, though. He might be enjoying it. He's very quiet as we ride and I can't think of a smart remark to make after seeing him with my mom, so I just drive in silence until we get back home and try hard not to memorize the feeling of his warm, muscled body pressed against my back. It's not working. I could write midterms on this subject and get the top mark in the class.

I'm shivering by the time we get back and I smell like a pond, so that's lovely.

"Look, umm, I'm going to hit the shower, okay?" I say when we pull in. Because this totally isn't awkward. "I can show you where you can get clean."

He gets off the quad and my back is suddenly freezing cold with his warmth gone. He stands there looking at me nervously, biting his lip and rubbing the back of his neck with a palm. It makes all his muscles flex and makes that clinging T-shirt cling even more and I have to swallow and look away.

Wow. And to think, if he wasn't Ian's buddy we might still be making out beside a taco stand. And I might never know that he's half amazing and half a jerk.

"I've handled this all wrong," he says, and well, yeah. That's pretty obvious. "It was a mistake to kiss a stranger but I made it way worse afterward. I'm sorry."

It kind of stings that he calls that kiss a mistake.

It's a mistake I'd quickly repeat if he wasn't who he is. But there's a ghost of that twinkle back in his eye again. It must be from my mom's kiss. I swear she's a healer right down to the core. How can I deny him this joy or whatever it is?

"Yeah, me, too," I say a little ruefully. And I actually mean it. It's not his fault that he's taken all my opportunities or that I enjoyed that kiss and am seriously annoyed that there won't be more kisses.

"Fresh start?" he asks, holding out a hand.

I clasp it, determined that I won't mess this up a second time. But when I touch him, a buzz of familiarity goes through me and settles somewhere in my belly. I end up holding his hand for a breath too long and I can tell he notices when he inhales sharply.

Great. The last thing I need is for him to think I'm in on the Tessa and Brent marriage conspiracy.

I drop his hand like a dead fish and laugh awkwardly just as my parent's quad roars into the garage.

Whew. Perfect timing.

"Mom will show you where the towels are," I say with a wave, flipping my pond weed hair out of my face and practically running from the garage, into the house, and upstairs to the bathroom I use whenever I'm at home — which is all the time now that I live here again like an adult failure. At least I have my own shop. If I had to share that, too, I don't think my ego could take it.

I jiggle the trick lock to make sure it really latches, and then I strip out of my pond filth, toss it all in the hamper, and hop into the shower.

I will not think about Brent while I'm in the shower. I will not wonder if he's in the downstairs bathroom buck naked and showering off pond smell. I won't think about what those calloused hands look like when they spread soap all over his body or how his body looks when it's completely naked with water running in little rivers over it.

Eyes on the prize, Tessa, I coach myself. Get through dinner. Tomorrow you get to race.

I can't wait. It's going to be spectacular.

My mind fills with daydreams about winning and qualifying for the bigger races and then getting so much traffic to my online channel that I can support myself and move out and I'm so deep in daydreams that I hear nothing but the swish of hot water cleaning me until I turn off the taps.

I squeeze out my hair and draw in a deep breath. I need a moment to compose myself before I move on. I stand in the silence and the steam and I think about racing and everything I'm working toward.

It helps.

A lot.

I draw in a shaky breath, twist my hair one more time, and then at just that moment, the bathroom door creaks open and a voice in the hallway — my mom — says, "The extra towels are just in there. Go ahead and grab one."

My eyes go wide. Oh crap. That trick lock! It's betrayed me!

I hold my breath. Does that mean it's Brent out there? With only a thin shower curtain separating us? Uh oh.

The polite thing is to make myself known. He must think I'm finished and the bathroom is empty. I open my mouth to call out but I hear the slide of the towel basket and then the door shuts. Crisis averted. Whew.

I'm about to step out of the shower to get my own towel, when a phone rings.

And that's not my ringtone.

Panic surges through me. Shit.

I bite my lip as I hear Brent's voice take the call. He's still here. The realization is painful like stubbing your toe kind of painful

"Hello?"

And OMG he has it on speakerphone and a familiar voice — but granted, one I've only heard streaming online — floods the bathroom.

"Brent! Amazing to connect with you. This is Big Daddy Boom from Boom Enterprises. Ian told me that you're in for the race tour!"

It's the billionaire online vlogger. Right now. On speaker-phone. In my bathroom. I would kill to be in Brent's shoes. And instead, I'm hiding naked in the shower. If my life had a narrator he'd be groaning right now.

"Wow, yes. I'm very excited about the opportunity," Brent says. Lucky dumbass.

"Look, we're hoping to make it a mini-series on BOOM Motorsports," Big Daddy BOOM says. "We're thinking nine episodes. One about preparation, then one for every race. Including repairs afterward and lots of narration over racing b-roll."

"That sounds dynamite."

"Great! We're looking at sending you a camera operator, but you might have to do all the filming. How do you feel about that?"

"That would be fine. I do my own filming already."

So do I, but you don't hear me bragging about it. Though you might hear my teeth chattering soon. It's cold in here when you're wet and naked. And vulnerable. And about to be discovered.

Sweat breaks out on the back of my neck. I wish I could rinse it off.

"Perfect. I'll send you contracts and details to the email address Ian gave us. Is that all good?"

"Absolutely."

"We're thinking about calling the mini-series 'False Start' since it's about your career in Australia and then switching gears to racing here. And let me tell you, son, we are excited to have you on board! This is going to be amazing. This will be the first mini-series we do on BOOM Motorsports, but if it takes off, we are thinking about the possibility of adding a third show to the channel and you'd be our number one candidate. How does that sound?"

How does it sound? It sounds like my brother gave him the damn keys to the kingdom. That's how it sounds. You know that old myth that you go green with envy? If it were true, I'd be full-on chartreuse right now.

I feel ill.

"It sounds amazing. I'm thrilled to be part of it."

"Great! Enjoy your family time and watch for my email."

The call disconnects and I hold my breath, certain that now Brent will leave, but instead, I hear a shuffling sound like clothes sliding over each other. He must be getting more towels. How many does he need? Well ... he is rather large in the sexiest way. Maybe those broad shoulders take a towel all of their own. I indulge myself in a quick memory of his chest under that clinging shirt. What would it look like fresh from the shower and being dried with a towel?

It's a pleasant enough thought that my lips are starting to twist into a smile when suddenly the curtain is snatched back and I realize the sound I heard was not towels sliding across each other at all. It was Brent undressing.

# Chapter Six



I OPEN THE SHOWER CURTAIN, still happy from my call with BOOM.

And she's standing right there, completely naked and dripping wet — like something out of the dreams I'm sure I'll be having later tonight. I feel my mouth fall open.

"Fuck," I gasp, backing up until I hit the towel rack on the wall behind me. The word wrenches out of me strung through with awe. She's ... she's ...

The towel rack collides with my back in a way that's definitely going to hurt tomorrow morning but the blinding pain forces me to sobriety.

My eyes are wide. I lick my lips without meaning to. I manage to snatch my gaze up to her face. Be a gentleman, Brent. Fuck. Be a gentleman.

A shuddering breath tears out of me like I've just been dealt a blow. Maybe I have been. Or been given some kind of gift. I can't process it.

Tessa shoots a wince toward the door and I realize with

sudden horror that my curse was louder than I would have intended. I drop my voice.

My mouth is so dry that my voice comes out sounding strangled and a bit pleading. "What are you trying to do to me, Tessa?"

My eyes drift down again like gravity is too much for them and I'm looking. Of course I'm looking, she's like ... right there ... and I wouldn't be able to rip my eyes off her if I wanted to. Fuck she's lovely.

Her wet hair hangs down in the kind of ribbons I want falling around my face with her on top of me. Her lips are parted, cheeks flushed with our shared embarrassment, but even embarrassed, her eyes are still twinkling and her gorgeous cupid's bow lips purse and then curve upward in suppressed amusement.

I could look at her face all day. I'm trying to keep my eyes there instead of letting them fall to the soft swell of her breasts or down that taut rib cage and flat abdomen to where her hips swell outward like they're made for coaxing caresses and reverent kisses that grow slowly more fervent.

Fuck, Brent, get a hold of yourself.

I thought she'd squeak and grab a towel or do something equally ladylike. Or maybe scream. Or punch me. Or something.

But she doesn't. She just tilts her chin like she isn't even the slightest bit humiliated at being caught not only naked and dripping wet but also hiding in the bathroom while I took a call and eavesdropping on the whole thing.

She's like some kind of mind-blowing gift to mankind. Not for me, obviously, not meant for me, but fuck.

All the curves her wet T-shirt and jeans suggested are right here in front of me. The little flare of her waist that my hands caressed when I kissed her looks *exactly* as I expected it would. This is like a feast for the eyes that I shouldn't have, but like a dirty orphan off the street, I've snuck in and shoved my face right into it.

Bad metaphor, Brent. Now I'm thinking of shoving my face in other places.

"You shouldn't take your calls on speakerphone. That's just awkward for everyone." Her tone is mildly accusatory with a hint of teasing.

I swallow and wrench my eyes back up to hers. I feel like I've been caught in the middle of a crime. My cheeks are hot, hands clenched at my sides. I draw in the longest, trembling breath and I know my body is betraying me right now. I can feel the heaviness in my lower abdomen as things thicken and harden.

Shit. I forgot I was naked, too. I have nothing to hide behind except the chain I always wear with my lucky washer strung on it. That's not much help right now. There's nothing to conceal what she does to me. I look frantically for a towel and see Tessa, with enormous dignity, swipe one from the basket, shake it once to unfurl it, and then wind it around herself before giving me a once-over.

I scramble to follow suit, trying to avoid the tiny succubus smirk on that teasing bow-shaped mouth. I want to press my lips between hers. I want to taste her amusement at my expense. I'm the worst.

Something inside me relaxes as she covers up as if I've been given a reprieve, but the disappointment flooding over me snatches any relief. One tiny glimpse and now it's all gone and it has to stay gone forever.

"Why?" I ask in a pained voice, closing my eyes like I should have at the start and running a hand over my face as if I can wipe the frustration away. I need to think. "Why are you hiding in here *spying* on me."

Now that we're covered, my mind is racing, turning to other things. She met me at random at the bus stop, right? We were both confused about who we were to each other, right? That kiss was natural attraction and an honest mistake. It had to be.

I look up at her desperately, hoping she'll say something like that. Because she's in this bathroom naked and she didn't say a word to warn me. Just let me strip and open the curtain and imprint her naked beauty on my mind forever. I feel like she took out my seams and sewed me into something different and I'm still not sure what that thing is.

"I wasn't hiding, and I didn't mean to spy."

At least she speaks in a whisper, though her dark brows are turned downward, her cheeks pink, and her eyes bright like she's the one who is mad here. Ha.

Something shifts in me from surprise and wonder mixed up with chagrin to a sudden flare of anger.

Is she making a fool of me?

I'm furious. I can't even really explain why, except I feel like I've been duped. I don't like that she's put me in this position. She's made me vulnerable. She's made me want her so badly that it's clouding my mind and making things physically painful.

I step toward her and she has nowhere to go when I lean in so we're pretty much nose to nose. Am I trying to intimidate her? Maybe. The emotions raging through me are a terrible mix of wonder and betrayal.

Any intimidation I'm trying to effect is annoyingly ineffective. She simply narrows her eyes at me.

"I don't know what your deal is," I hiss.

"My deal?" She snorts. "Do you see how ridiculous this is?"

"But it isn't going to work on me." I must be resolute. No matter how much I secretly want it to work on me.

"It's not?" She sounds like she's mocking me. Like she knows exactly how conflicted I am.

She's going to ruin everything. The family that wants to accept me and Olivia. This amazing job opportunity. My friendship with Ian. Everything. Because no matter how much they're eager to see us as an item, I can guaran-fucking-tee you that none of them wants us naked in the communal bathroom while they're in the next room making goddam turkey.

And don't tell me I'm hysterical. I think I've earned a little hysteria.

"I am un-seduce-able," I whisper, and if my voice sounds husky that's just the anger.

She looks down at the tent pitched under my towel and I feel so hot that I think I might combust right here. Her gaze feels like a touch and it sends a little shiver of pleasure straight through me that is impossible to suppress. I think she sees my shiver.

Her eyes rake their way back up my body and her eyes are wide when she says — equally breathily, but I am immune to that now, "I can see that."

Okay, maybe I'm not immune. My breath catches and I have to swallow when her eyes darken and she licks her lips.

Fuck.

And then she puts her hand over her mouth and her shoulders start to shake and the towel slips enough that I see most of one of her tiny perfect breasts and I swallow hard, feeling ill because now I've made her cry and I don't know how this can get any worse. I rake a hand awkwardly through my hair. But then I meet her eyes. They're dancing. Mocking me. She's not crying at all. She's laughing ... at me.

I clench my jaw as the fury returns. It is not helping. It merely fuels the confusion and desire swirling through me.

She recovers her composure, gives me a wry look, and then steps past me with all the dignity of a reigning queen.

When she's right beside me she leans in so close that I can feel her breath on my neck — a feeling that is not helping at all with my growing arousal — and she whispers, "Whatever you think is happening here — it's not. Trust me."

"I do not trust you, you ... you marmot of a woman." That was a reach.

"Marmot?" She presses her lips hard together like she's suppressing laughter again.

"Always popping up everywhere," I explain. "Listen. I'm going to shower now. And you are going to go." I'm still mad, but more than that I am desperate, and I can hear it leaking into my voice in the form of pleading. "And please, please don't come back. Or show up in my bed. Or tell your family. Or do any of the terrible things you are thinking of doing, because Tessa, I am not going to fall for you. I am not going to sleep with you. I am not so much as going to kiss you ever again, no matter what you do. I swear it."

She salutes. She fucking salutes me in the most mocking way possible.

"Whatever you say," she says, and then she slips out the door and I'm left in the foggy bathroom with my shame and fury.

At least I can shower in peace now.

I hope.

# Chapter Seven

*TESSA*

I SLIP out of the bathroom in a towel and scuttle to my room up in the attic. My pulse is through the roof. Not just because I'm afraid someone will find out that I was in that bathroom with Brent completely naked, but also because I'm in information overload.

I just saw Brent Bolt naked. And he's *gorgeous.* His skin is a warm light brown and totally beautiful. His body hair is a bit darker than the hair on his head — just a sprinkling of light brown across his firm chest and then racing in a line down between his hard abdominals to that lovely patch below that makes me bite my lip just at the memory of what I saw.

He's hard muscle and hard work, calloused hands, and little white welding and grinding scars. He's all man. Young, lean, masculine-scented man.

And he wanted me. That was pretty obvious. I press my lips together firmly as I dress just thinking about it. Mmmm. That was ... well, it's making it even harder to say no to the idea of him and me together. Let's just say I'm very persuadable with that memory burned in my mind.

I should be ashamed of myself.

Or something.

But honestly, at this point, it's all so ridiculous that it's just become pure funny. I wish I could tell Dad. If this were happening to anyone but me he would die laughing. But because I'm his little girl and Brent has seen *all of me* and made out with me — two separate incidents, for the record — I don't think he'll see the joke.

Even Brent didn't see the joke. He went from humiliated to angry lightning fast and I desperately wanted to pause the scene, step out of it, and get him to step out, too.

"Look," I would say if we were watching ourselves. "Can't you see how a ridiculous series of mistakes got us here? It wasn't intentional. And you shouldn't take it so personally."

Since I can't do any of that, I text my bestie, Kati. She's been pretty distracted lately since she recently got married, but she tries her best to keep up.

> Day from hell. Or maybe heaven, I don't know ... You'll laugh so hard. Can't wait to tell you tomorrow.

She sends me a thumbs-up. At least I still have one ally.

I slip into my usual outfit — jeans and a T-shirt (this one has a purring Mopar on it) — and head out the door to my shop. It's the old garage that came with the house. It's detached, has electricity, and a huge washtub. Those are the pros. It's also cold and drafty and really tight inside so that really all I can fit is a workbench, a single project, and a welder. There isn't even space for a large compressor. I have to sandblast somewhere else. And I have to do all my video editing on my phone.

But it's home sweet home to me. There's a pit in the center of the shop, like someone dug a grave for a car but didn't quite make it wide enough. My stock car is squatted over the pit and I hurry down inside to see if I can figure out what is causing that slight oil leak I've been hunting all week.

This is good. I feel like I'm settling into my happy place again. I get that for some people that's a book in a cozy chair or a favorite tv show with pizza. For me, it's wrenches, and the damp pit, and creating online videos.

I set up my camera and narrate my opening.

I'm as far as, "So now we're going to hunt down that pesky oil leak!" when someone opens my shop door and I see Ian's shoes in the bright outdoor light. With a sigh, I turn off the camera and climb out of the pit, looking a question at him. He kicks at a washer on the floor of the shop with the toe of his shoe and doesn't quite look at me.

"Hey, Tess," he says.

"Hey, Ian. Need something?"

He doesn't answer right away. He just frowns.

"You look pretty low for a guy who is about to consume his body weight in Mom's classic roast beef dinner," I say, laughing.

He still doesn't meet my eye. "Look, I only had one chance to pitch someone, so I pitched Brent. I get why that bothers you, but it was my choice to make."

"Sure," I say. What's done is done. Explanations are just going to make us both more agitated. "Want to help me find an oil leak? It's so slow that it's taken me all week to figure out where it's coming from. Like, show yourself already, leak!"

He looks up, finally. It's the first time he's been in my shop since he got here four days ago. The first time he's seen my car. I feel all warm and fuzzy when I note the impressed expression on his face as he takes her in.

She's bright white and lovely. My biggest sponsor's name is right on the door. "Heart Throb Hot Sauce." The dude on the logo is buff and winking at the camera, painted like a 1940s pinup girl, but he's a shirtless dude. It's a great logo. There's one on the other door, too. I've also got a sponsorship from Hook Lumber with their logo across the rear quarter of the car, Bill's Towing and Patrick's Tacos have little stickers on the front quarters and my last sponsor — an indie romance author with a huge following who offered me a sticker with only her website on it. She's the reason why the bottom of the door has big black letters that say "www.alicedukeauthor.com." I'm still not sure why she's sponsoring me. I can't see many race fans reading her tales of love-lorn woe, but hey, I won't say no to sponsors.

"Your car looks good," he says, swallowing.

"Right?" I grin. "I can't wait to race her tomorrow."

"About that," he says kicking the washer again. "It's going to be Brent's first race in the Hurricane."

"Yeah, I bet he'll do really well," I say generously.

Nothing can kill my vibe right now. I'm thinking about tomorrow, and my sweet car, and the chance to finally race her, and I can't wait. I've been on the track, obviously. Even driven laps for practice. But I haven't driven in a proper race. I know that's a whole new world. I know it will take more than one race to even get used to the methods, but I can't wait. I am ready.

"I think so, too." He pauses. "Which is why I think you shouldn't race."

"What?" My jaw falls open.

Rude. Like, stab me in the heart already. Not you, Heart Throb.

"Why not?" I ask, trying to keep the confrontation out of it.

"Well, he needs to be the center of attention his first time racing here."

"He will be," I say and I can't keep the belligerence out of my tone. "He's straight off the racing circuit in Australia. Everyone will be thrilled he's there. If he's worried about having to buy his own drinks after the race, he shouldn't be. The other racers will be buying all night."

Ian lifts an eyebrow. "Will they, though? With a girl racer to be excited about."

I feel my cheeks heat. "There are other girl racers. And the way you say that makes it sound like I'm twelve. I'm twenty-three, Ian."

He shrugs like there really isn't a difference. "Look, you'll distract from him on his big night."

And look, if you're here for my story then I think you've probably realized by now that I'm pretty easygoing. But this is a bit too far.

"Ian," I say, trying to be reasonable. "I've been preparing for this race and building my car for months. After you wouldn't let me drive yours, by the way. I've been dreaming about this race that whole time. I'm not going to just not do it so your friend can get more attention. It's not even like I'm going to win. With a first race I'll be lucky to make it through the whole thing without crashing so bad I have to get dragged off the track."

"Well if that's the case, then why won't you just give it to him?"

"Because it's mine and I don't want to," I say and now I can't help the emotion in my voice. I'm hurt. It's one thing to hook his friend up instead of me. His very hot, very amazing-looking-naked friend. It's another thing entirely to try to sink my chances of succeeding at all.

"See? That's why I didn't offer you this opportunity and I offered it to Brent instead. You're disorganized and impulsive, but worst of all, you aren't a team player. You're too independent. It's always got to be about what works for Tessa."

"That's unfair," I say but my reply is weak. Part of me is worried it might be a *bit* fair. After all, I am fairly disorganized, but the rest of me is too hurt to even let that part breathe. Who is Ian — my brother! — to come into my shop, fling insults around, and insist that I don't race? Wow, that takes nerve. And not the good kind.

"Well, you can prove it's an unfair assessment by sitting this one out," he says.

I blink back tears. I hate that I cry when I'm mad. It's the most humiliating reaction. I dash them away, put my wrench back on my tool trolley and leave the garage.

"I wish you'd stayed in Australia, Ian," I say grimly. "You could still go back, you know."

I like that I see hurt in his eyes. It makes me feel a bit better about how much his words hurt me.

For half a second.

And then, after that, I just feel guilt all the way into the house.

# Chapter Eight

*BRENT*

Usually, I love a hot shower. It unwinds all my muscles and makes me feel hopeful and ready for life. Today, it does none of these things. I'm so tense I jump when a door slams somewhere in the house. I towel off as quickly as possible when I hear footsteps outside the bathroom door. Everything feels like a threat. Like I'm about to be discovered. My heart is racing.

I just keep seeing her completely naked in this exact room, laughing. I mean that image is distracting enough all by itself. She was like some kind of religious revelation opening up the world to me for the first time. If she'd just been the girl I'd met at the taco stand, I'd be smitten. I'd be so far gone there would be no coming back. But instead, I'm a man who found himself trapped naked in a bathroom in what had to have been a setup.

My experiences with women in the past are pretty unanimous about one thing — beautiful women are very unlikely to show their naked bodies to me for no reason at all.

Have I been played from the moment she met me?

It seems impossible. I kissed her first. I teased her first.

But I feel like a big buck being stalked through the forest. She knows what I'm going to do before I even do it. And I don't know what to make of that. I'm not the kind of guy girls find irresistible. I know those guys. They're charming and successful and when they sneeze money flies out of their noses.

I just don't get what her motivation is. Why try to trap me? Especially with Olivia and Ian already pushing me toward her. She could have been a lot more subtle and still likely had *me* if that was what she was after. Just the thought of that clears my head for a moment because I'm not stupid enough to think she wants me for myself.

I breathe out a long sigh. Confusion might be my primary emotion right now, but this girl has done a number on me and my mind is all tangled up. She was heart-sinkingly beautiful. I feel a squeeze in my chest just thinking about her and how I can't have her under any circumstances.

My hands are shaky and jittery as I pull my clothes on. Images of her keep flashing through my mind and when I get to the one of her soaking wet in a clinging T-shirt, I think that maybe I need to get a breath of fresh air.

Yeah, that's it. Fresh air.

But my mind won't stop the replay of her — teasing me, kissing me, laughing at me, naked with me. I can't believe I met her only hours ago. It's like someone branded her right onto my brain and it burns and burns and burns.

I leave the bathroom confused but determined. I'm not going to let this girl get to me. I'm going to hold my course and win over Ian's parents and make this BOOM opportunity work. And no amount of naked surprises are going to change that.

Naked. Her with those bright, shining eyes and all that long hair — I'm a sucker for long hair — all slender curves and softness. I want to press my lips to that smooth freckled skin. I want to taste every inch of it.

Dammit, Brent, you have to get a hold of yourself before dinner.

Maybe that's what she's after. Messing me up. Making this BOOM deal impossible. That doesn't feel quite right, but honestly, nothing does right now. I don't even feel like I fit in my own skin.

I go down to dinner with my teeth on edge and my mind racing.

Dinner is like something out of a movie. The food glistens and steams on the spread table where Diane has outdone herself. The smell of roast beef — rich and warm — permeates everything. Golden potatoes, crisp pickled beets, bright salads, and round, warm rolls make my mouth water before we even get to the table.

Ian helps Diane bring food from the kitchen and Olivia smiles and draws me in for a quick hug.

"Have you been to Canada before?" Steve asks me when we sit down, and then we talk about my bus ride across the country.

Yeah, I took a bus. I just wanted to see the place that way, to get a feel for the size of it, and what kind of people live here. It was amazing. I get that most people wouldn't consider a sweaty bus ride with strangers amazing, but I met a First Nations woman and her grandchildren who taught me about local wildlife, and then I met a guy named Rich from the east coast of the country who was out west welding on the pipelines, and he talked for hours about east versus west and what life in the trades here is like. And I saw so much country.

It was truly amazing, even if it was kind of an oddball move instead of coming right here with Ian and Olivia, but I really hadn't been to this country before and I wanted to see it a bit on my own terms while I had the chance.

Now, I'm wondering if I made the right choice. If I'd been here from the start, would Tessa be doing whatever it is she's doing to me? Maybe she's spent these four days plotting this whole thing out. That devilish sparkle in her eye might be more than teasing. It might be actual plotting.

As if I've summoned her, she arrives at dinner with a smile. My heart does some kind of weird stutter at the sight of her, which I'm pretty sure is just panic. If she messed up a simple ride and a shower, what can she do with prime material like dinner?

She's always smiling, it seems. But now that smile has me jumpy. Every time I catch a glimpse of it, I'm transported right back to the bathroom and to her naked loveliness, and my cheeks are so hot they could double as a forge. Seriously, it's not like I've never seen a naked woman before. But there was something about the vulnerability of her all mixed up with teasing laughter and irritation that made her more than just any woman to me. It made her like some kind of drug designed to ruin me and I'd taken my first hit and now I was hooked forever.

She finds the open place between her father and Olivia. Am I mistaken, or is she avoiding Ian's eyes? I mean, she's avoiding me, careful not to get involved in any conversation I'm having. Probably, she's saving her next trick for the exact moment that it can ruin my life completely and it makes sense for her to be patient waiting for that. But why is she avoiding Ian?

"I bet it was fun quad biking with Brent, wasn't it?" Olivia asks her and I freeze. "When you met him at the bus station were you surprised? Was he what you expected from everything we told you?"

"He's not at all what I expected," she says and her eyes meet mine defiantly as if I would challenge that. Ha. "For starters, no one showed me a picture of him first. And then on top of that, you said he was a sweetheart."

"And he is!" Olivia gushes. "Honestly, Tessa, you two would be so perfect together. You could support him at all his races just like I support Ian."

"I'm right here," I growl and Diane laughs like my discomfort is tonight's entertainment. Maybe she and her daughter share a dark streak.

And my sister's comment makes me blush harder because yes, I'm annoyed as hell at Tessa, but they say she built her own car. That means she's serious about racing even if she's a complete psycho when it comes to me, and it's not fair to act like she has to be on the sidelines just because she's a girl. If this had happened before she entrapped me, I'd probably be standing up for her.

Instead, Steve does.

"Have you seen Tessa's car, Olivia?" he asks gently. "I think you'd like it. She's worked so hard to get it ready."

"Oh! I can't wait to see it," my sister says with a smile. "Will you give me a tour, Tessa?"

"Yep. Right now," Tessa says, leaping up from her seat.

"We're still eating, honey," her mom says as her dad hides a laugh behind his napkin.

"I'm not hungry," Tessa says, a wild expression on her face

I look over at Ian, expecting to share a look with him over his crazy sister, but his eyes are glued to his plate and he's shoveling roast beef into his mouth like he's being paid by the bite.

"Umm...I'm still eating, Tessa," Olivia says sweetly, nudging Ian with an elbow. "And I'm sure Ian will want to come to see it with us."

"I got the grand tour before supper," Ian says stiffly, looking up with a smile so fake it practically has mustache-glasses on it.

What is going on between these two?

I wonder that all through dinner — which Tessa stays to eat. She jokes with her dad the whole time in a way that makes me wish I'd known my dad. They have a steady riff that involves more puns than I thought were possible. But I also notice it means she doesn't have to talk to anyone else. Or even look at them.

Her mom is a sweetheart, quizzing me about growing up in

Minnesota and then the big move in my teens to Australia. She can relate ... sort of. She grew up on the West Coast of Canada and only moved here when she married Steve. She gets a twinkle in her eyes almost as bright as her daughter's when she talks about the towering trees there and I can't help but smile with her. Diane is like that. Completely infectious. She makes me miss Mom worse than ever.

My mom was a worrier. Sometimes, I can't believe she packed us up and moved to another continent when everything seemed to make her nervous. But she tried so hard and at her best, she was infectious like that, too.

And I don't understand how this family can all be so incredible to me while Tessa is so ... nerve-wracking. Insanity inducing. I have to bite my lip and look away from her more than once.

I'm going to be keeping that promise I made to her if I have to take cold showers for a month. No more ... anything. Not even kisses. She's not safe.

My eyes keep snagging on her by accident and when she folds her napkin discretely and slips away at the end of dinner, I don't think anyone but me notices. But I notice and it bothers me.

But that's only because I'm worried about what she might be up to. I mean, that girl is a walking menace.

Even with Tessa off doing whatever she does, I'm distracted by her. I keep hearing her laugh just around the corner or being sure I've caught a glimpse of her long black hair.

Ian takes me out to the garage to show me the ins and outs of the Hurricane. But he seems annoyed and I'm distracted and it makes it hard for both of us to concentrate.

"There's nothing here you haven't seen before," he says.

Oh, there's so much here that I haven't seen before. A series of images flash through my brain to confirm. I push them aside.

"Hell yeah, brother," I say with a confidence I don't feel — not because I have any doubts about the car but because my brain is on something else entirely. I manage a firm nod. "Thanks, man. I really appreciate it."

"We'll get it loaded up tomorrow and do a shake-down video for BOOM," Ian says, and this time we're both grinning, reminded of why we're here.

I'm so ready for it. I can already feel the adrenaline ready to come to the surface at just the thought of racing tomorrow. I was born to fly along the ground, to be fast, to use my reflexes to guide a car through every turn and land her safe past the finish line — preferably ahead of everyone else. And I'm ready to finally be the one in front of the camera as well as behind it.

"You won't regret recommending me, Ian," I say, crossing my arms over my chest. I can live up to that promise. I know it.

Ian's laugh, though, is hollow. And I don't know what that means. *Does* he regret it? Already?

"I'll show you to your bed. It's getting late," he says, leading the way into the house. "Mom is giving you Tessa's bed. She's going to sleep in her shop."

"Oh, I can't impose like that," I say, suddenly panicked. I can't imagine trying to sleep in her bed after everything else. It might just be the death of me. I can imagine a little divot in the mattress from her small body and the scent of cinnamon and apples between the sheets.

"Nonsense," Ian says. "If she's at all uncomfortable, then she can learn to stop dishing it out quite so hard."

I'm worried about the salty edge to my good friend's voice. Worried enough that I stop objecting and take the bed. And if it smells like Tessa, then I don't know, because when I go to sleep at long last, my thoughts are so full of her that *any be*d would hold her scent for me.

I try really hard not to dream. Any dream is certain to be tainted by this sudden …. longing? Anxiety? Attraction?

I go to sleep in the certain knowledge that I am fully ridiculous.

# Chapter Nine

*TESSA*

"I can't believe you're finally doing this!" Kati says, practically hopping up and down as I get the car off the trailer. I got here early to set up my tools — boy do I hope I don't need them but I'd have to be the most naive racer ever to really believe that.

Andrew, her husband, let me set up beside him, which was really sweet and I can tell by how he's talking to me that he fully expects to have to be my pit crew when things go sideways. He's so shy that he doesn't come out and say it, but it's just like Andrew to be silently kind.

We're racing in different classes. Andrew just does this for pure fun and only locally. He doesn't want to travel the circuit or run the really fast cars, but his Hornet class car is amazing. He let me practice with it all this past year and even drive a qualifier with it once.

I was lucky — no smash-ups or anything — but the Hornet class races a lot slower than the Midwest Modified that I built and comparing the two — well, it's safe to say that I'm not really ready for tonight even though I've done everything possible to get ready. My heart is racing through the roof. I'm already in my race suit even though it's way too hot. And me and Kati can't stop grinning.

"I can't believe I am, either, Kati!" I say.

"I'm going to have to get much better at turning a wrench now that I have two of you obsessed with this," Kati says with a grin.

Both Andrew and I laugh. Kati is ah-mazing at anything mechanical. She's just so calm all the time that people don't realize she's worked magic until so long after it's happened that they forget it was her.

"We're both lucky to have you," I say, a bit choked up, pulling her into a side hug.

"And because you're lucky, you're going to listen to me," Kati says, adjusting her glasses. They are huge cats' eyes and they make the roundness of her face look more pointed and skeptical, and less happy-go-lucky.

"Of course I am," I agree enthusiastically, as Andrew is swept up into a group of friends and drawn away from us.

"Don't forget," Kati starts, and then she runs me through all her race advice again. She's already given me this speech twice tonight.

It mostly centers around not doing anything stupid or impulsive on the track — yeah, she knows me — keeping it low-key for this first event — I can build up a reputation later when I'm better at it — trying my best to finish without crashing rather than to win for this first run, and just to have a great time because she loves me and she's cheering for me ... and Andrew, but that goes without saying.

She winks at me. Kati might be the quiet one in her huge Indian family, but she's still vibrant and loud next to Andrew — who is back now and wrapping an arm around her shoulders.

They share one of those disgustingly happy looks and then both turn their smiles to me.

"You'll do great," Andrew starts to say, and just when I'm getting all warm and fuzzy feeling because these two really are in my corner even if other people who should have my back have abandoned me — just at that moment, a car comes rumbling through the pits, showing off, of course, and my smile goes wooden.

"Is Ian driving tonight?" Kati asks in that Kati way that tells me her very calm demeanor is covering for surprise.

"No," I say with a scowl as I look down the pits and see everyone stopping to watch the Hurricane roll by.

"But that's R38, his car," Andrew says.

"And that's Brent, his best friend and brother-in-law, who has apparently replaced me forever as the better sibling," I say and there isn't any bitterness there, obviously.

Brent is driving around without a helmet on since these are just the pits. By the time he gets close, it's easy to see he isn't Ian, but that doesn't stop everyone who ever knew Ian from running over to say hello and chat with him — including Andrew.

"He's pretty attractive for a nemesis," Kati says, tapping her chin as she watches her husband fanboy over my brother's stupid Modified class car.

"The best villains are hot as hell," I agree. But honestly, I'm not mad at Brent. I just can't get over that he gets everything just handed to him while I have to work my ass off for it. "With or without their clothes on."

Kati turns to me with her eyes huge. "Talk to me about without."

"Trust me," I say, rolling my eyes, "it's exactly as good as you're imagining."

It really is. It's probably a good thing that I shivered all night in my sleeping bag on a camping cot after Ian gave my *fucking bed* to

Brent, or maybe I would have had the energy to dream about how great he'd looked naked. Instead, I'd had to pretend I hadn't seen his hotness while I hid under two sleeping bags and that's on my brother because I didn't see him giving up *his* bed in the guest room — although I will grudgingly admit that I wouldn't subject sweet Olivia to a night like I just had. Between the cold and the smell of fuel and the squeak of furry visitors, I had not had much sleep.

"I'm going to check everything over one more time," I say darkly.

"Really? You aren't going to give me any more details?" Kati sounds as hurt as I'd be in her shoes.

"There are no more details," I say with my face practically on the pavement as I visually check my brake lines for the three hundred and thirty-seventh time. "We kissed. It was amazing. I found out who he was and swore not to do it again. Then, he caught me naked in the shower while he was naked, and that's it. We haven't spoken since."

I look up to see Kati with her mouth forming an "O."

"What?" I snap. "It's not a love story. He thinks I'm trying to seduce him."

"Are you?"

"Obviously not." I poke at something that doesn't need to be poked. "I'm not really the seductress type, unless seductresses have turned in their lacy black lingerie for racing suits and their enchanting perfume for a row of ratcheting wrenches."

Kati looks past me toward the Hurricane. "I don't see what's so obvious about not wanting to seduce him, Tess. If I wasn't married to Andrew, I wouldn't need much convincing."

"You only say that because your brother hasn't handed him everything and told him to have fun while he gives you the cold shoulder."

I say this and I sort of mean it, but even as it leaves my lips all I can think of is him standing there totally exposed, eyes blazing as they met mine like he was going to set the whole world on fire.

"My brothers were both trying to marry me off to college friends before I married Andrew," Kati says absently. "You know that. If I'd married Anjet like they wanted, then my mother would stop crying whenever she thinks about how I might have red-headed babies."

"Then you understand," I growl. "It's not fun to be treated like a car someone can just lend to their buddy."

"Oh, I don't know," Kati purrs. "I think I could give him a ride."

I hear Andrew clear his throat and look up in time to see Kati's blushing cheeks and her husband's tolerantly wry look.

"I was talking about you, of course, my sweet," Kati says.

"Of course," Andrew agrees. "It's time for me to queue up for qualifiers."

But he can't be too mad because he kisses her before he takes off and after that, she's too obsessed with watching him — and eating the poutine she scores at a food stand — to tease me anymore.

My first qualifier comes before I am ready — despite all my dedicated devotion to getting ready — and I'm in my car and forming up in line with everyone else who's running in this qualifier before I see Brent again.

To my surprise, he's not in a gaggle of adoring fans anymore. And he's not with Ian, who I catch sight of as he helps Olivia find a good spot in the stands. Brent's leaning against the barrier, staring intently into every car as they go by and when he stares into mine and our gazes catch, I swear something lights off in me like a flare. By the way he clenches his jaw, I'm pretty sure it's lighting off in him, too. He looks away sharply, but he can't hide from me. He feels it, too.

Well, that settles it. I'm just going to have to ace this run.

Butterflies are racing around in my belly when I pull onto the track and then, just as I creep up over the edge of the hill and drop down into the bowl, the wind rushes in the car, cooling my face, catching my breath, and all the nerves from before morph in exhilaration and I'm just laughing with giddy joy as we fly around the circle track.

Here we go. Buckle up, people. Tessa Harstone is about to show you how it's done.

# Chapter Ten

*BRENT*

I'M BACK, people!

Back under the bright spotlights in the pit. Back to the sounds of generators and impact guns, of engines revving, of the announcer warming up the crowd. They're pumping country tunes on the loudspeakers from the local station and the stands are filling up so fast that it gives me that rush I always get knowing I'm going to compete.

I did a loop around the pits getting to know everyone. That's what I always do. No need to be a stranger, right? And then Ian and I did a once over on the car and set everything up the way we like it in the trailer, filmed a little, and now all I have to do is watch until it's ready time for my class. With a car in the Modifieds, that's going to be a while. Every other class runs first, and while there are only twelve cars running in my class, Street Stocks have fifty alone and have to run in waves.

I'm jazzed with the energy of it all. My racing suit is tied around my waist, ready to be untied and zipped up when it's time to go. A guy named Tony who I met during the drivers' meeting waves me over. He's in a restricted area wearing a high-vis vest and talking into a radio right where the cars ramp onto the track.

When I make it to where he is, he leans on in. "You can watch from here, Brent. Get a feel for our track."

And then he claps me on the shoulder and replaces his hearing protection. I think I might be grinning. There's something addictive about this. My own ears are thrumming with the sound, the smell of fuel hangs in the air, and already the red dust is rolling off the track into the stands, coating all the cheering people of Thunder Bay in a skim of dust. I don't think they care — or maybe it just adds to the flavor of their stand food. The food looks good. I'll have to grab a bratwurst later.

And then the cars reach the ramp and are slowly heading in and I know that Tessa drives one of these. Diane whispered to me that this was her first race in a car she built.

"It's white," she whispered to me. "38DD. It's a joke."

As if I couldn't spot Tessa's sense of humor right there.

I'm watching every racer as they go. I don't want to miss her and I don't know why. Ian didn't seem to care much.

"I want to make sure Olivia is comfortable," he'd said when I suggested watching from right down by the track. "It's important that she feels like she fits in here."

As if my sister hasn't watched a thousand races in Australia. She'll be fine. Ian needs to stop fussing over her so much or she'll start to feel smothered. I never do that.

And then there Tessa is, coming over the rise, her eyes laughing through the slit of her helmet. They catch on mine, still dancing, and I think my heart has stalled out. Then she guns it and bursts onto the track like a complete psycho — I mean who didn't see that coming? — and I'm laughing so hard that I miss the last car heading out.

I shouldn't laugh. I should be wary about what she might do. But I'm not. No one is watching me down here by the ramp.

No one knows me. I'm just one face in a crowd and it's okay to find her funny in her enthusiasm for this. It's okay to let myself watch.

And I do watch. Her acceleration is perfect. She's digging into the first half of the corner just right and staying in tight to the inside, tires elongating with the force as she moves through the turn.

She's good.

If this really is her first time racing this then she's really good. Better than Ian, maybe.

My eyebrows are climbing as she runs the first laps with the others and then when the green flag drops it's madness. She's hard on the accelerator even though she's starting at the back of the pack. There's no caution here, and I wouldn't expect any from her. But what I definitely didn't expect is her natural talent at this. I can see just the slight delay between when she should do a thing and when she realizes it — that's her lack of experience — but by the fifth lap she's passed everyone right up to the third position and she's hanging in tight on the heels of the others. If they aren't careful, she might squeak into second and qualify for a feature spot.

I'm impressed. And it's hard to impress me.

And for some reason, this really gets under my skin. Why? Because I've kissed this girl. I've seen her in her skin. I've heard her dumb puns. And now I've seen her race, and everything about her is screaming "the perfect woman for Brent" and she's the one woman I absolutely must not allow to get close to me. It almost feels like a huge cosmic joke — and I'm the butt of it.

In a flurry of speed at the very end of the race, she places second and is going to move on to the feature for her class. I feel like a lead weight is in my belly.

I heard her parents whispering this morning on the front deck.

"Tessa is upset because Ian gave his car to Brent to drive

when he wouldn't lend it to her," Steve had been explaining to Diane. "And he set him up with a job with this Boom guy. That could have been her."

"It's no life for a girl," Diane said. "She should have been a nurse. I've told her a thousand times. All that care she has for cars could have been for people. Aren't people more important than cars?"

Steve had made a noncommittal noise. And I brushed off the whole thing as silliness. I came here all the way from Australia. Of course Ian had known I needed something serious before I'd want to do that. And, of course, Ian hadn't offered the things he'd handed me to Tessa. She wouldn't have been able to do anything with them.

But now that I've seen her car and seen her drive? I think maybe I was wrong.

And I have this terrible sick feeling in my belly.

It might be guilt.

But that's stupid, right? It was just one race. Anyone could get lucky in just one race. I've already seen how headstrong and impulsive she is. Actually, placing second at all in her first race probably shows how unsuitable she is. She should have held back and just let herself get a feel for this speed of racing and then placed in a later race when she had experience. Her advancement onward is actually a sign that she's not right for this.

I'm trying to tell myself all this. But myself is not listening.

Something prompts me to abandon the stands and head to the pits. The next line of Midwest Modifieds is in line waiting for the track to clear for their run. I skirt around them and into the puddles of light that dapple the pavement. There are more fancy rigs here than I expected in a place like Thunder Bay, but honestly, this is a world-class track, even if it's only a few years old.

I push my way past a guy scarfing down a hotdog while he fiddles with the pressure in his tires, past another guy stripped down to his skivvies so he can tug his race suit on, and straight to where I know her trailer is. I saw her there, brooding, on my way in. I think that maybe I might know why she's brooding now.

There's a lump in my throat and I'm not sure what I'll say, but there's no one there waiting to help her like there is at the other trailers and when her car rumbles into her slot, I'm the one who is there.

I don't know what motivates me here, okay? I'm a bit of a mystery even to myself.

But when she stops the car, I lean in through the narrow slot of a window.

"Tess," I murmur, and then I lean in more to help her out of that five-point harness.

It puts my fingers where they graze her thighs through the cloth of her protective suit, and I have to lean in so close to reach the harness that my cheek presses right against the swell of her breasts like a lover collapsed on her.

My cheeks are hot and blazing. My lips are parted with my breath coming in little agonized gasps. I didn't think this through, did I? And then she's unclipped and I slip back out the window and she grabs her helmet off and looks at me with stunned, fiery eyes.

"What are you doing?" she asks me breathlessly. We are both breathing like we're on fire. Maybe we are. Maybe hell has caught up with us.

"Helping you out," I manage in a rasp. "Damn, that was a really good run."

And then I turn and abandon her, wincing and flexing my fingers as I go, because they're still burning with the touch of her thighs through her racing suit.

*Chapter Eleven*

"I'm here! I'm here! I'm here!" Kati calls and I hear her flip-flops slapping on the pavement. "I'm so sorry, I got caught up. Oh. You're out."

Kati usually helps me to get all the gear off and unclip. I could do it myself, but she makes it much easier. Now, she pulls up, stunned to see me with my helmet and gloves off, tying the sleeves of my suit around my waist.

"I was hung up in line," Kati says, offering me a paper basket of nachos with cheese identical to the one she's kept for herself in her other hand. Kati's vegetarian and options at the races are limited for her.

"It's fine," I say and she must see how shocked my face looks. In the distance, I can still see Brent's profile pop up in one pool of streetlight only to be lost in shadow again. He's moving so fast that it almost feels like he's running away. And what was he even doing here helping me out of the harness? He was the last person I expected.

"Your run was amazing!" Kati beams, "Even though I'm

pretty sure I told you to take it easy the first time and not try to place."

"Yeah, sorry," I say, frowning as I eat a nacho.

That was so weird. And so incredibly sexy. Like even more sexy than seeing him naked had been. Maybe it was because he didn't look like he thought I was trying to kill him.

I mean it's not sexy when Kati helps me out of the harness, which she does sometimes because it's a pain to do on your own.

But with Brent doing it, it felt ... intimate. Like an act of devotion he was performing rather than just a regular thing friends can do for each other. It felt like affection. It felt like foreplay.

I'm crazy. That's the problem here. He's probably helped unclip my brother when he had an issue. And that wouldn't have been sexy at all.

I shake my head.

"Still stunned by the results?" Kati asks me, wrapping an arm around my shoulders. Wow, she's the best friend. I'm not even responding and she's carrying our whole friendship.

"I must be," I say with a gust of a laugh. "Wow."

"Wow, is right," Andrew says, coming up from behind us. "Eat fast, ladies. We need to check this car over and make sure she's up for another run.

It doesn't take us long. I might not have a ton of experience racing this class, but I've been helping in the pits for ages and I know this car I built like no one else. We run through our checklist quickly while Andrew lectures me.

"It's a race, Tess, I get that. But it's not about winning for you today, okay? You need to get your experience levels up first. You lucked out on that qualifier. Don't you dare do something stupid in this next race."

"Yes, Andrew," I say mildly and both he and Kati look at me with suspicion in their eyes.

Okay, mildness might be out of character for me. But I'm

feeling things. Brent watched my run and unclipped me. And Ian didn't. Even though I know he's here. And I'm all tumbled around with a feeling of loss and hurt mixed up with surprise and curiosity and a weird charge of attraction and I don't know how to untangle this ball of feelings. I resort to scarfing down nachos.

When we're done, we hit the stands to watch the next few races together. There will be a Hornets feature next, which Andrew didn't qualify for, and then a Street Stock feature and I'm eager to see both. I don't need to get back to my car until after the Super Stocks run.

I catch a glimpse of Ian close to the track, filming the races for his YouTube channel. He likely did a huge intro and interview with Brent first and now it's action time. I ignore it. I set my own action camera up in my car and filmed the first race and I'll be filming the next race, too. I don't need him.

Besides, I love being a spectator. Not as much as driving, obviously. But I cheer like crazy, gasp when things get hairy, and wince when a car goes spinning end to end and takes out two other racers.

"What a night!" Kati says as we watch the Modifieds zip onto the track for their qualifier.

Ian's car is easy to pick out. It's bright, shiny, undented, and stickered with not just his six sponsors, but also the BOOM Motorsports logo. I fight hard at my twinge of jealousy over that stupid orange sticker and instead I manage to join Kati in cheering for him.

Honestly, he doesn't need my cheers. He takes the lead in the first lap and keeps it right on through. They're on the last lap when Andrew comes to drag me away.

"They're staging for your feature!" he says, tugging me away from the race.

Surprisingly, it's hard to go, but the second I hit the pits my adrenaline takes off. I untie the arms of my race suit and start to slip them on and zip up. I feel like there are bees buzzing under my skin. I can't wait. The first race was everything I'd hoped for. It felt like I'd finally, finally come into my true self and now I get to do it again.

I'm behind the wheel and all buckled in again before I know it. I start my car, ready to get in line and she fires up like she always does … and then something goes wrong. It sounds like my sweet girl is choking on rocks. I kill the engine and yank off my helmet. I'm fumbling with my neck brace, my hands shaking too much to deal with it. Kati reaches in and gently takes it off for me.

"What happened?" Andrew's face looks pale in the bright streetlight above us. He's scrambling for the cotter pins holding my hood down while Kati reaches in to unbuckle me.

"It will be okay. It will be okay," she chants to me but she sounds panicked and I certainly am.

The second I'm free, I leap out, and the three of us lift the hood off and to the side.

"Try to turn the engine over," Andrew says, but I can tell by the look in his eyes that he's feeling sick for me — maybe even as sick as I'm feeling for myself. That wasn't a good sound.

I turn the key again and this time when it starts, it sounds like something is grinding in the engine. I turn it off immediately and put my face in my hands.

Fuck. Fuck. Fuck.

My engine is blown. My five-thousand-dollar-all-the-money-I-had engine is blown. The feature race is going without me and I don't even care. I stare numbly as Andrew grabs tools, expression deadly serious.

"You want to look now or later."

"Let's look now," I say, miserably. "We're going to have to push the car just to get it on the trailer."

Kati wraps her arms around her torso and I feel the first tear break loose and slide down my cheek.

Damn it. Not now. I swipe it aside, take the impact gun Andrew offers me, and get to work stripping off the air cleaner and valve covers.

"Shit," I say and it comes out as a moan.

"Oh, shit," Andrew says and his curse sounds horrified. "Someone put BBs in your engine. Look."

And I see them in there. In the valves. Everywhere. Little round copper beads are everywhere.

"They would have been sucked right in," he says as if he's a doctor breaking the news to me that I'll never drive again. And I might not.

"But who would do this to my car?" I ask Andrew, and this time, I can't stop the tears from leaking down my face. He looks miserable as he puts his arm around Kati who is crying, too.

"I've heard of it happening before. Not for years, and not around here, but I heard it happened to a buddy's friend down in Indiana. She was a clear shot to win. And she was a girl. And someone took that personally."

I hear the people in the stands cheering as the big feature of the night — Modified class — is queueing up to start. And I know Brent's going to be driving Ian's car and probably winning, or at least placing. I see his car get in line with the others in the distance. And I'm going to be pushing my car into her trailer and packing up, my season over before it even started because one thing I don't have is money to rebuild this engine.

I dry my tears, turn my action camera back on, and turn it to face me where I explain the whole thing and then set up to film us push the car onto the trailer. It hasn't even taken very long. We have the car on the trailer already when the line of Modified cars starts to move onto the track.

"Let's watch the feature race," Andrew suggests. "We can pack tools later."

His smile is just a bit too bright and I know he's trying so hard to cheer me and Kati up that I smile back — a wobbly smile, but a smile — and follow them to stand at the nearest point from the pits that spectators can watch from.

The green flag drops just as we get there and the cars race down the track. I feel sick as I watch Brent passing and weaving, making his way to the front of the pack again. I see where Ian is in the stands — not because I'm looking, but because he's jumping up and down so enthusiastically that he's impossible to miss. His camera work on this is going to be appalling.

And then just when I think maybe I shouldn't torture myself by watching this, Brent hits the apex of the turn, accelerates, and ... somehow doesn't turn?

Oh no.

He crashes into the wall, his car spinning like a globe. He bumps four other cars, sending them pinwheeling, and he catches the fifth one in such a way that it acts like a wedge, scooping his car up over the hood and tumbling through the air to land on its roof.

Silence floods the stands.

And then the announcer is speaking calmly over the loudspeakers as the red flag goes up and the support people go running out onto the track.

But my heart is in my throat. Because that wasn't a mistake. No one, not even a rookie like me, would have driven like that. Something has happened to Brent.

## Chapter Twelve

*TESSA*

M Y  E Y E S  G O to Ian first. He's already running, leaping over the barrier and into the track. No one stops him. The crowd is frozen, the emergency crews all leaping into action. Trucks from track maintenance are there immediately as well as the EMS truck on standby. The medics scramble out to Brent's car.

My hands are covering my face, and I'm peering through my fingers.

The crowd is frozen.

And then, after long seconds, the announcer speaks.

"I'm getting word from the men on the ground, ladies and gentlemen. All of our drivers are in stable condition. We're going to work to clear the tracks now."

And I feel like I can breathe again.

The track maintenance trucks are pulling the damaged cars off the track. Those that can still run on their own power limp off the track. Those that can't are towed. And I'm biting my lip when I see Brent pulled out of the car, put on a stretcher, and hustled into the back of the ambulance. My brother is right there with him but my heart hitches in my throat. Where is Olivia?

She's in the stands. Standing up. Looking lost.

I clench my jaw and hurry.

I circle the track and get to the stands and fight my way up the crowded stands to where she's standing.

"Olivia?" I say gently and then she crumples into me, and if Kati hadn't been right behind me she might have knocked me onto the people a step below us.

It's ages before she can pull herself together enough to let go of me. The debris is already swept away and the remaining cars are lining up to go again.

"Let's get you out of here," I suggest, and at her nod, Kati and I guide her through the crowd and to where I'm parked in the pit.

"Andrew and I will get any tools you don't have packed already," Kati says as we help Olivia into my truck. She's clinging to her cell phone, staring at the screen. I think Ian is texting her.

"He'll be okay," I say as I hop in the driver's seat. "Do you want to go to the hospital?"

"Ian says I should go home," she says, finally looking up at me, her big eyes so wide she looks like a cartoon puppy.

"Yes, but what do you want?" I ask wryly. My brother isn't a god. Does she know that?

"I want to do what Ian wants," she says and her hands are shaking, so yeah, she should probably be delivered to my mom ASAP.

I drive home in silence and the second I park in our driveway Mom is running out of the house and opening Olivia's door so she can scoop her into a hug and bring her into the house.

Good. I'm not great with upset people. I never know what to say. I sit with Dad on the porch instead, hunching over a cup of coffee he pours for me. It's understood that none of us will be sleeping tonight.

"How was your race?" he asks eventually.

It's a warm night and the crickets are chirping like mad.

"The qualifier went great. I would have run in the feature but some jerk sabotaged my car," I say, taking a long sip of coffee.

"Slashed a tire?"

"If only. I have spare tires. They poured BBs into my engine. It's ruined."

I clench my jaw and drink more coffee and Dad drinks his. He doesn't need to say anything. And I don't need to hear it. We both know this is a huge blow to me and that even though it is, it's not the thing to talk about tonight.

After about an hour, mom and Olivia come out to join us. Mom has her arm around Olivia's shoulder and Olivia is sniffling over a mug of tea.

A couple of Ian's friends show up with his truck and trailer and I help them park it and secure everything and thank them for bringing it home to us. I haven't even looked at my car yet and I feel sick at the idea of both of our cars wrecked. This is the worst, worst, worst-case scenario.

Kati and Andrew come by next with my tools and worried looks. I thank them, stash everything in my garage, get a second round of hugs, and then they're gone, too.

It's another two hours before we hear from Ian. Brent is a bit banged up but generally fine. They're going to release him home, but we'll have to watch him for a concussion. They're doing some tests before they release him because according to Brent, he blacked out in the middle of that turn and that caused the crash.

Dad leaves for the hospital to drive them both home when the tests are done and Mom convinces Olivia to take a shower and go to bed.

"He's going to be okay, honey," she says, sharing a look of commiseration with me before helping her into the house.

"He's all I have," Olivia says, crying again.

"Not anymore, honey."

And that leaves me on the porch alone, watching the darkness and tense as a serpentine belt. Will Brent be okay? Sometimes concussions sneak up on you.

And will Ian blame me for this? Because I wouldn't do what he asked and refuse to race? What if I can't patch up my relationship with my brother?

I hug my knees to my chest, twisting with emotion. I'm worried about Brent. I keep thinking of him coming to the pits and helping me out of my car. Had he wanted to say something to me? Maybe I should have been more friendly and less ... whatever I was. Maybe he was distracted and looking for help and I didn't give it to him. Guilt worms its way through my belly and I am miserable with it.

When the headlights wind their way down the driveway, the tension in me ratchets up higher. I stand, awkwardly — one of my feet is asleep — and I swallow down my nerves as the men move in my direction in a huddle. Dad is first, the other two cloaked by his shadow. He gives me a half-smile and opens the door for the others.

Brent is next. His eyes are glued to my dad's back and I feel a spike of awareness as he passes me. At the very last second, his eyes shoot up and meet mine, and his cheeks heat, and then he's through the door and my heart is racing like I just finished a race.

Ian is a step behind and he pauses to wrap me in a sudden, totally unexpected hug.

"I'm sorry," he whispers into my hair.

"It will be okay," I say, patting his back. I'm not sure what he's apologizing for. "He'll be okay."

He nods and swallows but then his face crumples. "It could have been you."

"It's okay," I say and give him another quick hug. "I think Olivia is waiting for you."

He nods, visibly pulling himself together, and then he's gone through the door. I follow them all reluctantly.

Whatever we thought our futures held a few hours ago, it's all washing away like sand on the shore and I hate the feeling of being out of control. I hate the feeling of sitting in the rubble of all my dreams. But at least my brother is my friend again.

# Chapter Thirteen

*BRENT*

I FEEL MISERABLE. I have a dislocated rib, and a headache like none other, and every time I stand up the room rocks and I feel nauseated, though the doctors said that was totally normal. They figure the adrenaline is leaving my system and my body misses it.

Guilt is my main problem. Guilt that I wrecked Ian's car. Guilt that I'm dependent on him and his family. Guilt that I've ruined everything.

Olivia hugs me before I head to bed. She doesn't say anything to help with the guilt, but I'm glad she's here and glad she's safe.

I don't sleep. Every hour from eleven to one, Diane dutifully checks in on me right on the hour, popping her head in the door. I wave to her every time and she smiles, but she looks worried. I left the nightstand light on. It's faint and I can't sleep anyway.

I don't know what I'm going to do or how I'm going to

replace Ian's car. I don't even know how damaged it is. I'm mostly fine. The roll cage kept me from the worst impacts and my helmet and neck guard kept the essentials safe, but I don't know what caused the blackout in the first place and the tests last night were inconclusive.

At 2:05 a different head looks in on me. One with long black hair. I don't so much as twitch, just meet her eye and clench my jaw. The only thing that makes this worse is that I did it all in front of her after that embarrassing display after her race. She saw me lose control. She saw me wreck the car her brother wouldn't let her drive. I bet she wouldn't have wrecked it. Guilt wrings my stomach like a bar mop.

At 3:07 she looks in again. She's not punctual like Diane. I wonder if she's sleeping in between check-ins. And if so, is she out in the garage again or in the house somewhere? This is supposed to be her room.

She's wearing loose grey shorts cut so high that they have to be pajama shorts and a spaghetti-strap tank top. She's magazine cute.

She looks me over, and again, I meet her gaze and refuse to say a thing.

I don't know what to do. But it will be better in the morning. I'll go over Ian's car and make a list of parts and start tearing it apart and that will make it better. Even with sore ribs, I can do that.

At 4:12 I stand up. No point pretending to sleep anymore. I'll just go out there and start. But when I stand, I feel suddenly ill, nausea washing over me, the room swimming. And then small hands grip my forearms and guide me down to sit on the edge of the bed. It's not helping.

"Lie back," she says quietly, helping to lift my feet onto the bed.

After a moment, the worst of it passes and I open my eyes.

"You were in a crash you big dummy," she says, shaking her head. Her tone is kind even if the words are not. "You can't be jumping out of bed. The doctors said to watch for a concussion."

"This isn't a concussion."

I don't like being nursed. Well, I liked it when Diane did it, but not when Tessa does it. I have the worst feeling I'll end up naked and helpless in her hands.

"You don't know that. What were you trying to do?"

"Race the feature, what do you think?" I say miserably, fighting another wave of nausea.

"No, I mean just now." There's amusement in her tone.

"I want to go look at the car."

"Oh." No amusement now. She understands.

I force myself up and sit for a minute until the room stops spinning.

"I'll help you, but we have to be quiet," Tessa says. She's sitting beside me on the edge of the bed. Her legs are small beside mine and so are her feet. They're kind of adorable. "If we aren't quiet, then someone will come and stop you."

"And you won't stop me?" I ask, my mouth turning into its usual smirk. But I'm really wondering what her answer will be. I still don't understand what motivates Tessa.

"I wouldn't dare," she says dryly. "I've already seen how rotten it is to be on your bad side. Which side is your injured rib on, by the way?"

So she knows what's wrong with me, then. I gesture to my right and she comes over and stands to my left.

"You can lean on my shoulder."

I grimace, but I put a hand on her shoulder, trying not to think about how delicate it is even under that firm muscle. She smells of cinnamon and apples still. Maybe she chews gum.

I'm never going to smell apple pie and not think of her.

We make our way slowly and silently down the stairs and out the door. The cold air hits me hard. I'm wearing casual soft pants and a T-shirt but the night air is cold enough that it tenses the muscles around my hurt ribs, making them ache painfully — painfully enough that I have to take a moment to catch my breath.

I glance down at Tessa and see she's shivering, too, but refusing to admit she's cold by doing something like wrapping her arms around herself. She's cute and perky looking even though it's the early hours of the morning but the cold makes her look vulnerable and I have a sudden urge to wrap an arm around her protectively.

My breath is quick and my face feels hot, and none of it is the injury.

Tessa makes me feel like a live wire just by watching me the way she's doing right now, like she's trying to take me apart with her mind to see how I work.

I look away, annoyed. I made her a promise, and I plan to keep it, hurt or not, soft and curving under my arm or not — I will not enter into any kind of a relationship with this live grenade of a woman. And she doesn't need any protection I can give her. I'm the broken one here.

Fortunately, all she does is lift an eyebrow at me before she guides me to where Brent's truck and trailer are parked. I see they're both fine. All his tools are neatly packed, too. It's the car ratchet strapped to the trailer that looks bad.

When we get to it, I try to jump up on the trailer, wobble, and have to sit on the edge of it instead.

To my surprise, Tessa hops out without so much as a glance at me and starts looking over the car.

"Do you want to know how bad it is all at once or as I go?" she calls down.

"As you go," I say miserably.

"Well, the body is terrible. This whole thing needs hammering out or straight-up replacing."

As if I can't see the body panels are completely crumpled.

"New sponsor stickers, too. These are illegible."

She crouches down and I get a long, clear view of smooth legs. I swallow and look back at the car. It's going to be hard to keep that promise if I keep letting my eyes find Tessa. She's absolutely beautiful — and I'm sure she knows it or she wouldn't have been flaunting herself to me this whole time. She's also ... right. Like she fits in the world in a way I never have. It's part of her charm. It's like finding a tree exactly how it should be on a rocky point along a lake, or seeing a creek turn just right in the way it flows. It's beautiful but it's also beautiful because it's right. It's meant to be that way.

She flips her hair over her shoulder when she turns to me, and when her eyes sparkle, I have to bite back a gasp. My head is swimming, but that's probably still the concussion.

"I think the frame is bent. Which is bad news. But this frame is pretty simple. We can probably cut out the bend and replace it or replace this whole side."

"Okay," I say. That's a huge job, but I'm distracted by the curve of her little shell of an ear and it's making it hard to think about the frame.

"The roll cage saved your life, obviously, and it's gnarly. Tough as nails. There's a little tweak right here," she taps the roll cage, "that might need attention. Otherwise, it seems good. Hood is a write-off. Tires and wheels look fine, though the steering and suspension will all have to be gone over because who even knows what's tweaked on it."

"Can you start it?" I ask hoarsely.

She meets my eye and then swallows. "We might wake someone up."

I just shrug.

"Sure," she says, worrying at her lower lip.

The engine cranks over without an issue and she lets it run for a few minutes before killing it. She climbs out of the car and comes down to sit beside me. "We should run diagnostics, but it's probably fine. It's ironic. My engine is trash but my car is fine. Ian's car is trash but his engine is probably fine." She pauses and then pulls a face. "Oops. I didn't mean to say 'trash.'"

I snort. "You aren't wrong. We're looking at weeks of work to fix this."

"Mmm," she says like she doesn't want to outright agree even though it's obvious.

"Did you say there's something wrong with your car?" I must have heard that wrong. It was driving great last night. *She* was driving great. A total natural.

Wow but I'm attracted to this woman.

"Someone dumped BBs in the motor."

"What's a BB?"

"You know, like a pellet? For a gun? Like not a real bang bang gun but a target-shooting toy-ish gun? They're small and round like a bearing."

"Why the hell would they do that?" I ask, meeting her gaze and I see all kinds of anger and devastation suppressed under the tight smile she offers. It pierces right to my heart and something rough forms in my throat. I want to hug her. I don't know if I should.

"Some people don't like being beaten by a girl."

Anger rises up in my chest and I'm growling before I realize it.

And she's so miserable looking that I move without thinking. I reach for her and she lets me draw her in and hold her against me.

I keep my hands light, gentle, so she won't think I'm trying to do anything I'm not. I keep my hands closed in fists so they won't go exploring off into Tessa territory like pith-helmet-wearing British colonists. She feels so good even in this light embrace that I close my eyes for a moment and breathe in her cinnamon apple scent.

"Fuck," I whisper into her hair, trying and failing to express that I understand what she's saying in a way most people wouldn't — that I know how gutted she must be. "I'm so sorry."

"That's pretty much the size of it."

Her voice is a little muffled in my chest. I let go of her and immediately feel the loss. The sad smile on her face feels like a kick to the gut.

The night breeze blows over us. I can't even see the edge of dawn yet.

"Do you want some coffee?" she asks me suddenly, wrapping her arms around herself like she can hold her little body together with itself.

"Don't you need to get back to your cot in the garage?" I ask, lifting an eyebrow and she laughs. She likes being teased. And dammit, I like teasing her.

But I'm feeling light-headed — worse than before even — as if all my energy is slowly dripping out around my feet. I'm not sure I have access right now to my best comebacks.

"I scored the couch for while I'm making sure you don't do whatever people with bad concussions do."

"And what is that?" I ask as I stand, but the world rocks again and she has to catch my arm and help me sit. I clench my fists and set my jaw. I don't like playing patient to her nurse. It's not my kind of role.

"I'm starting to worry that it's this."

I flick a look at her, expecting emasculating pity, but all I see is humor.

She bites her lip around a smile. She looks so cute when she does that. And somehow it takes the edge off the insult that I need her help to do simple things like stand.

I like her. I really like her. Like, really, really like her. If I ordered a custom girl from a girl builder, I'd order this one.

Wow. Was that really a thought I had?

I don't think my brain is working correctly.

"I don't think so either," she says, laughing as she helps me stand again and lets me lean on her while she guides me to the house. I must have said that last thing out loud.

"You said that out loud, too." Now she's laughing, snorting as she tries to hold it back. She needs to be quiet.

"Shhh!" I say, raising a finger to my lips and blowing. I get distracted by how my breath makes little goosebumps on her skin. I do it again.

I have this sudden desire to see if I can do that everywhere on her whole body. Why didn't I try that in the bathroom instead of complaining? Missed opportunity.

Wow, do I feel foggy.

I hardly even realize she's sat me down in the kitchen until I hear her making the coffee. Her parents have this great padded window seat. I put my feet up on it and lean my head back against the window so that I can think more clearly.

"The problem is," I say muzzily. "We have two halves of a car, but not a full car. We could mash them together to make one, but then what? You wouldn't have a car."

"That's some good math there, Brent."

I like how she says my name, like it means something more to her than it does to other people. I smile sleepily.

"I won't have a car now, anyway," she says after a moment. I hear her pouring the coffee. "What do you take in it?"

"Two sugar. I like it sweet," I say, eyes still closed. "It's a helluva thing you getting sabotaged. You were amazing out there. A natural. Better than Ian."

"You don't have to say those things." She sets the mug on the counter. This whole kitchen smells like apple pie and love. I could live here on this kitchen bench. I think I will. I wonder what my address will be and if they'll charge me rent.

"I'm not saying them," I say before I pause and realize that makes no sense. "I'm meaning them."

"Okay, brainiac," she says, laughing. "If you say so. Keep talking. I like you high on whatever they gave you. You're so much nicer to me than when you're sober."

I am sober, though, aren't I? They didn't give me any drugs at all.

"I admire you," I say thickly. Wow, that draft through the window feels good. "You're amazing. That car you built. That body."

"It's just sheet metal."

"No," I pause and open my eyes enough to gesture up and down her. She's sitting at the kitchen table, feet up on one of the other chairs. God have mercy but she looks good. "That one. That one there."

She laughs, covering her mouth to keep it quiet. "Keep going. I love this."

I think I might be making a fool of myself but when I try to think of why my forehead scrunches uselessly and more words pour out.

"Those kisses. Wow. Do you practice?"

"Yes, every night on my pillow. You wouldn't believe the hours I've logged."

"Lucky pillow," I say despondently, reaching out and taking my coffee so I can nurse it between leaning my head back on the cold glass of the window and little hot sips. Just like dealing with her. A hot sip and then you need to cool your head for a bit. "I used to dream I'd meet a girl like you."

"And then you completely flubbed it," she reminds me.

I open my eyes to meet hers. Wow. They're so big. And hazel. And twinkly. I love them.

"Can we have a do-over?" I sip my coffee loudly. Do I always sip this loudly?

"Sure, Concussion King. Whatever you say," she says, sipping her coffee a lot quieter than me.

"Good. I say you come over here and kiss me again."

"I thought you said no more kisses." There's no laughter in her voice this time. I think there's tension but whatever is going on in my brain can't interpret it. I give up and make kissy lips instead.

I hear her sigh and then hear the floor creak and then her hand is on my knee and I feel sudden butterflies in my stomach and then her lips are on mine.

They're hot and soft and my mind might be drifting right now, but something very hard and certain runs through me straight to my abdomen. I shift, reaching to catch the sides of her tank top in my fingers and draw her closer, and then sliding my hands around her neat little waist to gather her in while my mouth slowly, gently opens hers, tasting, drinking her in. I lower her onto my lap, half smirking at how the flare of her hips kicks out under my palms into a perfectly curved pair of thighs. She's amazing.

I'm lost in velvet kisses. They make my head spin. Or maybe it was already spinning. I don't remember or really give a care. I'm too deep into sinking pleasure, like falling into a bed of cushions. Like a shower with the exact perfect temperature of water.

I'm not sure I'm breathing. I'm not sure I care. I'm lost in the rhythm of her lips on mine. The soft slide and clasp. Lost to the feel of her tongue leading the dance and my slow reactions following. I kiss, and kiss, and kiss, and I think I'll just go ahead and do this forever.

Everything feels good. My lips, my hands, my chest where her hands are planted, right down to the warmth gathering low in my body and thrumming with expectation. All of me agrees with one thing. This is good and I want to keep going.

And then a throat clears and Tessa is off my lap, leaving me gasping and suddenly feeling very empty. I open my eyes and she's gone.

And the only one in the room is her brother looking down at me.

"Fuck," I say.

"I'll say."

# Chapter Fourteen

*TESSA*

I HAVE my engine pulled and fully disassembled by noon. Look, I'm not hiding.

Okay, I'm hiding. My brother caught me kissing his best friend. What did you think I was going to do?

I know it's Ian in the doorway before he speaks. He just stands there a long time like he's waiting for me to look up. Eventually, he gives in and speaks first. Tessa one, Ian nothing.

"So, it's not a concussion, but the doctors don't know what was making him so ill this morning. They think it might pass. But it also might not and until it does, he has to stay sitting or lying down pretty much all the time."

This is not what I expected. I look up.

"What?"

"That's why Brent was acting so funny. He told me he pulled you into his lap and kissed you. Is that not how it happened?"

"To the letter," I say gravely. Let Brent take the fall for that.

It's his turn, and he has an excuse much better than my "I just really wanted to, okay?" excuse.

"I hope you don't hold it against him," Ian says, frowning, and I turn back to the engine so he won't see me flush. He sounds stressed.

"Of course not."

"It's hard enough on his ego to have to sit around. He's twenty-five, not eighty." He pauses. "Is your engine actually screwed up?"

"The block is trashed. I don't even have enough here to rebuild it." My tone is grim — as it should be.

He's quiet for so long that I look up and see him wincing.

"Okay, so, don't get mad," he says.

"Okaaaay." I am wary.

"Olivia and I still have to go to Utah. I called Big Daddy Boom this morning and hashed the whole thing out with him. He needs me sooner than we expected."

"That's great, Ian," I say tonelessly.

"I gave him your race footage. It was just sitting there with your laptop."

I stare at him. I feel like this should mean something other than anger that he took my work without permission, but I don't know what.

"I gave him mine and Brent's too," he says and now it all comes out in a rush. "And he thought you did really well in your race, and I told him that between this car and mine, we definitely could still pull them together into one car in time to get Brent on the road."

I feel my mouth fall open but I shut it tightly and clench my jaw.

"Look, I'm sorry," Ian says and it's only the misery in his voice that is keeping me from shouting.

Wow, so I was really promising, hey? So now he's going to take what little I have left.

"I'm sorry that I didn't let you drive my car. I'm sorry that I asked you not to race. I'm sorry that I gave the show to my friend instead of you."

I could rub his wrong decision in his face, but instead, I just nod. I know what's coming next. He needs my car. For Brent.

"I need a favor from you," he says, wincing.

Of course he does. I want to be mad. I want to rage at the unfairness of life but what the hell is the point? Without an engine, I'm screwed anyway.

"You can have the car. Put your engine into it," I say miserably. "I'll even help you."

He wanders over to the car and leans on his forearms on the roof and turns to look at me. "Thanks."

I nod and keep working, sorting parts. I feel like I have bees under my skin stinging me. I want to get out of here and shake them off. I want to let tears of disappointment fall. I don't so much as flinch. I'm Tessa Harstone. If I can't take a hit and stand up again and keep going ... well, I won't be me if I do that.

"I talked to BOOM and they still want to do the show."

I'm careful in my response.

"Brent will like that."

He says nothing for so long that I look up. "What?"

"You saw Brent. He can't go on his own. He needs help." I wait while he squirms until, eventually, he says. "I pitched you to BOOM. That's why I took your footage." He holds up a hand. "Not as a replacement, so don't get too excited. As a team. You'd help Brent. You'd be the pit crew. You'd film and do narration. The whole thing you already do." He pauses and kicks at an imaginary rock on the floor. I know it's imaginary. I keep this floor clean. "And if he's not well enough, then you'll drive."

I swallow. Wow. I'm both flattered and insulted all at once.

"It's a big ask," he says.

It is, but not in the way he means. I'll get everything I ever wanted. At Brent's expense.

Ian rubs his face with his hands again. He's not going to need to shave if he keeps doing that.

"I know it's a lot to ask for since I should have asked you in the first place and now I'm asking you to do the scut work for Brent's show. But I don't really have anyone else to ask, Tessa. Who would drop their entire life in just three days to hit the road with a trailer and a man who just got in a wreck?"

"Lots of people would," I say breezily, bagging bolts as I talk.

"No, they wouldn't. But that's why I'm asking. Will you?"

And when I look up he has puppy-dog Ian eyes and there's no way I can say no.

"Yes," I say. "But you're helping me swap out the engine and the drive train on your car."

"Of course," he says with a grin. "Keep your phone charged. I told BOOM they could call you anytime."

He winks. Jerk.

But it's hard to be mad. In fact, it's hard not to be pitifully grateful. When he comes over to give me a hug, I let him. But my mind is racing because in just a few days I'm going to get the opportunity of a lifetime and I cannot afford to screw this up.

No more sleepy drugged kisses. No more accidental naked bathroom meetings.

It's business now.

*Chapter Fifteen*

*BRENT*

THE NEXT FEW days go by in a miserable blur. Ian and Tessa get to work on Frankensteining one car out of two — it's going to run in her class, Midwest Modifieds, and carry stickers for all ten of our combined sponsors. I've gotten to look at it twice and both times ended up with me collapsing and being hustled back to bed.

I'm furious and frustrated in equal measures. Any level of activity leaves me nauseated and loopy. I've gone to the hospital twice, had tests done three times, and been told firmly that this is now something to take up with my own doctor. I'm going to have to live with it forever. It's like they think I'm making it up.

I've caught little bursts of conversation between the others here. They all believe me, but they're divided on what to do about it. Olivia and Diane want me to remain here with the Harstones, where Diane can mother and nurse me — possibly forever. Steve seems to think that isn't going to happen but doesn't give an opinion on what *will* happen. Ian believes I'll be fine with a few days' rest as long as my car and trailer are ready for me, and who even knows what Tessa believes.

She's been so caught up in her car project that I've only seen her at meals, and half the time she doesn't show up for them or she grabs hot food with her bare hands and then runs back out the door. She doesn't so much as look at me when we are in the same room and every time she ignores me, I feel like a splinter of something is caught in my throat.

Yesterday, a gift arrived from BOOM Enterprises. Well, I say gift but it's more of a loan. I haven't gone to look at it because the thought of it makes me feel ill. I'm useless, and guilty from being useless, and cranky at being guilty, and then guilty because I'm cranky, and then ... well, it's a never-ending cycle and I know it's messed me up. I know it's taken me from a confident, happy person who was maybe just a little tightly wound, to this uncertain disaster. And I hate it.

And I can't do anything about it.

"You just have to learn to accept that you have limitations right now," Diane says to me as I sit on the couch, exhausted from showering.

"It could be forever," I say. It's the closest I've come to saying it out loud, but everyone else is outside admiring how Ian and Tessa have set up the BOOM gift and I need to confess this fear to someone.

She puts down the dishes she's drying in the kitchen and comes to sit with me.

"Maybe," she says. "Or maybe not. But if you sit around despairing, then it will only be worse." She takes one of my hands and pats it. "You don't need to panic. You can have a home here with me and Steve if you don't get better. But I think you shouldn't think like that. I think you should go out there and give it your best with the capacity you have right now." Her jaw firms and for the first time, I see her daughter in her face.

"Prove you can still live your life. Don't give up before it's even over."

And that lights enough of a fire in me that I get up and make my way out to where everyone is. I have to do it slowly. But I do it.

BOOM has sent the most high-end blaze orange car hauler with living quarters that I've ever seen. It's forty feet long, for starters. It arrived by independent courier last night. I have to swallow down nerves as I make my way toward it for the first time. The BOOM logo is emblazoned across the side of the trailer and right now the back ramp is open and I can look right up into the pristine garage portion of the trailer where Tessa has already loaded up her car.

Our car?

Whatever it is now.

It doesn't feel like mine when I haven't turned a single nut tight on the whole project, but it fits nicely in the garage space and the built-in cabinetry has been supplemented by additional well-worn tools that I'm sure Tessa and Ian picked out from her shop. I swallow, make my way inside, and lean against the workbench for a moment. I need a second — both because I'm light-headed and because this ... it feels amazing and yet it feels like it's not for me at the same time.

Everyone else must be in the living quarters portion of the trailer. That's fine. I'll just chill here for a moment.

I hear her voice coming toward me and I don't mean to eavesdrop. I just assume she'll see me standing here, but she's talking intently on the phone and the volume coming through the other side is easy to hear — Big Daddy Boom is always easy to hear.

"Honestly, Tessa, we're really excited for this pivot, and sending you the trailer is our way of telling you that," he's saying. "False Start will only be a more accurate title for this show now, and we think that you and Brent Bolt will make a fabulous team. We prefer teams in general as they make better tv with all the back and forth and byplay. You've seen Nicola and Ada's show, right?"

"Absolutely, I love it!" Tessa says enthusiastically. She moves further into the trailer and leans against the car, her back to me. She must not see me. I should probably move, but my head is spinning.

Besides, I like the view. With no one watching, not even her, I can run my eyes up and down her, letting them catch on her rounded ass and gently dip down her shoulder and trace the outside of her arm. Who would have thought elbows could look so good? They do when they're part of the rest of this package.

"For this miniseries, we want the raw feel, so you'll do your own camera work and narration but your brother will edit the clips on this end. If it takes off and becomes a full series, then we'll hire you and Brent full-time for the show and send you a cameraperson to film it."

"Wow. I can't thank you enough."

"You don't need to! We love what we're seeing with you. You're going to be massively inspiring to our audience. They love underdog stories and with you just starting out in a car you built yourself, being advised by Brent who has had a massive medical setback — this is pure gold for us."

My heart kicks up a notch. People are going to hear about my medical issues. I don't know what to think about that. I don't like it ... but do I have any other option other than tanking my chances at being a part of this? I doubt it.

"Just don't get married," Boom jokes. "Don't fall in love with each other and become a couple."

Tessa laughs, "Of course not."

My mouth feels dry. I already promised her the same thing but it seems more ... certain ... when she promises it to someone else. I don't know why that bothers me so much.

I mean, the groggy kissing was amazing. It made me want so

much more. But I was in no condition to be starting anything with someone and I'd had to lie to Ian and pretend it was all a mistake to keep the pair of us from scrutiny. That's not exactly an adult way to start a relationship. Not that that is what this is. Obviously.

"You say that now," Boom says wryly through the speakerphone. "But you have no idea how common that is around here. Okay, film the race this weekend in Thunder Bay and then we'll get this show rolling. I have to call Brent next. You're my star now, Tessa. Don't hesitate to reach out. I've got your back."

Tessa signs off and my phone is already ringing. She spins and looks at me, wide-eyed. I don't bother trying to act apologetic or whatever. Look, this is my best right now. Leaning on a workbench barely managing to answer a phone is my best. It sucks, but it is what it is.

"Brent," I say when I pick up but I don't take my eyes off of Tessa, and she must think that's funny because she smirks, wiggles her hips like she thinks I'm checking her out and she's teasing me. I glower at her and she thinks that's funny, too. She's still laughing when she leaves.

My pulse, on the other hand, is in my throat and it makes me more light-headed. I swear she's going to be the death of me. That girl spins me up with a single look. I watch her walking away through the door of the trailer garage as if I didn't already get enough of watching while she was here. Her pretty ass and thighs curve just perfectly and I feel my tongue slip out and circle my lips as I watch. I don't even realize she's playing me until she looks over her shoulder and winks.

Dammit. The phone has been talking and I've heard none of it.

I let out a strangled, "Yeah."

"Okay," Boom's voice is on the line. "So I've set the whole thing up. Ian will drive you down to Minneapolis tomorrow and my buddy will do the MRI, run any other tests he can, and sort you out. We're gonna get you driving again, son, as soon as possible. And if it takes more than a weekend, Tessa has agreed to support you, even if she has to keep you in bed most of the time."

My cheeks flame at that and I swallow. I know what he means. But I'm imagining ways she could keep me in bed and all of them are good.

"Is it a plan?" he asks me.

"Yes!" I say too quickly. "Thank you so much. I'm enormously grateful."

And I am. Medical help when no one else believes me? This is huge.

"It's not a problem. I see so much potential here. It's going to be amazing. And don't forget to go check out the site. We've got your prep video and Tessa's spliced together and up in the subscriber-only section with footage of your crash and narration. It's the best possible beginning to this. It's going to grab subscribers right by the throat. We'll be popping up teasers of it on social media all week, so don't freak out if your numbers skyrocket. Just go with Ian, get fixed up, and then help me make this the best new show on BOOM Motorsports."

"I will," I agree. Because even if the idea of exploiting my crash and illness makes me sick, this is still the best opportunity I've ever had and it's hard to believe that he's still offering it to me. It's even harder to believe that BOOM is paying for me to see a specialist — a friend who let us hop his long line to see me tomorrow. I owe him forever for that.

It's all so much that I can hardly take it. I wander through the man door into the human compartment of the trailer and stop dead. And not just because my sister is kissing Ian with one of her feet popped up in the air like this is a romcom on tv, but because it's flipping palatial in this trailer. The kitchenette is sleek and clean and through the frosted glass doors on the cabinets, I can see Tessa has already stocked it. There's a big leather couch with a pair of throw pillows on it that I'm pretty sure she added because they are not BOOM orange, a small but very nice bathroom, and a bed — also covered in throw pillows. There's only one bed, and I'm pretty sure Tessa doesn't plan to share it with me, which means my bed is the plush couch.

"Brent!" Olivia says happily while I'm still looking at the couch. "You look so much better!"

I'm not, but I'm fine with her thinking so. I nod and agree to everything she says and everything Ian wants me to do before tomorrow, and before I know it, I'm back in bed, resting up for the long drive the next morning. It's hard to sleep. Harder still when I think about how Tessa will be racing that night without me here to watch. She's going to drive the car. She could wreck it before any of this ever begins, which worries me.

I know that's pretty hypocritical since I wrecked it first, but I still can't sleep until I get up and write a letter to leave for her. I try three times before I get it right, and even then I almost don't leave it for her at all, and almost text her and tell her not to open it when Ian and I set out at four in the morning. It's an eight-hour drive to Minneapolis and my appointment is at noon.

I don't text her, though, and the tension of wondering what she thinks of it eats at me all through the appointment, all through the scans, all through the part where Boom's specialist friend tells me I'm a lucky bastard to have been sent to him because apparently I have a spinal fluid leak and he's an expert in them and willing to do something called a blood patch tomorrow morning before I have to leave.

"You'll have to take it easy for six to eight weeks afterward," he says calmly.

"Six to eight weeks?" I repeat, appalled.

He snorts. I think it's a laugh but not a ha-ha funny kind of one.

"You think that's bad? Sometimes it takes years for people to get diagnosed, never mind treated. Years of having to lie down constantly, of bringing a walker with you so you can sit down when you're out and about and you get lightheaded. Years of never knowing if you'll be okay again. You only have to fuss for eight weeks. You should be thankful."

I am thankful. But I'm also very worried when he gives me a long list of restrictions and emails a second set of them to Boom. I get a text immediately afterward from BOOM Motorsports.

> Have tasked Tessa with making sure you follow these. So glad to see an end in sight! BOOM.

Great. She's going to be my warden now as well as my nurse, rival, and coworker. Boom might have warned her not to marry me, but I have a feeling she is going to feel an awful lot like a wife for the next while. I just hope that when this is over we can still be friends. I'm starting to worry that even that might not be possible.

"Cheer up," Ian says as he drives me to the hotel. "Just a few hiccups and then all our dreams will come true, right brother?"

"Right," I say, but my mind isn't on my dreams. My mind is on the girl racing tonight. I feel very tense for a guy who is an eight-hour drive away. And I know it isn't just about keeping the car safe.

No matter how hard I try to be reasonable, I keep seeing that wink she sent me over her shoulder and worrying that I'll never see it again.

# Chapter Sixteen

*TESSA*

I STARE at the crumpled letter in my hands. It's on yellow legal paper which tells me he swiped the pad from beside the phone where my dad likes to keep it to scribble down part numbers. Yeah. Dad still has a landline.

Of all the things I expected from Brent, it was not a letter. The second I saw it wedged under the shop door I'd been uncertain about what to do with it. I mean obviously, I should read it, but we don't really live in a time of letters except as legal notices. Is this something like that? Some kind of legal notice of "Tessa Harstone, I solemnly swear we won't kiss again and I make this statement formally and have had it notarized because last time a verbal agreement was not honored."

Was that what this was?

My name was written in surprisingly neat, round handwriting. With Brent's precision, I'd expected block letters like a drafting student. Or possibly something highly spiky and masculine. Instead, his are loops and whorls in a round, confident hand.

I had meant to read it immediately, but moments after I grabbed it off the floor, there had been a knock on the door and my mom had come in, so I'd jammed it into my boot and forgotten all about it. Until now when I'm dressing for tonight's race and I go to tug my boot on and there it is.

With a sigh, I unfold the letter and move so the window is behind me and the light illuminates what's written.

Tessa,

I feel like I've dropped the ball with you in a lot of ways. I should say sorry, but I'm not sure which parts I'm sorry for. Actually, I'm not sure I'm sorry for a lot of it, even if I should be. But if we're going to do this thing, then I think we should hash out what it looks like between the two of us rather than letting BOOM and Ian negotiate for us.

Coffee?

When I get back?

This time when I'm not loopy from a brain injury and don't try to kiss you.

You can tell me what you want. And I'll try to honor it.

Note, I said "try."

Brent

It's very him. Slightly charming. Mostly infuriating. No gratitude for what I've done for him so far or what I've agreed to do for him in the future. Uh-huh.

So if it's so infuriating why is it on my mind the whole way to the racetrack?

Why do I keep hearing "I dropped the ball with you in a lot of ways" while the local racers all come and look at the new fancy trailer BOOM has loaned us and stare at it while they try to avoid getting in the background of the video I'm filming?

Why do I think about how he's probably not sorry for kissing me or walking in on me naked or unbuckling me in a really intimate way as I unload the car and show her off to everyone?

Why is it his face I'm seeing while I hug Kati and Andrew and talk shop with them about the trip ahead?

"Four different states?" Kati's eyes practically have stars in them. "You'll text me from every one right? I want selfies in front of landmarks. I want selfies in front of your growling companion. I want selfies in front of the orange trailer. I want all the selfies!"

I give her a huge orange foam hand with "BOOM" written on it. The trailer was stuffed full of BOOM merch and Big Daddy Boom told me to use as much as I liked. I'm wearing a BOOM tank under my race suit tonight and a guy who works for him named Tanner sent me a creepy email asking for my measurements that I didn't much care for until it turned out he was ordering me a custom orange BOOM racing suit.

There were even coozies stuffed in the drinks fridge in the trailer (yeah, it has a drinks fridge! That's high-class right there) and branded condoms in the bedside drawer — which, yuck, I'm blaming Tanner for those. And I'm not going to admit where my mind went when I saw them either. Not even if you bring in one of those bright FBI lights and a grim man in shades who thinks giving someone a soda is how you make friends and influence people.

I'm in the car before I know it and this time the nerves are gone and I'm all anticipation. I can't wait. This is what I'm made for. I practically feel like I *am* my car when she rumbles to life under me and joins the others in line to get onto the track. She was great before, but I don't have so much ego that I can't admit she's better now with Ian's engine. His has a beefier cam and it sounds really lopey on the idle. I love it.

I feel like I'm flying when I hit the track. My heart is swollen with happiness, my eyes darting as I try to look for everything at once, my breath catching and uncatching with a combination of excitement and concentration, and through the whole thing, in the background, my mind keeps repeating one thing from the letter.

*You can tell me what you want. And I'll try to honor it.*

What if what I want isn't what he expects? What if it's all the sexy things I've been thinking of since I first read those words. But it can't be, right? It would be crazy stupid to start anything with him — especially given he's the most prickly hot-and-cold man I've ever met. Especially when we have to work together and BOOM made me promise not to start something.

And exactly none of that makes a difference when I win my qualifying race with my mind fixed on what he looked like naked in that bathroom and how much fun it might have been to step up to him then and kiss him the way he kissed me when he first met me.

It's a good thing that I can't leave my car for even a second between races — no BBs this time, you bastards — because I'm useless for anything else. I'm staring off into the mid-distance when Kati brings me a poutine, and Andrew has to remind me twice to check my tire pressure before it sinks in. I'm a mess. A dreamy, dopey mess.

And that's over an invitation to coffee. So what does that tell you? It tells me that anything more than that could be a deadly mistake.

Though maybe not for my racing game because even if I drift into the second race with my eyes still full of memories of tanned skin and light brown hair across a particular chest and trailing down to some very interesting areas below, I still knock the race out of the park. I come in second. And I'm qualified now to run the next race out on the road.

We'll be grabbing our dreams with both fists all because of me.

But I'm still thinking about things that have nothing to do with racing at all.

## Chapter Seventeen

*BRENT*

WE HAVE coffee the morning after I get back home. Or at least I think it's morning. She sneaks into my room and yanks the covers off my torso to wake me up. I sleep in my boxer briefs, so it's actually kind of scandalous. I mean, not for us. Not compared to everything else we've been doing. But for normal humans, it would be.

I just realized there's an *us*.

"I'm supposed to rest," I mutter. I'm not a quick waker like some people are. My brain likes the happy lands of sleep and gets very cranky and very slow when it's forced awake early — like a diesel truck trying to crank on the coldest winter morning.

"You're supposed to have coffee with me." Her voice is a whisper and I can't tell what emotion is behind it, but she must really want this coffee if she's waking me up at ... I glance at the bedside clock — her bedside clock, yes — and wow, it's five-thirty. They have one of those in the morning, too. How precious.

"You know, you can drink coffee on your own first and we

can have more later. You do know that, right?" I ask, my voice muzzy and burred with sleep and sleepy sadness. "You don't actually have to wake me up for the very first cup."

The problem for me is that the bed is very warm and the room is chilly and I don't actually want to get out of bed. And my mind is still half-dreaming and it's suggesting that I could just pull her in here with me and wrap all these blankets around both of us to form a nice little nest and we'd be twice as warm and all that softness of her sweet flesh would be twice as comfortable, and then I could just go back to sleep curled all around her.

She leans in close to whisper her response — doubtlessly in an effort to keep from waking the rest of the house.

"Brent," she whispers. Her hand touches my shoulder so tentatively, like she's scared I might turn and bite it. I like the feeling of her touching me.

The more alert parts of my brain are lining up to remind me that we are definitely not supposed to be promoting any kind of touching or bed games with the girl who owns that warm hand, but sleepy me is as powerful as a mountain and is shutting down all logical argument. Still, practical-Brent might have won, but at that moment, Tessa slips, probably on the stack of car magazines beside the bed. Hers, not mine, because this is her bed, in her room, and if you think that doesn't turn me on every single time I lie down and smell her in the sheets, then I don't know if you're paying attention to this story.

Her slip makes her stumble and she tries to catch herself on the bedside table but instead ends up tumbling right onto the mattress beside me and half on top of me.

"Oof."

The breath is knocked from my lungs and my arms come up reflexively and then wrap around her without realizing it before I've caught my breath again. Not quite the cuddle I'd been imagining, but sure, fine, this can work.

By the time I can breathe, she's pushing up with hands on either side of me. By luck, or fate, or what-have-you, she has landed so that her body is flush against mine from where her chest meets my belly to where her belly meets my hips. Only our legs remain untangled. Unbidden, ideas flash through my sleepy mind twice as fast as lightning until the careful, wary parts give up trying to chase them down and stop them. Fine, yes, I want her right exactly in this position in my bed. There's no point in denying it.

"Sorry!" She whispers, but then she realizes my hands are still wrapped around her, and her eyes go really big in the faint bedroom light. "What are you doing?"

"It's really comfortable in this bed," I whisper back, teasing in my sleepiness and sudden desire. "You should try it sometime."

"I know. It's my bed."

"I think I've improved it. It's better than it used to be. Come try it."

"You've improved it?"

Now I can hear she's trying not to laugh. I think my favorite thing about her is how easy it is to make her laugh. Okay, maybe not my favorite. My favorite thing about her is currently struggling to push upward and clad in very tight hugging jeans that show its round outline perfectly. I have an urge to slap it gently that I desperately overrule.

"I improve everything I touch," I whisper confidentially.

"You're touching me right now." Her tone is dry. "I see no improvements."

"Not the way I want to."

It slips out before I can stop it, and it's tinged with all the dreaming lust that I'm feeling. That sobers me quickly. This would be a terrible idea on every level, not the least of which being that we are in her parents' house with them sleeping just below us.

"Shit. I didn't mean it like that."

"Disappointing," she says and her tone is so dry it could soak up more rainwater than a tree with a carefully cultivated root system.

"I just meant it was an accident."

There's a pause where we both realize that I still have my hands on her, only they've slipped and fallen down to cup her pretty ass.

"If you're coming to get coffee with me, you should know there's a dress code," she whispers, her eyes very serious and narrowed as she looks down at my black boxer briefs and the sleepy half-arousal she's given me.

"You mean I can't go in my underwear? Wow. What kind of hoity-toity place are you taking me to?"

"It's called Grandma's Truck Stop."

She slips out of my light grasp without any resistance from me. I miss her the second she's gone. And not just because she was pleasantly warm. In some other reality, she isn't Ian's sister and after that first meeting we've spent every night in bed all curled up around each other like fiddleheads. I feel homesick for that other reality.

"On second thought," I manage, "I'll stay in bed until a classier dame comes for me."

She laughs. "See? I told you I'm a dame. A lady knight with my racing charger bent on winning the jousts."

She steps back and crosses her arms and I realize she means to stay there while I dress.

Well.

This is interesting.

It would be even more interesting if it wasn't so damn hard to get out of bed these days. I have the patch, but it's going to be weeks of recovery. And since I only got it yesterday, I'm supposed to be taking it easy. I'm supposed to be keeping out of situations that might get my blood pressure too high.

Ha.

"Jousts, is it?" I grumble. "I was tilted right off my horse. Throw me my jeans, would you? They're on the chair behind you."

"You mean *my* chair?" she asks innocently. "In my room? Where you've been sleeping and waiting for me like a surprise gift?"

She's teasing, but it's almost too much. I can be her gift if that's what she wants. She can unwrap me and play with me until she gets bored.

I just hold my hand out and wait. Eventually, with a gust of something that might be a sigh or a laugh, she puts the waistband of my jeans into it. I dress slowly, watching her to show her she can't make me uncomfortable with all that staring. Unfortunately, she doesn't seem uncomfortable either. If anything, she seems to be enjoying the show.

She bites her lip, her eyes tracing my every movement and when her gaze meets mine her eyebrows lift in a question.

I growl wordlessly.

Suddenly, this game is too much for me. I grab a T-shirt and hoodie from my bag and pull them on hurriedly. Could I use a shower and teeth brushing? Yes. But I'm also not going to do any of that with her watching me like a lion wondering when it might feel like making a kill.

Will she be watching me the whole time we're on the road together?

I shiver.

She might be. I have to swallow down the thought. It makes my lower abdomen clench with anticipation.

When I run a hand nervously through my hair before I put on my hat, she leans in to say, "You don't have to look pretty. It's just coffee, not a hot date."

"You'd think so," I whisper as I follow her out of the room, "but seeing as I've already had women flinging themselves into my bed and it's not even six in the morning, anything could happen. Best be prepared."

"Maybe you'll go home with Grandma," she whispers archly as we slip out the front door. I grab my jacket and the plastic bag I have shoved in the arm of it is still there. Good.

"Maybe. Is she hot?" I ask as we sneak down the driveway to where she has her 4Runner parked.

"Is that your only criteria?" She starts her vehicle up and pulls out of the driveway. "Seems a bit basic. I expected more from you, to be honest."

"Look, can we just do this?" I don't mean to be irritable, but it's cold out here and the warm cuddles in the soft bed didn't happen and the combination has left me feeling cheated.

She snorts, but there is no more chatter as we make our way to a truck-stop that is, indeed, called Grandma's and order coffee. We take a lonely booth that looks out over the filling pumps.

"So, you wanted to talk?" She says coyly when we're both served weak truck stop coffee with stingy little cylinders of cream and packets of sugar. I dump four sugar packets in mine and sip like a man taking his medicine.

I clear my throat, trying to organize my thoughts as she sips her coffee and watches me with those dancing, considering eyes. It's hard to think when she looks at me like that and I don't like it. Okay, that's a lie. I'm lying to myself. I do like it. I want those eyes narrowed at me all the time. Weighing. Judging. I want to surprise them and make them laugh.

I asked for this meeting, and yet I have no idea what to say. All my carefully thought-through speeches are gone.

"Look," I say uncertainly, as if demanding that *she* look will somehow help *me* see. "I didn't realize."

"That the coffee is so terrible? I knew and I still came here. What does that say about me?"

I start to smile before I shake my head. She's interrupting my apology.

"I didn't realize that everything Ian was offering me should have been for you."

She looks away sharply and for just a flicker of a moment, I think I see hurt in her eyes. She's good at disguising it.

"I'm trying to apologize. I stole your spot. I took what should have been for you."

She tosses her head like it doesn't matter. "I didn't earn those things. I have exactly what I earned. Half a car and a promising vlog channel. A very ... well, I won't say comfortable, so a very much *real* cot in the detached shop at my parent's house."

This time I do laugh. I love the fire in her eyes. I love the way she looks like she might burst from her chair and go charging off to earn even more things all for herself.

My laugh makes her dissolve into a head-shaking smile, too. She's never far from laughter even when she's angry.

"I don't see why *you're* apologizing." She rolls her eyes at me like she's indulging me. "It's my brother who offered you the car. It's BOOM who offered you the opportunity. And it's both of them who have shackled you with me now as an unwanted addition to your life."

"Shackled?" I ask, looking down at her wrists. She shivers so faintly that I think anyone who wasn't watching her every move the way I am would never see it. And when her teeth catch her lower lip, I shiver, too. "I'd say it's safe to say we're both shackled. And now we have to manage this three-legged race they've given us or lose both of our chances."

She nods, her face turning serious.

"Do you want any of this?" I ask her gently. "Do you want this opportunity when it comes ... with me?"

I'm not an insecure man. But I need to know this. I won't force her and I never would.

"Yes." She says it so quickly that I laugh. She rolls her eyes again but this time I think it's at herself. "I'm not an idiot. I want to race stock cars. There's no money in that. In fact, it drains everything you have very quickly. Which means, I need another way to make money and that's my vlogging. You know as well as I do what a grind it is to fight your way to visibility with that."

I make a sound in the back of my throat. Do I ever. We're more alike than she imagines. I'm just starting to relax, thinking that we're on the same page.

"If this works out and we get to make a show for BOOM, that's our big break. Of course, I want it. Of course, I'll work with anyone to get it."

But that stings. She'll work with anyone, will she? Anyone. Even me? Ouch.

"Do you want it?" She takes a sip of her coffee as if trying to look like she cares less than she does.

I nod sharply. I'm still stinging.

"It was your chance before it was mine," she says carefully. "Do you still want it now that I'm part of the deal?"

"Yes," I say fervently and then feel my cheeks heat.

Has she parsed out that my enthusiastic yes is not just for the opportunity but for her, too? I can only hope she hasn't. My mouth twists in distaste, and yes, she's seen that. I clear my throat to try to control the damage as her face grows wary.

"I want what you want, Tessa. I want to race — even though I can't quite yet. I want this show. I want to do it with you because this is the best chance for both of us and because right now I need you." She opens her mouth and I raise a hand to forestall her. "And yes, I realize that puts you in a precarious situation when I get well again, but I promise you we are equal partners. I won't nudge you out when I'm well, just like I'm trusting you not to stab me in the back when I'm sick. Here."

I shove the plastic grocery bag at her and she takes it with an uncertain look in her eye.

"What are these?"

"Letters," I say and my voice is tight because I'm suddenly even more nervous than I was before. She seems to stiffen at my tone but I don't know how to joke through this part, so I stick to what I do know. "If we're going to do this together then we need to trust each other."

"And you think that will be a problem?" She quirks an amused eyebrow at me and I almost melt.

She's so ... in control of herself. It drives me wild. I want to break it all down and feel her vulnerable and gasping and spread out before me. Instead, I hold a tight reign on my voice and words.

"I do think so. We didn't have the most promising start."

"I'd beg to differ," she murmurs. "It had more promise than you know."

She's not looking at my crotch, is she? My face grows hotter and I feel that hunted feeling again. I'm going to pretend I didn't hear her.

"And I broke my word to you when I kissed you after promising not to."

"You had a brain injury," she says, but her voice is growing cold. Dammit, I'm screwing this up.

"So if we're going to do this together we need to trust each other. You need to trust I won't kiss you unexpectedly. I need to trust you won't corner me naked somewhere."

"To be clear are you worried about *you* being naked or *me* being naked."

That spark of trouble is back in her eye. Double dammit.

"Both," I grind out and it comes out hoarse because now she's brought back memories of her naked all over again and worse, my mind has layered in thoughts of me hovering over her, slowly rocking my hips to join hers. I run a hand over my face to clear my head. "We need to make promises again that nothing like that will happen. For the sake of our future."

She presses a single finger to her bottom lip as she thinks and something in my belly flips. She's ridiculously kissable like that with her small cupid's bow mouth and her twinkling eyes.

"Fine," she says eventually. "I promise not to intentionally try to seduce you, though I might do it by accident."

I clench my jaw, but I manage to push the words I don't want to say through my hesitant lips.

"And I promise I will lay no hand on you, no kiss, no unwanted advance of any kind."

"It's like the opposite of a wedding," she muses and then holds up her hand sadly. "But no ring."

"You want a ring for *not* marrying me?"

"Well, you did make me say vows."

She's adorable when she's fake pouting. And somehow the vow makes it worse, as if declaring to her that I will not cross the line ... again ... has only made my mind generate more scenarios involving the two of us. I push aside one that involves a lot of heavy breathing and try to drink my coffee.

"And since we're vowing things, you need to promise not to tell Ian or your sister about what's happened between us so far," she says. "It was mostly accidental, but them knowing about it could ruin everything."

"Agreed."

She opens the bag. "You wrote me letters. So. Many. Letters."

I take a deep breath. "They're contingency plans."

"Why?" The word stretches out across her lovely lips.

"We might be separated at key moments. You might need to know what to do."

"I think I manage it on my own." She doesn't seem too impressed.

"This way you will know what I want, and you can choose whether or not to honor it," I say grimly.

*"In case I pass out in the bathroom',"* she reads and then looks at me. "Are you really afraid of that?"

My face flushes brighter. "The doctor revealed a lot of things which now make me afraid."

She shifts the envelope like she's going to open it but I throw up a hand.

"Please don't read them unless the condition is met." She stares at me. My heart sinks. "You're going to read them all right now, aren't you?"

She sighs. "Fine. I will attempt to honor your wishes. There must be a hundred of these. *'If I can't get out of bed.'* Hmm. *'If Ian tries to override my choices about the car.'* Ha. Well, at least you know my brother. What is this one? *'When the guy who beats you in qualifiers starts flirting with you.'* That's oddly specific."

"Lots of them are. Just promise to wait until they happen."

"And what, am I supposed to carry these around on me for every contingency?"

"That would be great." I nod.

She shakes her head. "No."

"Please?" Everything we're doing is just so uncertain. I need some kind of insurance. Some kind of way to be sure that she'll at least have access to my opinions along the way if I'm stuck in bed or something.

"Do I get to write letters for you, then?"

"I ... I ..." I hadn't even considered that she might want that.

"It's only fair," she says coyly.

"Yes. Fine. Certainly."

"Can I write one for what to do if you find yourself secretly longing for me?"

She's teasing me, her eyes twinkling like twin stars. But she's way too close to the mark.

"Knock yourself out," I grumble. If such a letter existed, I'd have to open it right now. All I see when I look at her is peerless-ness. And I've always wanted the best.

"This is going to be fun." She stretches out the word "fun" to its maximum length.

The sound in my throat is more growl than anything else. But she smirks, pulls out a pen, and scrawls on a napkin, shoving it at me before she gets up and saunters away.

It says, *In case she gets up to go to the Ladies' Room* in the sloppiest handwriting I've seen since elementary school.

I flip it over and laugh. In the same sloppy writing, it says, *"Order her a cherry danish."*

Maybe this will be fun even if I have to behave myself. I certainly haven't had anyone to joke with in a while. And if I'm really lucky the jokes will keep me from drowning in unrequited angst. Maybe. Hopefully.

*Chapter Eighteen*

*TESSA*

HE DIDN'T LEAVE me a letter for if I thought the goodbyes were taking too long. If he had, then I'd be opening it. It's six in the morning ... well, more like half past six since we've been out here for almost half an hour shivering in the dawn light. My mom hugs me for what feels like the five-hundredth time. My dad is giving Brent some last-minute advice about the truck.

"It's easy to forget to keep an eye on your truck when all your attention is on the race car," he's saying, as if he hadn't given me the same lecture before he hugged me goodbye.

My things are already inside the trailer and so is Brent's duffle. I've already hugged Olivia goodbye and promised her three times that I will take care of Brent. She seems more worried about him than the situation justifies. Either he's sicker than I think, or she's a natural worrier. Or maybe she senses the tension between the pair of us and she thinks she can bind me to help him instead of murder him, which, come to think of it, is kind of a clever scheme.

Ian dances uncomfortably from foot to foot and I know he

wants to come with us, even though his plane is leaving later today out to Utah.

"This is all on you now," he whispers to me. "You need to make sure nothing falls apart, that the schedule is kept, the car maintained, Ian doesn't need to get rushed to emergency, and that the filming is done and the races run — and won, if possible."

He's practically twanging with worry.

"Seriously, Ian," I say. "You used to be fun. What happened?"

He leans in even closer and his eyes are intense. "I fell in love and married the most beautiful woman in the world."

I laugh. "And that sucked out all your fun? Or did you have to give it up in a deal with the devil to win her?"

"I realized," he says, frowning at me the way only big brothers can, "that I had someone whose happiness depends on me. I realized that I have something to lose. You should be so lucky."

"Well don't worry. While you're busy keeping Olivia beautiful, I'll keep your car safe. But I'm not making deals with the devil."

Ian looks over his shoulder and then back at me. "Maybe you should make one of your own. Seriously, Tess. Would it be so bad?"

I think my family is finally winding down. Harstone goodbyes are some of the longest in the world. But Olivia is hugging Brent tearfully, which means we're almost ready to go. I'm trying not to look at him. His dark blond hair is particularly glowing in the dawn and he's definitely too lovely to be headed out on a road trip with gremlin me.

"Listen, Ian," I whisper, "This opportunity had better not be an elaborate scheme to get us together."

He raises his hands. "Does that sound like me?"

"No," I hiss. "It sounds like Olivia."

He smiles in that way he does whenever her name is brought up, like she's a secret pleasure he keeps all to himself.

"She does like that idea. A lot."

I roll my eyes and he laughs.

"Fine then," he says. "Win all the races. Keep the car rolling. I'll be viewing all your footage and I'll try to edit out the embarrassing parts."

"You'd better," I say with a smirk.

And then we're off, and I'm not watching Brent at all as we pull out of the driveway. I'm not noticing how close these seats are together as I get used to pulling the world's most orange trailer. It's huge. It takes so much concentration that it's not until we're on the highway that I see Brent's face is pale and drawn.

He's fiddling with the radio despondently, the muscles in his forearm rippling as his fingers twist the knob. Wow. I'm fixated on forearms.

I jerk my eyes off his arm and back onto the road. It's really pretty. Not the road. The arm.

Wow, I'm a mess.

It's just any time Brent is this close to me I can feel it, like a magnet feels another magnet. Sometimes it seems to push me away like he's carrying a forcefield with him, but other times it draws me close — fast and inexorable like two magnets with opposite poles. I can't stop looking when it does that. Can't stop all the hairs on my arms from rising or all my thoughts bending in his direction like the great circles of an airplane's flight path. I'm drawn to him without meaning to be — even when I'm meaning *not* to be.

I fight the desire to look at him and lose.

He's even paler, the bones on his face sticking out jarringly. He sees me looking at him and tries for an unsteady smile.

"Are you okay?" I ask him, worried. Wow, I'm already failing at taking care of him.

"We have two days to get there," he says as if he's coaching himself.

"That's right," I say uncertainly. "It's a twenty-hour drive. We should be able to do it in one shot."

He moans.

"Or ... not?"

"Not," he says miserably. "I'm going to need stops, Tessa."

I knew he was recovering from illness and couldn't drive, but one look at him with his head in his hands tells me this is worse than I thought.

"Do you think you can make it an hour?" I ask him, biting my lower lip.

"Talk to me," he moans. He's very boyish when he's unhappy. "Talk about anything. I just need to think about something other than my swimming, miserable head."

His hand reaches for me, misses, grabs hold of nothing, and then falls between us. I watch it there for a moment not sure whether I should take it or pick it up and put it back in his lap.

"We put a few boost improvements on the engine when we rebuilt it," I start.

"Not cars. Tell me about you. Do you have a boyfriend?"

His hand crawls across the seat like a tarantula and then one of his thick, blunt fingers snags at the edge of my front pocket and hooks inside. He seems to settle at the physical touch, so I don't remind him that he vowed not to touch me. Maybe it doesn't count if it's through clothing.

"You're asking me that right now? After you've already kissed me and thrown me in a pond and told me that we can never be together, you wonder if there might be a man out there somewhere who I'm dating? Are you worried about retribution?"

He looks up at me a bit pitifully. He's very young-looking when he's sick and I can't help myself. I want to indulge him.

"No, I don't have a boyfriend. Is there a letter for if I acquire one?"

"There isn't," he says with a moan. "Maybe I'll write one."

"Do you have a girlfriend back in Australia?"

If he does then he's a cad. Yes, I know that's an old-fashioned word. It's still applicable.

"Who has the time?" He looks very pale. Green almost.

"Well, most people find some time," I say, starting to laugh now. I shouldn't laugh at him. He's so sick, but he's also hilarious.

"Have you?" He grits out. Maybe his misery is worse? I can't tell with his face in one hand. "Have you found the time for a long line of lovers?"

"Yes, I have so many that I needed this huge trailer to fit them in."

He snorts but I can tell his head is still swimming. The finger in my pocket spasms like he's fighting nausea or dizziness.

"Honestly, I haven't had a serious boyfriend since high school."

He scoffs. "Fine, you don't have to tell me things if you don't want to."

"I'm not lying."

"You don't kiss like a girl who hasn't had a boyfriend since whatever poor spotty turd dated you in high school."

I keep my tone light. He's wiggled a second finger into my pocket. "Wow, that's flattering. I'll tell Jason you said hi."

I'm good at making him laugh. He clutches the dash as he chuckles, white-knuckled like he's barely staying conscious.

"I just meant that you seemed ... experienced."

"I don't need to have done something a lot to be good at it," I say tossing my hair. "You saw me racing. I did just fine."

In truth, it's been a long time since I dated. Thunder Bay really doesn't have a lot of options. And I'd only date a car guy, anyway. How else would someone understand why I care so much about something that doesn't make money?

Although I might make an exception for someone with fingers like Brent's. I don't know why the backs of them just touching me are sending little tingles down my thighs but I'm not averse to it at all.

"You did more than fine in that race," he grits out. "When can we stop? I need air."

"Can you make it at least until the first rest point by the lake?"

"I'll try. Tell me more about why you don't date."

"I like men with big knuckles because they've busted them wrenching. I like men with work ethics and sober thinking. I like fidelity, honesty, and keeping your word about things. It doesn't seem like a tall list, but you'd be surprised."

I hope I don't sound bitter because I'm not. I'm just a realist and I know what my options are. And I'm just not bored or lonely enough to need to settle.

"Wow. Who would have thought? I like the exact same thing," he teases.

"Really? So I'll need to call dibs when I see a hottie with a chiseled jaw, unshaven face, and a So-Cal Speed Shop jacket before you scoop him up first?"

"Exactly."

It's fun and light between us today and I love it.

"Keep talking," he begs me, fingers flexing and unflexing in the edge of my pocket like he's unconsciously caressing me.

So, I tell him about my childhood pets and hobbies — I've had quite a few over the years from growing pumpkins to drawing, to welding. And about growing up with my parents and Ian here in this little out-in-the-middle-of-nowhere Canadian city.

He joins in with stories about his mom and Olivia in their tiny midwest town. Apparently, Pineville is as boring as

Thunder Bay but about one-tenth of the size. Who'd have thought it?

When we finally reach the rest stop and I carefully park the truck and trailer he stumbles out of the truck. I expect him to take a bathroom break or be sick, but instead, he makes his way out to the little strip of pink sand along the bright water of Lake Superior and plops down between white strips of driftwood, and then lies right back so that he's looking up at the sky.

He's beautiful, of course. Like a statue cast by some rich city as a focal point on their splendid beach. He's bronzed and lovely, muscled, and draped across the sand like a Greek god or a Michelangelo statue.

"Is this an invitation to walk all over you?" I tease, looking down at him with my breath caught in my throat. I miss his fingers in my pocket already.

"No," he says miserably, turning his head back and forth until his hair is full of sand. "I feel awful."

"You don't say? And here I thought this was just your way of sabotaging our trip."

"We're only an hour out of town," he moans. "How am I supposed to take twenty more?"

How indeed? I clench my jaw suddenly worried about making a deadline that is still two days away.

"We'll get through it," I say, instead, and I choose to let the cool lake breeze wash over me and try to enjoy looking at the bright water as far as I can see and the gorgeous windswept shore instead of stressing about what I can't change. "You can spend the next nineteen hours telling me about your stream of girl-friends since you mocked poor Jason so cruelly."

"I can't," he says and his words are faint enough that I have to lie down on the sand beside him to hear him at all. His voice has the timbre again — the one that settles into my bones.

It's funny how lying on a cold beach fully clothed always feels so different than lying on hot sand in a bikini. In the cold,

I'm more conscious of the earth under me. Of how dense and firm and real it is. Like a solid foundation rising up to meet me. The ground seems friendly. The trees seem to want to shelter me. The waves sing a lullaby and even the driftwood feels like a gift just waiting to be claimed. And somehow together they make the man beside me feel more real. More firm. More like a constant.

"Did they make you sign confidentiality documents after they realized what a monumental mistake it was to date you?" I tease.

"Yes, that's it." His eyes are closed and he throws his forearm over them as if to protect them further from the morning sun.

"Well, I'm not signing one."

"I'm not dating you."

"Clearly."

There's a long pause before he says, "I had Mom and Olivia to take care of. I didn't have time for girlfriends. I didn't really want one. It would just be one more person to worry about."

"Wow, savior complex much?"

I want to tease him more but his silence feels heavy. His thick brows knit together.

"Everything in life always feels like so much work," he says eventually. "I'm working, working, working all the time, and failing at it. Even when I seem to be winning at racing or in my small business, I end up losing. Even when I seem to be doing a good job with Mom or with Olivia, then I do something stupid. I don't have anything that just comes easily to me, and girls are part of that. They see me and they see the worry and the exacting standards and they don't want to get involved. You want to know why I kissed you when I first met you? You were laughing with me. No one laughs with me. No one thinks I'm funny. They just see this serious guy trying really hard. And failing to charm them only makes me try harder and seem more serious."

That is ... some very accurate self-analysis.

"Quite the hole you've dug for yourself. Now, who's the marmot?"

"Ha ha."

We're quiet for a long time, just lying there side by side in the sand. And yeah, our schedule is pressing on us but I find I don't care like I usually do. I'm enjoying just being here with him. Just soaking in this moment where we have the same goals in mind and the same hopes and dreams.

Just loving how my whole body warms knowing he's lying beside me. I can only imagine what it would be like with him in bed if *not touching* is this intense.

It's nearly an hour before he feels like he can try again.

"Let's do it before it's too much," he says.

We slip back into the vehicle and drive. I like this highway. It's not very challenging. You just follow the road through the curves and dips and up the hills and down the other side. And I chat idly with Brent. I want to know more about him than just the surface. I want to dig in deep and find out how this Tessa-magnet works.

I find out he's a history buff. He likes to read anything to do with history, but he's particularly obsessed with anything to do with the history of cars or manufacturing. He watches a lot of tv — but it's all videos from other car guys and girls. He's never had a pet. He was a good student, but not top of his class in anything. Went to university for one year to study engineering and then realized it would mean an office job for life, so he dropped out and started racing cars. He has a lot of friends in Australia who he misses already. He's happy Olivia has Ian but it feels weird to him that they aren't traveling with him anymore.

And through it all I keep wondering if it's possible that no one sees what I see — an intent, focused, driven man who adores racing and motorsports just like me, and is endearingly obsessed with caring about his family and friends. It makes my mouth kind of dry and my heart kind of achy and I don't like this softening toward him. If we're going to be partners in this business endeavor then we can't afford to get too tangled up personally. We've already made things less stable with all the sexual tension. If I find him endearing as a friend ... won't that make it worse?

When we stop so I can make us sandwiches for lunch and eat them at the rest stop, I flip through his letters frantically looking for one that says, *"If you find yourself becoming my friend."* But there isn't one and I'm not sure what that means or what I should do.

Earnestly, I text Kati.

> I think I'm becoming friends with Brent.

> Isn't that a good thing?

> It feels dangerous.

> MMMM danger.

She sends me a lip licking emotion. She's not getting this. I try Ian.

> Could Brent and I be friends?

> Um, isn't that what we've been trying to make happen? I hope you're keeping an eye on your load. That's a big trailer.

> My load is fine.

> Talk later. Plane's boarding.

I sigh. Am I the only one who sees what a disaster this is? Apparently.

With a weak smile, I bring Brent his sandwich and sit with him on a rock looking out over the lake. It's fucking romantic.

Dammit.

I could get used to this. And then where would I be? I'd be all tied up with him and that makes my stomach flutter nervously. I don't like it. It's not what I planned.

But I can't seem to stop seeing all the ways he's beautiful — not just because of his lovely body but because of his everything. And it's making things very complicated.

*Chapter Nineteen*



IF TWO NORMAL people were faced with the difficulty of a twenty-hour journey that must accommodate an invalid, I doubt they would have done it as we do, but this is working for us.

We stop every three or four hours and Tessa, biting her lip and white-knuckling her way through maneuvers, parks the trailer for us along beautiful Lake Superior shorelines or between the green laden branches of provincial parks. She has a knack for finding me the most idyllic spots to rest.

The first time we stopped after lunch — along the shores of Superior — she hopped out of the driver's seat, came around to my side of the truck, wrenched the door open, and looked at me with a long dry stare.

"Bed. No excuses," she said.

"But what will you do?"

I couldn't follow up on the question when she didn't answer. My head was swimming, extreme drowsiness dragging me down. I barely knew where I was going when she helped me out of the truck, guided me into the trailer, and then chivvied me into the bed there.

"The bed's for you," I'd tried to protest. "I'll take the couch."

But she was immovable, and I had no energy to push back. I was bundled swiftly into the bed, though I must admit that even through the dragging claws of exhaustion and the dizzy tilting of the world, I memorized the touch of her hands as she spread covers out over me and smoothed the hair from my forehead.

I wanted to snatch her hand and drag her in with me. Or just hold it. Or just touch it for a fleeting moment. But I had no power to do any of that. Instead, I drifted off to sleep.

I woke a few hours later and found her in the garage bay of the trailer, filming video for BOOM. She was giving a tour of the garage bay, having apparently, already rolled the car out, explained the ins and outs of the engine, and credited our sponsors. When I looked through her clips I was impressed.

"The park makes a perfect spot for this. The light is fantastic," I'd said while she grinned.

"I know, right? I'm glad we stopped here."

I helped guide her while she drove the car back inside the trailer and then we were off again.

Every stop has been pretty much the same since then. We wait until my body starts to fall apart, then Tessa pulls us over and lets me sleep. When night falls, I think we'll just sleep for the night, but Tessa shakes her head.

"Wake me when you're up again," she whispers as I curl into the blankets. "We'll keep going like this through the night."

I try to ask where she will sleep, but exhaustion sweeps me away. Six to eight weeks. That's what the doctor said. I sure hope it's not six to eight weeks of this. I'm embarrassed by a single day of it. She's been nursemaid and mother to me.

I fall asleep dreaming of the childhood she described, chasing a dog with copper fur and a laughing young Ian.

I wake to darkness.

I can think again. Always a good feeling. Muzzily, I find my phone on the mattress beside me. Someone — Tessa — has plugged it in and it's charged up. I have a text from Ian.

> Made it to Utah. Olivia says "hi." BOOM is putting us up in his guest house. You wouldn't believe this place.

My sister is safe. I let out a sigh of relief at that. She's terrible about texting, but thank goodness Ian isn't.

There's another one from Steve.

> Be careful driving. My weather app says there's a storm on its way.

I don't hear anything outside the trailer, so it can't be here yet. I stretch my muscles. Waking up is always when I feel the most mentally sharp.

I slip out of the trailer bed and down to the main area. Everything is lit by moonlight spilling in through the windows. It casts dark shadows across the main living area like drifts of black snow.

Tessa hasn't bothered to fold out the leather couch. She sleeps sprawled out across it, a sleeping bag half tangled around her lower half. I can't help the smile that quirks around the edges of my lips. She sleeps exactly like she lives — wide and open as if she has not a care in the world. She's wearing yoga pants and a tank top with a stylized cartoon race car printed on it and her hair tangles all around her. I lean in to brush a long strand away from her face and freeze when she swallows and turns her face into my hand. The warmth of her skin against mine makes something feel like it's smarting inside my chest.

Dammit. I shouldn't be touching her — not even her hair. I snatch back my hand from her face. It feels like I've been stung.

This is so ridiculous. It's like bundling a kid into a Hershey truck and telling him not to take a bite.

When I draw back I see she has one of my letters crumpled in her hand. I can't read it in the dark but I know which one it must be. It's probably the one titled *"When I have to sleep constantly."* I laugh silently and slip out the trailer door and into the night.

I need fresh air.

The sky is velvet washed with a bright swirl of crystal stars, like dust motes caught in a sunbeam but the opposite. I stand for a moment and look up and up and up into the infinite. On nights like this, I feel like I can reach up past my own life into the stream of history and into the thousand lives that came before mine and looked up into these same stars. Reach into the thousand lives that will come after mine, brimming with hopes and disappointments and burning aching questions.

Around me, the wind is picking up, sending the tree branches shaking and the leaves trembling. I wrap my arms around myself and tremble with them. What if I never recover? What if this is my life? Lived in snatches of a few hours at a time. I drag a hand over my face and fight back emotions blacker than the sky. I don't dare let them drag me down. I have a terrible feeling that if I do, there will be no clawing my way back up again.

I don't hear her slip out of the trailer and her hand on my arm makes me leap to the side, skittering away from her touch. My heart is in my throat.

She flicks on her phone, yawning. "We'd better get going again. There's going to be weather."

We get in the vehicle and drive. It's lonely and the highway seems less friendly now that we aren't skirting the lake. There are hours between gas stations or places to stop. I could use a coffee, but that's not an option, and it's two in the morning so I doubt much would be open even if we found something.

We drive in silence, both of us yawning, both of us feeling the anxiety of Tessa driving this huge truck and trailer in the darkness on a lonely road. It's three when it starts raining and three-thirty when the rain starts to fall in sheets so heavy that I can hardly see.

Tessa leans forward over her steering wheel, face screwed up in concentration.

"We should find somewhere to pull over," I say, tension ringing in my voice.

"Yes," she says.

"Somewhere off the road." I wish I were driving. I'm more equipped to handle this.

"Yes."

"Before this gets any heavier." My tone is urgent.

She shoots me a glare. "Brent, if you see a magic rest stop, or snowplow turnaround, or weigh station, or side road, feel free to point it out."

I don't see any of those but that doesn't keep me from thinking that I could probably be doing this better if I were at the wheel. I wouldn't be hunched half over the steering wheel peering through the dash like a blind old grandmother for starters.

I open my mouth to offer some more advice when something lets loose in the rear of the load. I clench my jaw at the same time that Tessa utters a low "shit," and fights the steering wheel to keep us on the road. My heart is in my throat, pulse racing. I want to yell at her but I don't even know what I'd yell. I can hear her breathing so loudly that it fills the cab of the truck.

And then — finally — we've stopped and I don't think we're in the ditch — not even the trailer — but we're definitely on the side of the road. I clutch my chest and draw in a huge breath. The world is spinning and flecked with black. I guess that's why the doctor told me to avoid an elevated heart rate. I can't even get myself under control enough to stop her when she leaps out of the driver's door.

Fuck.

She can't go out there alone.

I fumble for the door release and then leap out, stumbling after her and having to hold the side of the truck to steady my spinning head.

I'm in no condition to help with this.

I can't see a thing in the sheeting rain and it's so loud on the pavement that I can't hear where Tessa has gone. I hold the side of the truck as I make my way toward the back. The issue was in the rear. That's where she'll be. Hopefully, she has the damn sense to stay off the road. In the rain. In the dark. On the Trans-Canada Highway. Awesome. This is just great.

I look at the rear tires of the truck when I get there. Fine on this side. That's good. We always have the option to unhitch if we really have to.

We're on the side of the road, parked on gravel that is quickly turning to mud. I can't see any better place to stop up ahead in the headlights. At least this stretch is straight, so we're less likely to be hit by traffic but less likely isn't unlikely. I don't like this. At all.

I check the hitch next. Still attached. Looks fine. Properly locked. Not twisted or anything.

So far, so good.

I make my way down the trailer and Tessa's not on this side. The tires on this side are fine. Axle looks fine. We aren't in the ditch, though the rear of the trailer is very close to the edge of the gravel and the angle makes it look a bit precarious. I have to step into the ditch to walk around the back of the trailer. I find Tessa there, hunched in the rain looking at the rear tire of the trailer on the driver's side.

I don't like that. I turn on the flashlight app on my phone

and shine it down the road to try to indicate we're here if anyone comes along.

"Tire's blown," Tessa calls to me.

I can see that.

"I'm going to grab a jack and swap it for the spare." She has to yell to be heard over the rain.

"Bad idea. Let's just run it like this until we get somewhere safer," I yell back.

"On the rim?" She looks at me like I'm crazy. "We'll ruin the wheel."

"If you change it out here some yahoo might hit us both. Do you want to die for a fucking wheel?"

"What yahoo? There's no one here for miles."

She pushes past me and something in my chest breaks loose — some kind of filter that I think might have been more important than this trailer wheel.

I follow her, stomping through the rain. She already has the rear man-door to the trailer open and I follow her inside.

"This is crazy. Do you have a death wish?"

She already has the jack. She's tugging it along behind her.

"Seriously, Tessa," I practically spit. "Would you stop and talk to me?"

"The sooner I change the tire, the sooner we're safely back on the road," she grits out. She won't even look at me.

Dammit.

I huff as I move to block her. "Would you cut it out? You're being an idiot."

That makes her look up. "Wait, so because I'm doing things my way and not yours it makes me an idiot?"

"If this is your way, then your way is an idiot way." I'm not helping things. I know it but I don't know how to find my missing filter.

"Yeah, I have total faith in you, too, Brent," she says, and then she passes me, jack in tow.

I hurry after her and grab the jack.

"At least let me do the hard work."

I lift the jack out of the trailer and set it down on the pavement, but when I go to straighten, my body moves in the wrong direction. Instead of going up, it goes down. Hard.

I hit the pavement with my butt and the world swims all around us.

I hear the exasperated sigh even over the rain. Strong hands pull me up and guide me to the edge of the man door and then those same hands are laid on my shoulders right before she presses me down to sit on the edge of the doorway, legs hanging out of the trailer.

"Stay there and don't get in the way," she says, and then she's gone.

I see her when she comes back for the impact driver and torque wrench. And then again when she comes for the spare.

And my guts are all tangled in knots. And I'm so, so mad that she's out there acting like an idiot and I'm stuck here unable to straighten up and go stop her.

Then she's cycling past me again, putting back the wrench and the impact driver, the blown tire, and then, last of all, the jack.

When she's done, she grabs my hand and pulls me up unceremoniously, secures the trailer door, marches me up to the truck, opens my door, and shoves me in.

When she gets in her side, she drives away in silence. I want to scream at her. I want to accuse her of being an idiot. I want to cry because I have no strength. But a few minutes later, we pull into an empty, closed weigh station for haul trucks. There's plenty of room around here to park the trailer. Tessa takes her chance with it and then comes around to my door.

I don't want to get out. Both because I'm mad and because my head is still spinning, but it would be childish to refuse, so I get out with her and go to the living quarters part of the trailer.

We both go inside and she flips the light on.

We're soaking wet, shivering, and staring at each other.

Yikes.

She's beautiful when she's mad, and she's so incredibly mad right now that she's trembling. Her cheeks are flushed. Her lips just slightly purple from cold but they're curled up like she's about to tell me everything that's wrong with me and her clothes cling and stick to all her curves. I go ahead and take a long look at them. Why not? I don't get to touch. I might as well look.

Staring is not helping. I'm shivering and my vision is wavering like I might pass out and the trailer feels hot and I'm *still* turned on.

I can't help it. She's amazing.

"Fuck you, Brent Bolt," she spits out when she can finally speak. "Fuck you. I drove us this whole way and you just sat or slept, so you don't get to show up and order me around when you feel like it. I had that situation under control. I handled it. You don't get to backseat drive me."

Oh, she's mad? Imagine how I feel when my hands are tied and I can't even do anything about it because of my condition. I feel a matching fury bubbling up to the surface. To be clear, it is in no way dampening my attraction, or the way my heart just splits wide open and turns into liquid for her.

"I just sat around?" I say icily. "I just slept?"

I see her face twitch when she admits to herself that she's gone a bit far.

"Maybe you should be thanking me for that or you wouldn't be here at all. If I could do more than sleep, you never would have been offered this gig. And then where would you be with the kind of idiotic judgment that decided changing tires in the rain and the dark and the middle of the road is a good idea? Hmm?"

"I'd be just fine," she says, shivering.

I think half her trembling is fury and I want to kiss her so hard that I win this argument. I want to let her keep whispering "fuck you" to me while I lay her out on that couch and show her how she can do exactly that. I want a lot of things that I'm not going to get while the world is closing in to a single point.

I whip my shirt off. I just need to get out of these wet clothes before I collapse. That way I won't die of hypothermia while I'm immobile. Or whatever.

"What are you doing?" She sounds outraged.

I ignore her, kicking off my boots and wet jeans. Shit, I can barely see. I might throw up. The trailer is spinning around me.

"What are you doing?" Now it's a pained whisper.

Sorry sunshine, I'm way too close to fainting to answer.

I take a wobbling step forward and she takes a step backward.

"Brent," she gasps. "I'm not going to admit I'm an idiot just because you stun me with your naked body."

Stun her? That sounds promising.

I pass out while I'm still speculating.

# Chapter Twenty

*TESSA*

THE FIRST LETTER I opened from him was short. It said, *"If I sleep all the time"* on the front and then when I opened it, the letter said,

*Sorry.*

Pretty basic and to the point. No instructions or anything. The second letter I open has more to say.

I find it after I lift him from the trailer floor naked, wet, and shivering.

He's half-conscious. Enough to help me get him up and over to the couch but not enough to answer questions coherently.

"Tess," he slurs when I ask him if he's okay. Once I roll him into my sleeping bag he mumbles, "Sorry," and then after that, I can't get him to say anything at all. But he's shivering hard enough that I reluctantly strip down to my underthings and crawl into the sleeping bag with him.

He shifts, turning in his sleep so that his naked chest is against my side and murmuring in his sleep. He nuzzles against my neck with his lips, offering me semi-conscious ghost kisses and snuggling in as if every inch of him wants to find its matching part on me. He's still shivering or else I'd stop this.

I think.

But one of his big hands spreads out over my hip and I'm not sure exactly how far my self-control extends here and if I'd have the power to slip away when he's this big, soft, gentle-handed man drawn to me without knowing it.

I like it far too much.

I know exactly how bad an idea it is to soften to him and I still feel every inch of him against me and it's setting my blood on fire. I can hardly breathe. I think my brain is trying to memorize every sensation and it's running out of processing capacity because why waste brain power on stupid things like breathing and overthinking when you can memorize the exact way his thigh smooths over mine and clasps me in an unthinking embrace? Why bother with nonsense like self-preservation when I can shiver at the feeling of his hot breath on my throat, when he murmurs and snuggles in deeply until his eyebrow is pressed to my cheek and I can feel the flutter of his lashes?

Look, I've never experienced this level of vulnerable intimacy with a grown man before and it's ... well it's kind of intoxicating, to be honest. I just want to keep going and see exactly how far it goes and if I could ever find the end of this whole-body tingling feeling that's filling me with all the heat of desire and an almost indulgent affection.

I've always been a sucker for hurt things. Puppies with burs in their paws, bunnies with bare patches in their fur, and birds that flew into the window. There's an element of that all mixed up with this intense sexual attraction, and I'll be the first to admit that it's doing a number on me. Suddenly, the idea of indulging Olivia and Mom with beach vacations and family nights that end with me tripping into this man's bed are seeming more like a guilty pleasure I can dream about than a terror to be avoided at all costs.

After about ten minutes his shivering stops, so mission accomplished, Tessa, if the mission was to stop him from getting hypothermia while simultaneously making yourself the most frustrated woman alive. I have not been soothed by this closeness. On the contrary, I'm so turned on and wound up that I'm afraid one more of his sleepy ghost kisses to my neck might trigger an orgasm and humiliate me for all eternity.

Desperately, I reach beside me and feel on the floor for his stack of letters that I wedged under the couch. I can sift through them without moving too much and I do. I'm not sure whether I should open the one marked *"If I pass out"* or the one that says, *"If you find yourself falling in love with me."*

Let's face it, the hubris of writing that one makes my face flare hot with embarrassment and defiance — I don't like the idea that I might be so predictable or so easy to seduce — and in the end, I open it.

It says,

*Don't even think about it.*

Good advice.

*I swore not to touch you and I won't."*

Sure. Because he's definitely not touching me now with his sleepy fingers spread wide and kneading unconsciously into my hip. If I just rolled a little onto my side and they stayed like they are, they could tangle into a much more interesting place and the question of whether I would orgasm right here would be settled in about twenty seconds.

*I won't be thinking about you that way and you'd better not think about me that way.*

Liar. I feel how hard he's getting against my leg.

*So respect us both and let it drop.*

Wow. Arrogant much?

But also he's not shivering anymore and I don't really have an excuse to be here, do I? In fact, I might be taking advantage of him if I stay.

Well played, letter. Well played.

Carefully, and with a lot more regret than I should have, I ease myself out of his embrace and slip from the bed. I feel miserable already. I want to be in there with him. I want to stay where his eyelashes brush my cheek. I want him to wake up and sink into my flesh — to gasp and moan and pull at my hair and give me his pretty green eyes and dimples all hazy with arousal. But that isn't mine to take if he isn't offering.

Dammit.

I pull on yoga pants and a crop top with all the frustration of a girl so wound up that she's basically a bomb in a movie with a red timer reading 0:03 and counting down, and then I stalk across the trailer, climb the ladder into the real bed above, and sprawl there on my back looking miserably at the skylight. I hate this. I am not supposed to be falling for Brent Bolt.

In my pocket, my phone buzzes.

I take it out and see I've missed all kinds of messages.

Kati's text reads:

> I hope that you're okay. I saw there was a storm and I can't sleep because I'm worried about you out in it. Text me when you wake up.

I text her back.

> I'm pulled over at a safe spot and fine. Don't worry. Go back to sleep.

There's another one on my phone from Ian:

> Landed safe in Utah. Good luck on the roads. Keep a close eye out driving because with a trailer like that it will take longer to stop.

And one from Olivia:

> Hi Tessa, I hope it's okay to text you directly. I was thinking about you through my whole trip. I just really think that I wasn't as warm to you as I could have been. I really want you to know how welcome you'd be to join my family even more deeply by starting something with Brent. I know you think it's a joke, but you'd both just be so happy. Love your new sister, Olivia.

Wow. Can I just say that only people over fifty write texts like they're letters? Also, thank you Olivia because that was the bucket of cold water I needed. There's nothing that makes me want to do a thing less than having a bunch of people staring at me hoping to see me do it. Except win races, obviously.

There's also one from my mom that's no less insistent, though a lot more subtle.

> Honey, I hope you're having a great time. I'm
> sure you are because Brent is just a joy and
> so welcome in our family, don't you think? He
> misses his mom and now he'll miss his sister
> with her off married to Ian so he'll really need
> all your happiness and sunshine.

At least my dad didn't weigh in.

I rub my eyes and lay back on the blankets. There's nothing quite like your family rooting for your love life's success to kill it in the seedling stage. And maybe that's for the best, right? I shouldn't be with Mr. Cranky-pants Brent anyway, and reminders of that are exactly what I need.

I fall asleep with that in mind but it doesn't stop the dreams all night long, one after another. They're all on the theme of "what might have happened in that sleeping bag if I hadn't come to my senses" and it just shows that my mind hates me and is trying to ruin my life. Thanks, mind.

# Chapter Twenty-One

*BRENT*

I COME to some time in the middle of the night and just go back to sleep. I can't deal right now and I don't want to try. I just want to lie here in this warm sleeping bag and try not to dwell on my own humiliation. My body has betrayed me. One minute I'm giving her a very deserved piece of my mind and the next I'm mostly naked and passing out. If I had to choose a punishment to inflict on my worst enemy this would make the top five. I don't even think I have an enemy — unless maybe it's her, so that just complicates things more.

My dreams tumble over each other and I'm pretty sure I dream all night about her warm body mostly naked and me snuggling into it. When that dream ends abruptly, I try to snatch it back and end up with a tumble of other dreams of her scolding me and doing stupid headstrong things like changing tires in the middle of the night on the road and then ripping all my clothes off and taking her pleasure. Yeah. They're weird. I wake up disoriented and confused, not sure what was dream and what was reality.

I'm in the wrong bed.

That's the first thing that comes to mind. I look around furtively and realize that not only am I alone, the bed up the ladder is mussed but no one is in it. She must have slept there after she hauled my unconscious ass onto this couch.

Relief floods over me. Everything is perfectly respectable. Nothing beyond my humiliation has happened. I shower and dress hurriedly, make both beds, and straighten the trailer until it's tidy enough for a new day. I don't like mess. I never have. It makes my mind feel cluttered.

I even brew some coffee and carefully fix her a mug.

See? I can make peace.

I step out into the makings of a warm summer day. The morning light is hazy where it filters through the trees. Last night's rain soaks the grass and a warm breeze is already working on evaporating it, making the edges of my T-shirt flap. The air is so warm I'm already breaking out in a light sweat. It's going to be a really humid Southern Ontario cooker of a day.

I find Tessa checking the spare tire on the trailer.

The second she realizes I'm there, she stiffens.

"I made coffee," I say and something in me freezes when she pastes a bright and very, very false smile on her face.

"That's nice," she says brightly. "Ready to go?"

"Umm, yes?" I don't know why she won't look at me. Is she as embarrassed as I am about last night? Was it ... could it be worse than I remember? I mean, it's not like she hasn't seen me naked before. Or passing out.

I can't think of anything that would make her uncomfortable, though. I mean, if she knew what I'd dreamed she'd be jumpy maybe, but my dreams are my own and I plan to keep them that way. Even if mere glimpses of her seem to steal little snatches of my breath.

Oh, wait. She's probably still mad about last night.

Which means I should apologize.

Except that I was right and I don't want her doing something that stupid again and possibly ending up dead.

I growl in the back of my throat without meaning to and her gaze shoots up and meets mine, her face goes scarlet, and then her jaw clenches and she slips past me.

"Do you want the coffee?" I call after her, but she doesn't even reply. She just hops in the truck and starts the engine and I'm forced to throw her coffee on the ground and hurry to the passenger side of the truck to start our day.

We drive the first leg in virtual silence. I try to find a radio station but her white-knuckled hold on the steering wheel tells me I keep picking wrong.

Dammit.

Eventually, I give up and read the texts I'm getting.

Ian texts:

> This place is amazing. You'd love it here. Full of energy and you wouldn't believe what BOOM is building for SEMA this year.

I feel a pang of jealousy at that one but I fire back, *Live it up, brother.*

Someone should have some fun.

There's another text from BOOM and that gets my heart racing.

> On track for the race tonight?

I text back:

> Absolutely.

One way or another we're getting there. I get a thumbs up in return.

There's one from Olivia, too.

Dear Brent, I miss you but am happy to hear
you're safe and well. Ian and I are
establishing ourselves in Utah and hope to
see you soon. I should tell you that already I
have heard rumors that BOOM would like to
bring you on full-time but there are some
people here who are afraid that hiring a pair
of people who are both single can only lead
to trouble. Perhaps if you were married it
would make for an easier sell, Love Olivia.

Wow, that was not subtle at all.

I'm getting that itch between my shoulder blades again that reminds me I do not like being penned in like a prize bull they want to breed.

I shoot a sideways glance at Tessa. Not even if the girl they have picked out seems to be stealing little slivers of me as the days go on. I can't help that. She's a little sorceress, obviously. But she can just keep on stealing until she has all of me, that still won't force my hand, or make me play into this fantasy that our families have for us. I'm a free man, not breeding stock.

I think I might be growling again without meaning to because Tessa says, "Are you hungry? You sound like a man who needs something to eat."

"I need something alright," I snarl irritably.

Her eyes go very wide and her nostrils flare — like she reads some kind of significance into that. Okaaay, what happened last night?

"Look," I say, grasping at the straws of memory. "I'm sorry I passed out while we were arguing. It wasn't fair to escape a fight like that."

Her sidelong glance tells me I'm way off the mark in my guess about what's bothering her, but she says, "It's fine, Brent. There's a place to stop in an hour. I'll make you lunch."

"I might do that again," I press on. "I'm not really up to full physical standard if you know what I mean."

This time when she glances toward me her eyes land in my lap and she says nothing just jerks them forward and onto the road again.

I swallow uncomfortably. I wouldn't have come on to her while she was helping me, would I?

Maybe.

Shit.

If I apologize for it and it didn't happen, I could make things worse. If I don't apologize and it did happen she might hate me for it.

I'm not sure what to do, so I do what I always do when I'm unsure. I stare out my window and try my damndest to ignore everything.

We stop for lunch. An awkward, miserable lunch.

Her pretty eyes won't look at me and her kissable mouth is bent into a frown. I nap for an hour and then we start up again and we get to the track by mid-afternoon with plenty of time for Tessa to run the car out while I film her going over it and talking about it for False Start.

This, at least, is something I can do. As my camera tracks her pre-race check-in, tech check, testing, and set up, she relaxes, seeming to forget it's me behind the camera. The track is busy, even hours before the race, and with two hours until the driver's meeting, there's time for me to sleep, and time for us to whip up some food in the tiny kitchenette — in stony silence, obviously, though it's interesting to note that we work well together even when we're both furious.

The track here isn't really bigger or better than the track in Thunder Bay — even though we're much closer to big populations — but I've found that one track is much the same as another whether they're in Australia or Canada or the USA.

We have our Driver's Meeting and I get some filming in of Tessa looking stunning in her racing suit as she readies herself for her race.

I feel all prickly under my skin. Some of it is tight, strangling envy. That makes perfect sense. It was supposed to be me in that car, me with the chance to race on this track and make a name for myself on BOOM Motorsports. But oddly enough, though envy makes me short and tight it's not what has me twanging like a bowstring. Attraction and tension do that.

I see the bright gleam in her hazel eyes as she looks at the track and it sends sparks shooting right through my veins. I see her tighten her jaw and narrow her eyes in determination during the Driver's Meeting and I feel an echo of that desire inside me and it's for her to win, win, win.

I check over the car silently with her. It's a beauty. The mods they made to the engine and set-up are exactly what I would have chosen. And as I lean on the car to catch my swimming head and watch Tessa efficiently circling it, checking everything as if by mental list, her single-minded intensity cinches my breath. When she leans in and tightens a bolt, I feel like I'm going to melt into a puddle.

Get it together Brent. You're not allowed to fall for this girl.

But what if I fell secretly and no one knew?

That would just be my problem right? I could keep it as a secret to take out and enjoy when no one was watching, like Steve's hidden treat cupboard. And if it hurt a bit, would that be so bad when I'd already enjoyed so much of it.

I know I'm bargaining with myself and the results are going to be disastrous but I can't help it. I'm doing it anyway. I'm sneaking little looks and hyper-aware of any time she so much as shifts around me. I'm masking my nausea and spinning head so I can offer little smiles of encouragement and find her best angle with the camera and make sure to get shots of everything in a way that shows her mastery. When it's her turn to race, I throttle back everything else, give her my warmest smile, and offer to help clip her in.

"Sure," she says absently.

Her eyes are on the track. She only cares about one thing —
clearly. And I love that laser focus. I love that passion. I click her
action camera on and lean in to snick the five-point harness shut.
It puts my fingers next to her thighs again. Puts my ear right
against her racing heart.

And when I'm done I wish her luck, and stand back and
adjust my camera filters to be just right for the race track conditions and if I have to lean really hard against the barricade to stay
upright, well it's been worth it. And if my head swims a little
while I keep the camera on her car that's fine, too.

There's no one here to see me wobble — well, there are five
thousand racing fans but they aren't looking at me. And there's
no one here to hide from, so I let my grin widen and my admiration soar and just watch her as she races her heart out like
nothing bad could ever happen to her. Ever.

And I hope it never does.

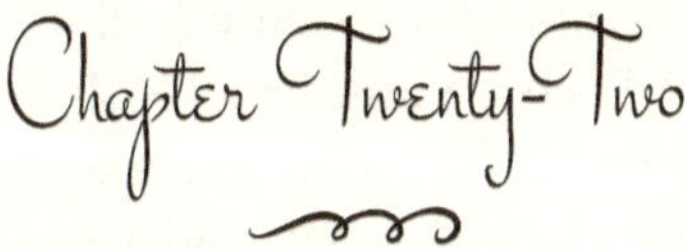

# Chapter Twenty-Two

*TESSA*

I LOVE WINNING. I love it. I come off the track having placed second in the feature race and my heart is in my throat. The car took a bit of a beating, I won't lie. We're gonna have to work like crazy to fix her up before the next race. But we can do it. We can.

I drive straight to our spot in the pits and I'm flying high. My smile won't wipe off my face. My mind is buzzing with dreams and hopes. This is it. This is what I've been working for all these years and I have it. Visions of the show taking off, of tens of thousands ... no, hundreds of thousands ... no, millions ... okay, that's reaching ... hundreds of thousands of views and subscribers and making it and keeping this as my full-time job, all of that is dancing in my head and when I stop the car and rip off my helmet my breath is ragged with excitement.

Brent isn't at our garage trailer and that's fine because I know how hard it is for him to get around right now. Which is why I'm surprised when someone is suddenly at my window.

"Need help getting out?" A low male voice with a heavy French Canadian accent rumbles in my ear.

"I've got it," I say, but when I turn, my jazzed smile is still on my face and it only grows wider when it's matched by a very pretty grin on a very masculine face.

"Are you certain?" he asks and he tilts his head and flushes bashfully even if this move isn't bashful at all.

"Umm, okay," I agree, a little breathlessly. My heart races as he leans in the car and unfastens me and now we're both flushed and breathless and I look over my shoulder to see another car parked behind mine. It's number 88 — the car that just took first in my class.

"Great race!" he says, approval as thick in his voice as his accent, and he steps back and lets me slide out of the car and past him.

"Thanks, you too!" I say excitedly.

"I'm Pierre Gagnon," he says, still grinning and offering me a hand.

"Tessa Harstone. That was a clever slide you worked in during the last lap."

"Oh, the lap where you tried to pass me?"

He winks. Why is that so adorable?

"Yes, that one." I laugh.

"Can I help you with your hood?" he offers.

"Thanks!"

The sooner I get a good look at how bad the damage is, the sooner I can be back to racing again, and after tonight, I want to win first. Second is great, but how mint would it be to win, win?

We slide the hood off together and set it aside and I lean in over the engine. Everything looks good inside. So maybe I'll just be beating out the dents in this body and fixing any alignment issues.

"Is everything you have hidden so sleek?" Pierre asks, leaning over me to look into the engine compartment.

I'm about ninety percent sure he's flirting with me, but honestly, sometimes I have a hard time telling with Canadiens, and I don't want to act like he is if he isn't and then end up humiliated. Before I come up with a neutral response, a call startles me.

"Hey! What's going on here? Engine trouble?" The words are gruff and snapped out like the speaker thinks he's a marine sergeant with a new batch of recruits to train.

I yank my head out of the engine compartment, nearly colliding with Pierre as he also rips his attention from what we were doing to where Brent is hurrying forward, camera up and definitely filming this.

"It seems your partner is worried I might steal your trade secrets," Pierre says, his grin widening as he nudges me with an elbow. He's about ten years older than me and when he smiles indulgently, he looks like he's humoring Brent, and being the bigger man. It's quite the trick.

Brent must think so, too, because he looks like someone is increasing his internal air pressure. He inflates up to his full height — taller than I've ever seen. Does he always hunch? — And his eyes widen slightly in a stricken look mostly hidden under a grimace, but I know him well enough that I know what I'm seeing.

"This is Pierre," I say brightly. "Number Eighty-Eight. He won first place!"

"And you won second," Brent snaps.

"She's amazing," Pierre says charmingly, offering a hand. Brent ignores it which is a little juvenile if you ask me.

"Thank you for your help, Pierre," I say with a broad smile.

He waves and starts to head to his car but looks over his shoulder to say, "Let me know if you need any more help. We're friendly down here at Flamboro. And maybe if you race at St. Croix next, I can show you around town."

I smile wider at the mention of the Quebec race track. "Sounds like a plan."

"We leave for the States tomorrow," Brent says coldly. "Farmer City Racetrack."

Pierre whistles. "The big time!" He salutes me, teasing. "Good luck, Tessa Harstone. And my offer stands if you come to Quebec."

"We're not going to Quebec," Brent snarls.

"Good luck, Pierre!" I wave cheerfully.

Brent's being a jerk, but I don't need to be. Pierre's been really friendly and that's kind of a nice change, if you know what I mean. And it's not flirting. And even if it was, it's none of his business since he's sworn not to touch me.

I say that to myself, but honestly, I'm totally lying my ass off and I know it. I *was* letting Pierre flirt with me because it felt good to have someone congratulate me and felt even better that it was a sexy Quebecois in his thirties. And I also let him do it because I'm sexually frustrated from sleeping virtually naked with a man who has vowed to have nothing to do with me. Maybe I want to rub his nose in it just a bit after he cuddled naked with me and then didn't say a thing about it for an entire day.

Okay, my reasons suck. But they're mine and I'm keeping them, thanks so much. If I need to jump-start my entire career with a hefty dose of spite, then I'll spite with the spitey-est.

"How's the car looking after the race?" Brent asks me tightly, pointing emphatically at the camera. Oh. Yeah. Reality check. We're still filming. I hope he got good coverage of the race, but my job isn't over.

I open my race suit and tie the arms around my waist so that it shows my BOOM tank — you're welcome BOOM Motorsports — and then I give his camera my best smile and start to run down the hits the car took in the race. The ones I remember, at least. There were a lot, if I'm being honest. I lay out my plan for how to fix the dents and how to check the suspension, and then I begin.

Brent sets up a camera on a tripod a little distance from me and if he's swaying and pale when he abruptly leaves, well, he's sick and it's going to happen, right? I finish checking the suspension and fixing the alignment — not easy to do without a partner — and then I turn off the camera and pack the car into the trailer. I can beat the panels out later. That's fine. I need to change out of my race gear and get some working clothes on before I start.

I bring the camera with me. I can send all the footage to BOOM before I get started.

In the living part of the trailer, Brent is passed out on the bed, literally snoring, his feet hang out over the end of the mattress. I feel a lump in my throat when I look at him lying vulnerable and broken on the bed. He frustrates me. And attracts me. And annoys me and all in equal measures.

On the little kitchenette counter, he's written me a note on masking tape with a permanent marker.

*You didn't read the damn letter.*

Wow. Angry much? He's drawn an arrow on the tape. It points to one of his letters.

*When Dudes Flirt With You At The Races.*

I smirk. Well, at least he anticipated that other men might like me. Should I be flattered by that? I don't know. I open the letter.

*Don't even think about it. They want something from you.*

Yeah, Brent. It's called sex and maybe even a relationship. Something that apparently I can't ever have with you, so how is it your business where I find it? Wow, I sound bitter even to myself. He's messing with my mind. I am not this person.

*You'll look cheap if you're a girl who just hooks up with other racers.*

Well, that's both sexist and offensive. My brother dated his sister when he was on the racing circuit. Did that make him look cheap? Hmm?

I pull out a pot from the cupboard, put it on the stove, light the paper on fire, and throw it inside the pot, making sure to arrange the masking tape so it points to the crumpled ashes on the stove.

There, Brent, enjoy the attention I've given to your letter.

Annoyed, I dress swiftly and then grab my laptop, phone, and camera, and go back out to the garage portion of the trailer. I like it better here. Maybe I'll set a cot up just like at home and avoid Brent forever. Home, sweet home.

I pull out the stool from under the workbench and set to work, checking my social media as I upload the video files to BOOM.

I freeze. Holy Mother of Moses.

This morning I had six thousand Instagram followers. Six thousand followers I'd slaved for a dozen at a time, chipping my way into the social media world. I have ten thousand now. I check my other platforms and they have similar leaps. All my uploaded videos have almost double the views. I can't see how many people watch the BOOM Motorsports channel, but I can read the comments on my own socials and they're all on one theme.

"I just found your show on BOOM! I'm now a fan!" one of them reads.

Another says, "Great work getting us fresh content, BOOM! Thanks to False Start I'm now a subscriber!"

As I watch, my follower count is ticking upward.

Shit. This is huge.

I don't dare lose it no matter how mad I am at Brent.

I check my texts with trembling hands.

Ian:

> Get me footage of tonight's race ASAP, the people are loving your show! Oh, and BOOM wants some reel of you and Brent each talking about what you like about the other person. Get me that tonight if you can. Sitting on the stool in the mobile garage would be great for branding.

I look up at the huge BOOM decal on the wall behind the workbench. Yeah, he's not wrong.

There are some other texts from my parents, mostly well-wishes and a few digs about how it would be nice if I married Brent and fulfilled all their hopes and dreams, a few from friends back home who found the show and are congratulating me, and one from Kati.

Kati's text is just emojis but the second I read it, I dial her number.

"Kati?" I ask when she picks up.

"I can't talk right now," she whispers into the phone.

"Is it true?"

"YES!" she whisper-screams.

"Congratulations," I whisper back. "Celebrate when I get back?"

"YES!" This whisper scream is mostly drowned out by her mother scolding her to put her cell phone away and I say goodbye as the line cuts out.

I smile down at the baby emoji on my phone. I'm going to make the best auntie.

And with that in my heart, I set up the camera to film myself telling the world what I like about Brent. It's tough to find words that don't include how I feel when his naked body is pressed against me or how absolutely insane he makes me the rest of the time, but every time I think I might be losing the spirit of the exercise, I think about Kati and a little baby and access the generous side of my heart.

When I'm done, I send it off to BOOM and turn my attention to something a lot more *me* than complimenting the man who drives me insane — banging body panels straight. It might not be the kind of banging I wish I were doing, but it will have to suffice for now.

# Chapter Twenty-Three

*BRENT*

I'VE NEVER GONE to sleep while my emotions were high and tangled. Which tells you this is not normal sleep. One moment, my guts are roiling and my chest is heavy and thick. Every glimpse of her feels like it's shredding something inside my chest, and then the next moment, I've collapsed in my bed and I'm fast asleep.

I wake up still upset and it's not helping at all.

I lie in my bed, miserable, my body shaking and nauseated. I think the patch is working. I'm not tired as often as I used to be, but that doesn't mean I'm completely free of effects. I've been pushing it too hard. I shouldn't be working myself up about this, but I am and I can't stop.

I'm spiraling through images in my mind of Tessa with Pierre, of *him* doing all the things I want to do with her — all the things I *have* done with her — and it makes my lip curl into a snarl and my fists clench. It makes me want to write her some *very pointed* letters. And I'd tell her that she has to fucking reserve herself for me. That I am the only one who really understands her genius and drive, not Pierre, not anyone but me. That I am the one who realizes she's the kind of person you only ever meet once if you meet them at all, that I recognize she's clever and funny and a fucking delight.

But I can't.

Because it would be stupid, right? It would sink what we have going here for our careers and it would trap me.

Oh yeah, it would trap me. That was what I was avoiding. Suddenly, that doesn't seem to matter as much. I could take smug looks from our family. If I don't like them I can just walk away, or drive away, or fly away. Was I really so stupid that *that* was what was keeping me away from her?

What if she went off with him while I was collapsed here? What if she's in his trailer right now? Look, it's not an unreasonable fear. After all, the pair of us were making out over tacos about ten minutes after we met. I'd seen immediately how wildly unusual she was in the best of ways. Rare. That's the word. Rare and precious. Maybe that bastard Pierre saw it, too.

I need to get up and start driving. I need to get us away from him.

I just need to close my eyes for one minute first.

When I wake the second time I feel like I can't breathe and this is ridiculous. I hate myself for it. If there was one thing I was not supposed to do it was fall for my friend's kid sister. I feel like my brain is a race car with a stuck throttle. It's flying down the track with no way to stop it, certain to crash in the most perilous way.

I manage, this time, to wrench myself from bed.

The trailer is empty except for a pot of ashes.

My letter.

Fuck.

She burned the letter. She's not taking my advice.

What does hyperventilating feel like? Not to be too dramatic, but I think I'm doing it.

I collapse on my ass on the couch and put my face in my hands. You're an idiot, Brent. You're acting like a hormonal teenager instead of a grown man. But she wrings my brain like a rag, and I hate it, and I'm addicted to it, and I can't live like this.

With an enormous wrenching of my will, I pull myself together, shower, dress, tidy the trailer — this is becoming a theme — and wander out into the night. The races are over. The lot is mostly empty, though some trucks are still pulling away.

I check the garage trailer and she's not there.

Dammit.

I could text her. And look like a needy fool.

I stare at my phone, trying to think of whether it's just being cautious if I try to text her now, or if it's being possessive and kind of dickish. In the end, I read my other texts and reply to them. The last one is from Ian. He thanks me for the footage — I guess she sent it out — and he needs me to film a video about how I feel about his sister.

Fuck.

How do I feel about her? I'm head over heels, okay? I fell off the fucking cliff. I'm a class-A idiot. I'd mock myself if I could.

But I'm a professional. I set up the camera. I set up the stool. I set my face in a serious expression. And I record the damn spiel.

I talk about only the facts. Her innate skill. Her great attitude. Her ridiculous capability and creativity. And I try like hell not to let the slightest bit of emotion leak into my words. If I do, the entire world will know this girl is gripping my naked heart in her hand like a gear shifter. And just like that car, I purr to her every whim.

And I think that maybe I always will.

Which is really going to suck.

Chapter Twenty-Four



*TESSA*

I SHOULD PROBABLY BE TIRED, but I'm flying too high. After beating a few body panels mostly flat, I'd gone out into the pits and met people, looked at cars, and chatted with pit crews. I was careful to keep my action camera on so I could record it all. BOOM will be excited to see how much extra footage I managed to get of some of this track's local racers. We talked about their cars and their histories and what they loved about racing. I think I've been patted on the back so much I'm going to be sore. It's been unreal.

"That's the way to do it," one older woman tells me from her vantage point sitting on a trailer wheel. "If I was young again, I'd do it just like you. Go see some of the world. Do what you love. Worry about money and responsibilities later."

I laugh uncomfortably because I'm well aware that I'm not as responsible as I should be. That I don't have much in the way of savings (I have two hundred and thirteen dollars in my bank account and if BOOM wasn't footing the expenses on this trip I wouldn't have been able to buy fuel to Sault Ste. Marie on that budget). I haven't done any of the things someone responsible should do. No full-time job. No home of my own. No long-term relationship or family starting up. By the time Mom was my age, she was married and pregnant with Ian.

"I'm serious," the older woman says, ruffling her short hair and taking a pull on whatever is hidden behind that can coozie. "People yammer on and on about being focused and starting your life up, but I've lived a bit, girl, and I know it's just as irresponsible to grab desperately at whatever seems close. If you don't try to follow your passions while you're young, when do you think you'll do it? When you have kids who need feeding? When you have a mortgage to pay? You're doing it right." She ends her speech by lifting her can to me. "Keep on racing, speed lady!"

I smile at her and carry on and after I've made the rounds and met more people than I'll ever remember, I go hit up the food stands before they shut down. With the features over and the crowd mostly gone, they're packing up, but I sweet talk a taco stand into giving me what they have left and I bring them with me back to the trailer. Maybe I don't know Brent well, but I know he likes tacos and after burning his letter, he'll be annoyed and maybe he'll let me buy him dinner to make up for it. They were also right within my budget — free — since the vendors just wanted me to leave and let them pack up. Look, I'm never above pity food.

I arrive back at the trailer just as Brent's leaving the garage portion. His light-colored hair is slightly mussed from sleep. His face needs a shave. His T-shirt and jeans are rumpled in a way that makes them actually cling a little more to his muscled chest and abdomen and drape around his lower half in a way that only highlights what's underneath rather than disguising it.

The harsh lights of the pits paint him in stark blacks and brights, sharpening his looks in a way that I feel like a punch to the gut. I kissed that man. I want to do it again.

I mean, that's stunning enough, but when he looks up suddenly and his eyes meet mine, they're searing as if they can see right through me.

I stumble for a step before I catch myself, suddenly uncertain. Maybe burning the letter was a bit too far.

"Tessa," he grits out and his voice is low and burred and it cuts into my chest.

"Brent," I try to sound bright and happy but it comes out a bit strangled. Look, it's not my fault that all my dreams are balancing on my ability to work with a man who is both molten-lead hot and also off-limits. I cross the rest of the gap between us and offer the paper plate I'm carrying. "I brought tacos."

The growl in his throat might be agreement that I have, indeed, brought him food, or it might be skepticism, or judgment. It's impossible to tell. I kind of like his grumpy guessing game.

"We need to get moving. The track is closing down," I say brightly. "I was thinking that maybe I'd take us to a campground I found online and we could spend the night there."

He steps forward, taking the plate and eating the taco in about three bites without saying a word to me. And I don't know why my eyes are glued to him. Watching a man eat a taco is hardly a sexy pastime. But I can't look away. There's some kind of weird energy about him every time he looks at me. Something intense and swirling that I can't name.

When he's done, he throws the plate in a nearby trash can and turns a look on me that makes my mouth dry.

"Where were you?" he asks in a low voice.

"Getting tacos, obviously," I say, smiling. What is with him?

"Before that."

He takes another step forward and there's finally something in his eye that I recognize. It's something between pain and tenderness and I almost flinch when his fingers find my elbow and hold it in the lightest grip I've ever felt — as if he isn't really holding or touching it at all, but more as if he paused in the act of caressing it. He's so near that I can smell his shampoo.

"Before what?" I ask, suddenly having trouble breathing.

"Before the tacos." Something like hurt is in his eyes. Something like jealousy.

Oh. Wow. So wait, I don't get to be near him but he also doesn't want me to be with anyone else? That's a bit sexy. But it's also ridiculously unfair. What about when he sees a girl he likes? Will he hold himself back or will he suddenly realize he has a double standard?

I give him a look to tell him exactly how unimpressed I am with this whole line of questioning and then I carefully unclip my action camera and hand it to him.

"Worried about who I might be … consorting with … Brent?"

He flinches.

I smile a bit dangerously. Usually, I can find whatever is funny in a situation, but being his virtual prisoner is not part of our deal.

"It's all on camera. Be my guest."

I swagger away so he can see I am unaffected by his suspicions.

"Tess?" He calls out, and I don't want to turn, but there's something sharp in his voice, so I do after all. "Keys."

He holds up his hand like he expects me to throw him the truck keys.

"What?"

"I just slept a few hours and you've been up all day. I'm driving."

I blink. "I don't think that's a good idea."

"You don't get to call every shot." His voice is tight. "We're a team."

I swallow down a flare of temper. I'd like to dress him down.

I'd like to establish with him that I am not going to be controlled by him. I decide — reluctantly — to pass on it for now.

I throw him the keys. "Great. I could use a rest."

By the time he gets into the truck cab, I've established myself in the passenger seat, balled a jacket against the passenger door, put a hat over my face, and I'm pretending to sleep. It's not easy in a truck cab that smells of road food and needs a good vacuuming.

He says nothing, starting up the truck and pulling out of the race pits. And yeah, it's a little annoying that there seems to be no learning curve for him to drive this truck and trailer combo. But it turns out I really am exhausted, and by the time we pull into traffic my lids are heavy.

The next thing I know a low voice is talking to me and a hand is on my arm.

"Passport," Brent says curtly.

I rub my eyes and look up to see him glowering down at me like an angry angel. I fumble in my purse and bring out my passport — barely in time for us to reach the window at the border crossing.

"Both Canadian citizens?" The guard asks as we hand our passports over and then runs through the normal spiel of checking passports and ID and questioning us about the food we might have with us.

By the time we're on the United States side of the border I'm fully awake and looking at Brent with pointed side-eye.

"We were supposed to go to that trailer park and sleep."

"I'm fine." His whole body is tense and he hunches over the wheel.

"You don't look fine."

"Thanks for that."

I roll my eyes. "I just meant that you look tired and maybe we should pull over so you can rest. Or at least so that I can drive."

"So that you can drive," he echoes.

What's got his goat?

"Yeah, so I can drive. You know, me, Tessa, the one who has been driving this whole time."

That only seems to make him more angry. "You know, I have a lot I can offer, too. I filmed you while you were racing and without someone filming there isn't a show."

I don't mention the fact that he was going to do this whole thing on his own and use the action camera footage for the racing.

"I'm the one who cleans up your perpetual mess in the trailer."

My eyes narrow at that. What, exactly, is his point?

"I have value here."

Oh.

"Of course you do," I say soothingly.

"Don't be condescending."

I snap my jaw shut. Well, if I can't be sympathetic, then what does he want from me? A fight?

Maybe.

"You should have consulted me before you drove us over the border," I tell him. "International travel shouldn't be accidental."

"We need to get to Farmer City Racetrack."

He's evading my accusation. I can tell by how the muscle jumps in his jaw. Honestly, he's kind of cute when he's all wound up. Which is most of the time. I wonder what he'd be like if he was able to blow off steam.

Unbidden, thoughts of sex with him like this fill my mind. Would he work out all that passion in the act? Would he kiss me furiously and place little bites all over? I think he might. Would he be just as demanding there as he is in everything else? Would this constant drive for perfection make him amazingly attentive?

And what about afterward? Would he mellow out for once

and just enjoy himself? I'd like to find out. Even if it would be a disaster, I'd like to try it just once.

But I'm too smart of a girl to do things just because I want to.

"Was there a reason we had to get to a racetrack two states away in the middle of the night a week before we're due there?" I ask instead. Maybe he can blow off steam arguing with me.

"I didn't want you to get any cute ideas about going off to Quebec," he growls.

I can't help the laugh that bubbles out of my throat. This is still about jealousy? He's driven this far on jealousy even though he's physically not really up to it and there's literally no other reason to go?

I've never had a man jealous over me before. I think I might like it. Or at least I might find it absolutely hilarious. All annoyance fades into the background as I catalog the little gifts he's giving me with this.

That little flicker of fire in his eyes is for me. That clenched jaw? Me, again. The flushed cheeks? Still me. White knuckles? Oh baby, those are me, too.

This is amazing. I kind of wonder how far I can push it but it seems like it might be irresponsible to do that.

"Don't laugh," he grits out. "Distractions on the road aren't going to help either of us. You didn't see me following girls around at the track."

"Yes, I was following him around," I say dryly, trying to keep the amusement out of my voice. "I followed him all the way to my parking spot and all the way to under the hood of my car."

He's silent. I can tell I haven't really dispelled his jealousy but he must realize how he's coming off in this.

"You do realize that you don't get to both swear to never so much as touch me again, while also being horrendously jealous of anyone who does, right?" I say gently.

"I do realize that."

But he keeps driving and he doesn't say anything else, just turns on talk radio and drives until we're halfway through Michigan.

I check my social media constantly. It's something to do other than fight with him. I can't keep up with the messages and notifications. I've doubled my following everywhere. My head is spinning. Hashtag False Start is everywhere and I'm getting nervous that I'll disappoint them all. I can't even keep a jealous partner happy. How will I keep this kind of fan base enthused?

Eventually, we find a nice campground that has an empty space for us. It's well into the small hours of the night when we park and head to our separate beds.

I can't get comfortable in mine. It's too short even for me, and the sleeping bag is too cold, and all I see when I close my eyes is Brent's burning gaze as he stares at the road.

I think he's asleep until I hear his whisper.

"Tess?"

"Yeah?"

"I'm sorry."

I let it hang in the air.

"For what, exactly?"

"For being a jealous prick."

I laugh at that. "Are you jealous, Brent?"

"Clearly."

"What are we going to do about it?"

"I was hoping you'd read the letter."

There's a letter for this? Is he kidding? I use my phone as a flashlight and find it in the crumpled stack.

*If I get jealous.*

I unfold it.

*You're a pretty woman and you're racing a hot car and gaining social media fame. So of course people will notice. And I'll probably get jealous Please know, it's not your fault. I'm an idiot.*

I bark a laugh. "How could you be so perceptive when you wrote these and yet so unable to help yourself now?"

"I'm only a man," he moans into his pillow so it comes out half muffled. I want to be that pillow. I want his face buried in my belly, moaning. And then, a minute later, he says, "It's freezing up here. Will you share a bed with me?"

He's killing me. Of course I want to.

"No."

"I promise to keep my hands to myself."

Nnngh.

I laugh. "Sure. Just like last time."

"Last time?"

"When we slept in bed together."

"That didn't happen." He sounds like he's in physical pain. Actually, this explains all of yesterday. He doesn't remember.

"Oh, it *so* did. It was literally last night. You were soaking wet and naked."

He moans.

"Go to sleep, Brent," I say repressively, and I don't know if he does or not but I do know it takes me an hour to fall asleep and I spend that entire hour reminding myself that the one thing I cannot afford to do is fall for Brent. Even if he is cute when he's jealous. Even if he is very appealing when he begs me to join him in his bed. Even if he's kind of everything I ever wanted.

*Chapter Twenty-Five*



BRENT

WHEN SHE'S NOT FLIRTING with French Canadiens or tying me up in knots, Tessa is easy company. We fall into a rhythm of sleep and travel and make our way to Illinois, stopping often on the way.

An easy one-day drive turns into a few very easy days and we stop at little cafes to eat — Tessa likes local places with a lot of character — and stop at lakes and scenic parks to stretch our legs, and work together on the car. We're a seamless team, to my surprise. Since we clash constantly personally, I'd expected it to be rough to work together, but it's not. I find her handing me tools before I need them and I answer her questions while she's still asking them.

How she does things feels natural to me. Maybe it was all that time working with Ian, or maybe we just sync up easily but I've hardly had a thought about something before she's starting to act on it and I can ease myself in to assist without her having to ask since I know exactly what she has in mind.

When I sleep along the way, she does little spotlights of our repairs for BOOM and if I watch them after that's just for quality control, right? Not because I'm fascinated by her charm. Not because I'm thrilled by how well she's doing.

Our social media is exploding. We post pictures and clips and honestly, I'm too ill to keep up with replying to people or follower counts or anything else. Tessa has fallen into the habit of taking my phone and doing it for me. Usually, she imitates my voice and gruffly says aloud whatever she's typing while I roll my eyes. She mostly does it when I'm driving. I think she gets bored if she isn't the one in charge of something and if it can't be driving the truck, then she makes sure she's driving something else.

"I have forty-thousand followers," she says as we drive through the northern tip of Indiana. "This is wild. You have sixty-thousand, you know."

I snort a laugh and smile at her. I do know. And I'm pleased by the fact that the show is going well, I need this. We both need it. But secretly, I'm more pleased to see her smiling so broadly, bare feet up on the dash as she sifts through our public faces and adjusts them to fit our goals. She makes any place she goes seem to form around her to fit. Right now, this truck cab is one hundred percent Tessa-domain. I'm not sure what role I play in that. Chauffeur, maybe?

When she isn't manning the socials, I ask her to review race footage and I offer helpful hints about how she can tighten up her turns and snatch a little more speed from the straightaways. They're things she'll hone in time, but the right tip might spark something in her, you never know, and while I'm much more experienced than she is, I've begun to admit to myself that she has more raw talent. If we hone it, who knows how far she'll go. Maybe I'll even get to go part of the way with her.

We still haven't seen any of the show, but Ian texts to tell me that it's a hit, and everyone loves it, and we're sure to be stars in no time.

My sister's texts are a little less fun.





The usual feeling of being boxed in doesn't come over me when I read it. Instead, I think of Pierre helping Tessa with the hood of her car. There are a lot of people who would be more than happy to help "take care" of Tessa and I think my new plan is to make sure that they don't get that opportunity.

I'm starting to feel at ease. It helps that I'm dizzy less often. I don't need quite as much sleep as I used to. It helps that I can start to laugh at Tessa's jokes. Maybe there's a constant underlying tension there, but I ignore it. If this is all I get of this girl, then I'm going to soak it in and love every minute of it. I feast on her silly jokes and revel in her laughter. She's slowly working her way under my skin and into my bones and I know I'm playing a dangerous game. I know this is going to hurt when it eventually must end, but I can't help myself. I'm addicted. And there's nothing else that can give me what I need but her.

We spend a few days at a campground outside Champaign, Illinois. It has a long dirt road where we can test and tune the car. My excitement to finally be well enough to help must show through because midway through tweaking the steering, I look up to find Tessa leaning against the trailer. Her arms are crossed over her chest and a speculative look is on her face.

"Solving the world's problems?" I ask with a slight smile. I love it when she looks at me like that, like I'm a problem she means to fix if she can just find the right wrenches.

"Solving one problem, I suppose," she says, her eyes dancing.

My smile grows. For just a moment, I let myself forget that I've been ill. I let myself forget about the pressure of this BOOM gig and the pressure from people outside, and I just let myself look at her, enjoy how much she pleases my eyes, how the smile on her laughing lips warms up my heart, how the glimmer of trouble in her eyes keeps me on my toes.

"You're twinkling," she says. Her face and hair are awash with the pink of sunset. It paints everything in a soft filter as if it, too, is caught up in the moment.

"Twinkling?" I'm too taken with her to form a proper thought beyond parroting her words.

"Your eyes are sparkling and your dimple has come out to play. Just like when I met you."

"Over the sweet siren of a car alarm," I tease and look down to wrench again before my heart breaks from too much watching. "What problem are you solving?"

"The Brent problem, obviously."

A laugh rips from my chest unbidden. "I'm a problem now?"

I look up a little coyly and smile at her from beneath my lashes. I like that she likes how I look when I'm happy because I like seeing that same look in her eyes.

"You've always been a problem," she says, launching off from the trailer and taking a step toward me. Her dark hair swirls around her like a curtain, first hiding, then revealing.

I stand automatically. My words are a little breathless. "No, *you* have been."

"What do you do with a problem you can't solve?" Her words are teasing, her smile playful, but that's the question, isn't it? It's the question I've been asking myself all week.

"Keep trying?" I suggest. My hands are grimy and I have a

wrench in one of them, but she's close enough that I could touch her. If I wasn't dirty. And if I hadn't made vows.

"No," she whispers.

"No?" My heart sinks hard.

She stands up on tiptoes until her nose is an inch from mine and I can smell her cinnamon and apple scent. I let my eyes flutter closed for a moment and just breathe her in. My arms are shaking from being held in place at my sides. I promised not to touch. I won't touch.

"Maybe you just let it be unsolvable," she whispers.

"That sounds like quitting," my voice sounds strained even to my own ears. "Maybe you should ask a friend to solve it for you."

"Mmm," she considers and the look in her eye is moving from teasing to challenging. "Then solve it, Brent. Solve it for me."

My breath comes out in a gust and I'm pretty sure that if she keeps teasing me I'm going to drop this wrench and leave grimy handprints all over her. Instead, I clear my throat.

"I have a gift for you," I say, reaching into my shirt and pulling out the chain I wear everywhere with the washer strung on it. I feel my cheeks heating. "This lock washer was the only thing holding a key bolt in place when my car won its first race." I smile inwardly before meeting her gaze again and something hot warms in my chest at the approval in her eyes. "The nut shook loose and it was a near thing. It's silly that I kept it, but it's become a habit. My lucky washer. I want you to have it. To wear it in the next race."

"What about you?" she asks, shifting her weight so that she's even closer. My skin tingles with the feeling of her so close. I could lean my weight forward just a little and our bodies would meet. It takes all my restraint to hold steady. "You're getting better. Soon you'll be driving."

I shake my head. "Maybe," I agree. "But Tess..." this part is hard and my voice betrays me, breaking roughly. I clear my throat and adopt a stern tone to keep it under control. "Tessa Harstone, I think you should be the one racing in this show. You're ... look," I run a hand through my hair. "You have more natural talent than I do. I can teach you the things experience brings. But you're more naturally ... just take it, okay?"

I pull the chain from my neck and slowly, so as not to startle her, I slip it over her head. It lies over her long hair and I feel a twist of possessiveness deep in my gut. I've put something of mine on her. It's practically crude the way that makes me feel satisfied inside.

"Let it guard you when I can't," I mutter, looking away so she won't see my eyes and read all the things I'm trying to keep to myself.

I turn away from her warmth — a warmth that isn't for me — throw my tools into the garage and wash up in the garage sink. When I turn, she's nowhere to be seen, so I head into the trailer. The awkwardness of my gift still hangs between us, but I'm done with the car and there's nothing else to do.

The shower is running in the little bathroom. I sit awkwardly on the couch and try to scroll through my socials. I feel oddly edgy and unsettled. I don't know what to do with this girl who drives me wild. I have no answer to solve this puzzle at all.

If I was a smart man, I would walk away from these feelings and just fulfill our agreement, but I'm not smart, I guess, because I keep miring myself in deeper. I must have looked like a love-sick fool out there to her. I'm ashamed of it. And if I push it, I'm only going to trip her up on her way to success. What does she need a broken racer for? She doesn't. She can do her own car work, her own filming, her own racing. She doesn't need me at all.

When I hear the bathroom door open, I don't look up. I just keep my head in my hands but then I hear her voice.

"Well, you're not going to solve the problem like that," she teases, laughter in her voice. "So, I think maybe I will. I swear, for a man who races cars, you sure do like tapping the brakes."

I look up at her. She's clean. And she's wearing my lucky charm.

And not a stitch else.

# Chapter Twenty-Six

*TESSA*

Do I know what I'm doing? Not really. They don't call me "dangerously impulsive" for no reason. Look, my head is telling me a thousand reasons why this is a terrible idea. And it's right about every one of them.

But my gut is telling me that if I don't jump now I'm going to lose my chance. It's the same feeling I get when it's the right time to make a move and go for the pass during a race. The same feeling I felt when I dumped my stupid job and decided to film car videos and live in my parents' garage. It's that part of me that assesses risks and payoffs and lets me know when it's time to leap.

This is the time to leap. Even if it doesn't feel right to my brain. Even if my heart feels all tangly. I do this now or it doesn't happen. I know that in the shower as I'm washing, my hands on autopilot, my mind spinning furiously.

Forget my family and his. Forget BOOM. Forget everything. I can feel us sinking into a routine. It's the routine of being friends and colleagues. And I'm going to watch some girl come up to him soon like Pierre came up to me — heck, I've been sending messages to his junk box all week from eager female fans — and he's going to smile at her with that patented dimple-sparkle-smile of his and she's going to swoon, and there will be no business deals or family in the way and he'll ask her to come to his bed and she won't say no and he'll press that ridiculously dear body of his to hers like he did to me and she won't go sleep somewhere else, she'll encourage him with warm touches and he'll sink into her and be lost to me forever.

I know it.

My gut is telling me that. It's telling me that this moment of vulnerability where he looked up at me through his lashes and then gave me a gift — this is a one-time thing and my last chance and suddenly, I know that I don't want to lose this chance. I just want to take it while I can.

I steel my spine, clench my jaw, and make my choice, and when I step out of the bathroom it's in nothing but his good luck charm.

I try a teasing opening salvo — something to tell him he can have fun, that he doesn't have to take everything seriously. But he looks up and just gapes at me like he doesn't believe what he's seeing.

"Shall I tell you how we're going to solve our problem?" I can't lose my nerve even if he looks more panicked than excited. I can feel my cheeks going scarlet. C'mon Tess, don't chicken out now.

"Problem?" he asks, breathlessly, standing so suddenly that I think he might be about to flee, but his eyes are all over me and he finally closes his mouth long enough to swallow. His eyes darken and the panic wicks away, replaced by something dark and tumultuous, something that looks like hunger.

"The problem of me and you," I say, smiling like we're sharing a joke. "I thought you wanted to solve it."

"Tess," he grits out. "This can't happen."

"Is that you saying that you don't want it to happen?"

He's flushing now, too. "Our families want it too badly."

"They don't need to know." I take a step forward. I have to hold my chin up a little higher to keep from freaking out. It's a terribly vulnerable thing to be here completely exposed to his eyes with no assurance that I won't be rejected.

"BOOM asked us not to start something. It will complicate things."

"Maybe I like complicated." I lick my lips and I see his eyes fasten onto the gesture, his own lips parting in response.

"You promised you wouldn't seduce me."

"Intentionally." I raise an eyebrow.

"This seems pretty intentional."

I take a gamble. "I've already seduced you ... unintentionally. This is just admitting what's already happened."

He doesn't fight me on it and my heart rate slows a little in relief.

"I vowed not to touch you," he says instead.

"Then don't touch me. I can touch enough for two."

A ragged gasp rips from his lips and I see his hands flex and unflex as his gaze rakes down me. I see the emotions rolling through him in waves of desire, frustration, concern, and then desperation. I can hardly take it. If he rejects me now, I won't ever be able to look at him again.

He sits down so fast that at first, I think he's rejecting me outright but then he looks up, laughing self-deprecatingly.

"They warned me not to get my heart rate up too fast. I guess this is why. Unless there are three of you gorgeously naked in front of me."

"There's just one."

He makes a "come here" motion with both hands and looks up at me with his lower lip caught between his teeth, a laugh bubbling out. It's that self-awareness piercing through this ridiculously sexy moment that melts me.

"Are you saying no?" I ask gently, kindly. "Because if you're saying no, it's okay."

He laughs again and his gaze meets mine. It's tenderness and heat in equal parts.

"Why the fuck would I ever say no to you, Tessa?"

I feel suddenly shy, my head dips and I'm watching him through my hair.

He swallows, and as if he's making a point, he rips his T-shirt off in a single motion, exposing all that lovely male skin sprinkled with dark blond hair. I step forward until I'm standing between his spread knees and put my hands on his shoulders, biting my lip a little shyly.

"Are you saying it's a bad idea, then?"

"You know damn well that it is," he says, but his eyes still aren't saying no, they're gazing a challenge into mine, as he clenches his jaw. "It's the worst idea ever ..." he pauses, letting that sit, "... and I'm hoping like hell that you don't change your mind."

"So you won't touch me?" I whisper, teasing him now as I lean in so I can kiss the top of his head. I hear his gasp as it puts his face into the softness of my breasts. "Just with your hands ... or is everything off limits."

"The hands do the touching," he growls.

I grab his wrists and carefully set them each up over the back of the couch on either side of him.

"So I do all the touching then," I agree, reaching down to open his belt and slide it through all the loops.

The sound he makes in the back of his throat is mostly a groan but partly still a growl.

"Can I touch you here?" I ask, placing two finger-tips under his chin to lift it up.

"Yes," he enunciates the word perfectly.

I smile and lean in, close enough that our lips are almost touching but not quite.

"Can I kiss you?"

"Yes," he grits out, and I do.

I slide my tongue over his lips and cradle them in my own as my tongue goes wandering and my hands move up to curl around his ears and then tangle through his tousled hair. I don't want to lose myself yet, but for a few minutes, I do, kissing, caressing, sinking into the taste of him like a glutton at a banquet. I want one of everything ... no, make that, two.

It's only his pained moan that draws me back. I place a hand flat across his chest and feel his heart hammering under my palm. His arms haven't moved a millimeter.

"Can I touch you here?"

"Yes."

It's barely a whisper now as my fingers spread wide and then trail down the center of his chest and abdomen, sliding through the silky hair forming a trail in the center, one fingertip catching on the edge of his belly button before my fingers meet denim. I sink to my knees to get a better look at things and a groan catches in his throat. He's biting his lip so hard that I think he's going to draw blood.

I release the button on his jeans and slide the zipper down with exquisite slowness before I peel him out of them and his trunks all at once. He bucks his hips up to help me, but his hands stay firmly on the back of the couch.

The moment his pants are off I slide back between his muscled thighs, tilting my head to one side. My hair slides over his leg and I feel his shuddering gasp. I let him fully enjoy it before I meet his eyes and then look pointedly at his thick erection as I speak the words I know will devastate him.

"How about here? Can I touch you here?"

"Fuck," he gasps, and his eyes are glassy, breath uneven.

"I'm going to take that as a yes."

I bite my lip and pause, to draw out every second of this and just when his expression turns from anticipation to pain, I lean in and soft as you please, I trace a barely-there-touch around the tip of him and watch as his eyes roll back in his head. Mmm.

And just when he thinks that's all I'm going to do, I lean forward and let my tongue do the exact same thing before I swallow him up in my mouth and his rough curse tells me it's doing exactly what I hoped it would, but it's not until I feel his hands finally touch my waist that I know he's mine entirely.

"Please," he begs me. "Please. I just want to feel all of you."

If he can't say no to me, I really can't say no to him.

"Take me to your bed," I whisper and his nod is all the yes I need.

# Chapter Twenty-Seven

*BRENT*

WE STAND TOGETHER and pause long enough for me to draw her in to my chest and wrap my arms around her tenderly. She looks up at me with that playful teasing look of hers and I'm drowning in wanting her. I lean into her warmth and softness, brush a feather-light wisp of hair from her face and press my lips reverently to hers. She's everything I've ever wanted and she's going to let me show her how much I treasure her.

I deepen our kiss, concentrating on showing her with my every movement. I gasp little breaths between soft, searing kisses. When I pull back, I brush her cheek with the back of my hand and look long into her eyes and I know mine are heavy with desire. I want all of this woman. Every last inch of her.

I think ... damn ... I think I might love her. That's crazy, right? It's been so fast. It can't be real. And yet it's there, heavy in my heart, bubbling up to my lips. It wraps me up in ribbons and demands that I present myself to her.

I open my mouth to speak it, but when I meet her eyes I see something in them that I didn't expect. Uncertainty. Weighing.

This, for her, is not a culmination of something that's been growing and won't be kept down. It's something else.

I let my arms fall and I step back. "What ...?"

I don't know how to ask her what she's doing. What we're doing. If it's what I think it is or something else.

Her expression shifts to sudden worry. "What's wrong?"

"You ..." I shake my head. "I can't."

"You can't what?" she asks deliberately, looking down to where I most certainly *can.*

"What would you say you feel for me right now?"

Her smile twists into laughing irony. "Enormous attraction. Come to bed with me and I'll tell you all about it."

I swallow, but my mouth is dry, not from desire but from the sure knowledge that I'm making a terrible mistake. I've fallen in love. I don't think I can fall back out. Or climb back out. Or whatever.

But that is clearly not how she feels about me.

My heart is racing with the knowledge of it.

It claws up my throat.

If I go to bed with her now, what then? Will it be a one-time thing? And then it will seal the possibility of anything more up in a neat package and lock it away. She'll have gotten me out of her system and she won't be able to work with me like we did before, right? I'll have traded everything for just one night.

I don't know how much of my thoughts are on my face. I feel stricken and I don't know how to go back to where I was just a few minutes ago.

"You're not ... you wouldn't say you're in love with me?"

Her laugh is a scoff and it's like a bucket of cold water thrown over me.

"Brent," she says, still laughing slightly. "Would you stop overthinking this? I'm drawn to you. I have been since I met you. I've wanted you all that time, and clearly, you've wanted me, too, or you wouldn't be so jealous when other men talk to me. We're living in this confined trailer and we're spending the night here one way or another. Why not spend it together? Why not take this opportunity while it's right here in front of us?"

Because it will probably break my heart, is what I don't tell her.

Because I think I'm too far gone on you already.

Because if I have sex with you then I'm never ever going to get the feeling of you out of every nerve of my body. I'll never recover. You'll fly free and far and I'll be left here ruined.

I don't know how to say any of it without sounding desperate or like some naive kid who just falls in love with the first girl willing to touch him. All my words stick in my throat and I don't know what to do.

I step back from her and I register the hurt and confusion in her eyes but I don't know what to tell her.

"I love you," is burning in my throat and I'm pretty sure it's the one thing I absolutely should not say.

I snatch up my shorts and jeans and shuck them on, refusing to meet her gaze again. If I do, I'm going to break into pieces. I'm going to take what she's offering and lose the rest. And I don't know what my plan is, only that this will ruin it. I can't love her only once when I want to hold her in my arms forever and never let go.

Fuck, I have it bad.

"What are you doing?"

She sounds a bit panicked when I bundle up her sleeping bag under one arm.

I'm only half dressed, my belt still hanging from the loops of my jeans in limp misery. I'm barefoot and bare-chested.

I risk one look at her. She's beautiful and devastating. I want to stop, drop everything, and kiss her all over and I can't. I can't because one taste of her will sink me if it's only going to be one.

"I'm going to sleep in the garage," I grit out.

"For fuck's sake, Brent."

Her laugh is disbelieving and she snatches my shirt from the couch and drags it on over her head. My shirt. On her perfect form. It twists something low in my abdomen that wants to throw my heart out the window and just take her right now.

"You don't have to go sleep in the garage. You can just say no and we both go to bed like usual."

"No," I gasp. She's so ridiculously sensible. It makes me want to curse, I love it so much.

"There," she says, smiling at me a bit sadly but also a bit fondly. "You've said it. Now let's go to our separate beds and think about what we've done."

She's teasing me and I'm dying. I'm already dead.

"I can't," I grit out and then I flee the trailer and dash into the garage portion, closing and locking the door between the two. I lean on the workbench and try to catch my breath.

And I think I made the wrong choice, because I was trying to keep from breaking my own heart, and it seems to be broken anyway.

## Chapter Twenty-Eight

*TESSA*

WELL, that went badly.

The door slams and I look down at his socks and shoes strewn across the ground and I know I've made a huge mistake.

But honestly, I don't know why. We've had a fun thing going for days. It's been light and easy. He seems to appreciate me. He gave me his good luck charm.

How could my gut have been so wrong? It's never wrong.

But I guess I was mistaken.

I run a hand through my hair. Am I humiliated? Well, maybe a bit. Rejection definitely stings, but I wasn't the one with my mouth slack with pleasure and my eyes rolled back in my head before I suddenly freaked and fled, so I don't think I need to be embarrassed.

My cheeks keep burning like they didn't get the memo.

And it's not like I asked for his hand in marriage or said I loved him or tried to make him fix my emotions, or neuroses, or relationships, like clingy girls do. I offered him fun sex.

And he slammed the door.

Okay, time for a game plan, Tessa. We'll call it, "Project Dignified Response" and keep our heads high. I feel the edges of my heart — or maybe my ego — crumpling, but I refuse the emotion. Return to sender. No such addressee. Or something.

Okay, what's the reasonable thing to do here? Well, it's definitely not chasing after him like a love-lorn fool. That's the surest way to scare guys off, if every friend drama I've ever observed is any indication.

I get a text as I'm debating what to do. It's one of those stupid sugar-sweet ones from Olivia. How are my brother's teeth not all rotten from being married to a girl like that?

Dear Tessa,

I know perfectly well that my uncharitable feelings toward my sister-in-law are not her fault and entirely a result of being flat-out rejected by her brother, but I can't help it. I'm annoyed.

I hope you are well. I have marvelous news. I think I may be pregnant. Too early to test, but never too early to tell family, right? xoxo Also, I'm so proud to start on our plans to be one big family together. How are things coming with Brent? Love, Olivia.

And look, I know my situation doesn't forgive what I'm doing, but that doesn't stop me from replying with sarcasm.

Swimmingly. We're picking out china.

I text back and then huff my way back into my own clothing, reluctantly shedding Brent's very masculine scented T-shirt, crawl into the bed — since he has my sleeping bag — and read the rest of my texts.

I chat excitedly with Kati for a while about her actual

confirmed pregnancy. (Okay, yes, I'm still bitter at poor Olivia). I think about telling her about my mistake and Project Dignified Response but I'm too embarrassed to confess this to anyone.

I get a text from BOOM just as I'm falling asleep.

> We have fresh racing suits with our branding for you to pick up at this mailing service location. Think you can get it before the race? We'd love to see you dressed in our colors!

I text back *"yes"* before going to sleep. If Brent doesn't like it, then I'll go without him.

I screw up my eyes and apparently, spite is like sleeping pills to me because I sleep the night away without a single dream. When I finally wake up, I hear Brent in the shower, and that's my cue to dress as fast as humanly possible and launch myself out of the trailer.

Okay, it's dramatic but I need a minute.

I pretend to work on the car. It needs no work.

When Brent comes out of the trailer looking terribly awkward and carrying two cups of hot coffee, Project Dignified Response is in full swing and I talk to him cheerfully about the weather, the schedule for the day, and the parcel to pick up from BOOM. I don't let him turn the conversation, even though I see the frustration and confusion and ... is that loss? ... in his eyes. That's right, Brent. You lost out. Good luck being offered that again.

But I'm a queen of cheer and optimism. I lay it on thick as we load the car together and pull out of the trailer park. Errands take most of the day, and then we're at the track, in the pits, and in the thick of things. I meet some fans — young girls mostly. Shake a lot of hands. Get to know people.

Everything is going perfectly until the moment that I open the box from BOOM. There are four racing suits. Two in a large male size — for Brent — and two in a petite ladies' size. They are bright orange with the BOOM logo on the breast and sleeve. Well and good. It's the name emblazoned on the back that's a problem because all four say "BOLT" in huge block letters.

"There must have been a mix-up," Brent says. He's looking pale. He's refused to nap all day. Maybe it's because he's feeling better, or maybe he's stubbornly refusing to be vulnerable around me the way I was around him.

"I promised to wear it and I will," I say, but my heart is falling. For some reason, wearing a race suit with his name on it feels … well it feels like splinters under my skin after last night. It's putting a real hitch in Project Dignified Response. But I can deal. I have to.

I pull on the racing suit and tie the arms around my waist. If I'm quick getting in and out of the car, no one will even notice the name on my back. Especially with the back rolled down and tied up the rest of the time.

"I'm sorry," Brent says gruffly when I come out to where he's checking camera batteries. "It's not fair for you to have to wear my name."

"It had nothing to do with you," I say tightly, but he won't meet my eye until after the driver's meeting right before my first race.

And when he does meet them, I can hardly catch my breath. He's outside the car and I'm inside. My helmet isn't on yet, but I'm checking my harness when he leans in past me to flip my camera on and I can smell his scent and feel the warmth of his thickly muscled arm so close to me. And I want to just breathe it in forever and then all of a sudden he turns and we're face to face in the tight proximity of the interior of the car.

And the look in his eye exactly matches the look that was in it when he was in my mouth and my lips part without meaning to, as the significance of that hits me full in the chest. He wants me still. Despite running away. Despite everything, he wants me.

"I don't mind wearing your name," I blurt out, desperate to make things right between us.

His smile is rueful. "Whatever I have is yours to take."

"Except not really," I challenge because I can never let well enough alone. It's kind of my thing.

He frowns. "What?"

I have to swallow before I say, "You didn't let me take you."

I think he wants to answer, but I rev the car engine, swallowing his words, and he pulls his head and arm back out through the window as I slip on my helmet and tighten the strap, and refuse to look at him again. So much for Project Dignified Response. It's on fire somewhere with my ego and at least half of my heart.

I'm full of roiling emotions and I channel them all into the race. I start at the back of the pack, but that's fine. I can pass, and pass, and pass all I like, and I do. I take every opportunity my gut throws at me and if it's terribly wrong about love, it's still genius at racing. I nab second place and qualify for the feature and then I'm driving back to the pits with my heart in my throat, and my whole body ringing with tension. I know I shouldn't have said that. I should have left things alone. I'm ready to eat my words.

I yank off my helmet as a blur of orange comes toward me. My mouth already opening and ready to apologize when I realize this isn't Brent coming to speak to me at all.

It's Big Daddy BOOM and for the first time ever, he doesn't seem to be smiling.

"Tessa Harstone," he says wryly. "On the one hand, it's great to finally meet you in person. On the other hand, I'm here with bad news. We have a big problem."

# Chapter Twenty-Nine

BRENT

SHE RACES like a pro and I watch her every move with a heavy heart. If my aim was to keep my heart from breaking, I've done a terrible job of it. All day, she's avoided my gaze and kept me carefully outside of her trust, moving every conversation to general pleasantries, turning every apologetic look I send her into a breezy smile. All day, I just keep seeing two things — her, kneeling between my legs and the look in her eyes just before I bolted.

I'm both intoxicated and terribly ashamed. I should have stopped her before it started if I wasn't going to go through with it. Or, if I was, then I should have confessed to her right there how my heart is all tied up in her smiles and frowns. Instead, I made two wrong choices like a fool.

I need to tell her. I need to confess. Then she'll understand and she won't feel awkward anymore, she'll probably just pity me. I mean, it will make things awkward in a different way after she lets me down with a bright smile and I'm sure that by the time we've completed these five races and BOOM picks her show up permanently and sends her a professional camera person, then she'll gently cut me loose. And that will be fine. It will. Because she'll be successful and happy.

I'll wait until after the race so that I don't distract her and then I'll tell her.

I finish filming her race from the barrier and turn my camera to the cheering crowds and feel a nostalgic smile tighten across my face. I love the feeling of celebrating with thousands of people — of light-hearted fun we get to enjoy together as we watch the cars roar down the track and take crazy gambles in their bid to win. That feeling we all share when the leaders are rounding the nearest curve and they're so close that I'm not sure I could squeeze my palm between their bumpers. Their tires elongate and seem to break all laws of physics as they angle around the turns at crazy speeds. We all get to gasp together, to let out laughing exhales when everyone makes it around the curve without crashing, and then cheers when they pick up speed on the straight stretches. It's the third-most intoxicating thing I've ever felt. Actual racing being second now that I've discovered that Tessa is number one.

Well, if I can't have her, I can still have this. I'm feeling a bit better every day. When she leaves me, I'll race again. It makes me snort to realize that my dream is now my consolation prize.

I duck my head, lower my camera, and turn to go to the pits when I feel a hand on my shoulder.

"Brent Bolt," a deep voice says, hand clamping down and I turn, ready to give a smile to a racing fan, but my eyes widen as I catch sight of the orange T-shirt with the cut-off sleeves and the towering form of Big Daddy BOOM right there and in the flesh.

"Boom," I say with a smile of greeting, and to my surprise, he grabs me with one arm and tightens it quickly in a one-armed hug.

He's bigger than he seems on camera. Taller than my six feet — he's six-two at least, and thick with muscle. It's not carved, chiseled muscle, but it's definitely more than you get by living an active lifestyle and working a blue-collar job. It's protein shakes and trainers kind of muscle. Fifty-ish but energetic and with his hair still dark and eyes bright, he's not a man you'd want to fight. He has a short beard he strokes on camera and it seems it's not just for show because he's stroking it now.

"You can call me Adam." While he isn't smiling, there's a kind of exuberant energy that rolls off of him like mist off the ground on a hot morning. He releases me and points toward the pits. "Let's go catch up with Tessa. We all need to talk."

"Sure," I say, and something feels heavy in my gut. Has he somehow found out what is going on between us? He was clear he didn't want a relationship from the start and I ... maybe I've slipped up and someone has noticed in our footage that I am completely smitten with the girl I'm supposed to be filming.

Once we're away from the noise of the crowd, Adam seems to relax a bit. He looks around us as if ensuring no one is listening and then leans in.

"I'm glad I have a moment to talk to you before we catch up with Tessa."

I nod. "I should thank you for the loan of the truck and trailer. They're absolutely amazing."

He waves a hand to dismiss that. "Listen, I know this was supposed to be you, and it's probably killing you not to be the one in the driver's seat."

I shrug. The thing is, it would be if it were anyone but Tessa.

"She's a natural," I say instead, and then force myself to say the true words that are likely about to kill my own opportunities. "She's going to be better than me. With some more experience and these opportunities, she'll be a better driver and you'll be glad you bet on her."

His sudden grin is fierce. "Oh, I'm already happy with my bet, Brent. Happier now when I hear this from you because I admire the kind of man who will tell the truth even when it means putting someone else ahead of him. Seriously, I do. And I want you to know that whatever happens here, you have a place with BOOM. We'll find you a spot to work, so don't let that worry you."

I smile and thank him, but my heart is sinking. He's going to break us up as a team, isn't he? Give her the crew she needs early and send me packing. I keep my jaw thrust out boldly and a confident expression on my face but I can't help the ball of emotions gathering in my throat. I'm not ready to say goodbye.

We catch up to Tessa as she's pulling into our spot in the pits. Adam races ahead of me to greet her. I look over the car while they're exchanging greetings, and after telling her he has bad news, he shifts suddenly into telling her to call him Adam. He gives her a hug and tells her how happy BOOM is to sponsor her races. I'm confused about what the bad news is, unless it's that he needs to replace me and he's worried about how she'll feel with new people backing her up.

I circle the vehicle while they're talking and then start to replace a tire with an air leak. By the time I'm almost done, Adam is squatting down beside me, assessing the vehicle. He makes a few suggestions that I hurry to enact, and then he looks at his phone.

"Looks like we have about twenty minutes before you need to get going again and the car looks ready to race," he tells Tessa. "Can the three of us head inside and talk?"

I expect him to lead us to the living quarters' portion of the trailer, but instead, he takes us into the garage and slides a few stools out from under the workbench, gesturing to us that we should sit. He stays standing.

It's only then that I realize that he looks nervous. He rubs the back of his neck and looks at us both before offering a rueful smile.

"We have a problem, the three of us."

In the pause, Tessa says, "I hope we haven't done anything wrong."

She's twisting her hands together.

Boom laughs. "Well, yes, and no. Not in my opinion, but public opinion is a different beast and ... well, so is gossip and that can cause some trouble." He takes off his ball cap and rubs the top of his head. "So, your show has been a huge success so far. Huge. Our streaming app has seen an increase in viewership of 20% that we can contribute just to marketing this show to prospects. That's huge. We love it. We had no idea it would be so popular so fast."

"That doesn't sound like a bad thing." I can't quite keep the question out of my tone.

"And it's not, of course. But we didn't quite expect the level of uproar when viewers realized that the pair of you are traveling in the same trailer — a trailer with only one real bed — and you aren't married. Bible belt mamas, am I right?"

Ooops.

Tessa looks confused, so I confess.

"I think I was the one who took a reel of the interior of the trailer and uploaded it. I thought viewers would get a kick out of what it's like to live on the road."

Adam nods. "And we chose to upload that to our socials, too, because we thought it was charming and surprisingly clean for a pair of people in their twenties." He pauses to smile, as if in apology. "It took off, getting us a ton of views and shares ... and a large contingent of people who thought it was a moral issue. Which would have just been online haters, except here's where it gets complicated." He pauses as if to gather his thoughts. "I like your sister Olivia a lot, Brent. She's a sweetheart. Reminds me a bit of my late wife Amy, if I'm being honest. But your sister was talking with the crew and there was some kind of mix-up. She seemed to imply that the pair of you were married."

He lets that sit and I feel my face grow hot. Damn it, Olivia.

What have you done?

"But we're not," Tessa says in a small voice. "We didn't lie to you. There's nothing between us."

And now my face is even hotter because that's a lie for me even if it isn't for her.

Adam nods and an odd expression crosses his face. He huffs an ironic laugh.

"I know I told you two not to start anything, but I have to say this might be easier if it were true. The thing is, my right-hand man Tanner heard her say whatever she said, and took it as truth, and started responding to comments online saying that you were in fact married. You might have noticed that he also went ahead and changed the name on the back of your racing suit to 'Bolt,' Tessa."

Tessa nods, biting her lip.

"And you wore it tonight," he says, letting that hang in the air.

"But we haven't submitted tonight's footage yet," I offer. "We could edit that out."

"Could we edit it out of everything everyone filmed?" Adam asks, spreading an arm to indicate the pits and stands outside the trailer.

"No," Tessa says in a small voice.

"Well, then that's the problem. People think you're married. Thousands of people. And with your show so fresh, it's in a vulnerable place. Any negative reactions at this point have the potential to spiral out of control."

Tessa shakes out her hair and draws in a long breath and I run a hand over my face. It feels like the three of us are passing an armed bomb from person to person and at any time it might go off.

"What do we do?" Tessa asks when she's composed herself.

"Well," Adam says, "We could cancel the rest of the show and the whole thing will fizzle out and that's that."

Tessa's face falls and I want to take her hand and tell her it will be okay but I can't. It will only make things worse.

"I don't want to do that," Adam clarifies and her eyes whip up to his. "But it would be the most honest route to take."

"What's the less honest route," I ask.

"Well, I won't lie directly to my viewers," Adam says. "I'm not that kind of man and also it's bad for business to base things on lies."

"So we can't just pretend to be married," Tessa says in a small voice.

And now my heart is sinking for even worse reasons because it's not just me who is about to lose all this — it's Tessa. And she doesn't deserve to lose out just because my sister is full of wishful thinking and spread rumors around that were repeated.

"There's got to be another way." I don't realize I've said it until I hear it echoing in the air.

"What? What other way?" I can tell Tessa is close to tears. Boom should have waited to break this news until after her feature. How is she supposed to race like this?

I glance at Adam and see his eyes laser-focused on me, like he needs me to be the one to say the obvious.

"We could actually get married," I say. "Quickly. Monday, when the government buildings open up again. And if we're actually married, then no one has lied ... really ... and we can just keep racing and doing our thing."

Tessa's mouth opens and closes twice.

"I can't *tell* you to get married," Adam says with an innocent look on his face and his palms held up and I nearly snort because he and I both know that's why he's here. "I'd never do that. I'm pretty sure it would be illegal to tell your contractors that, and besides, I don't set people up." He clears his throat. "Look, I like you two, and I'm sure I could eventually find you places somewhere in my company. Not right now, obviously, but eventually.

"But if you *did* choose to get married, then yes, it would

make all these troubles go away. And, we could plan to have you work your way west and have a huge party at my place to celebrate when the races are done. But that's just me spinning daydreams again. I know this is quite the bind and it's really unlikely that you'll take that option. More likely, you'll call me on Monday and tell me to send someone to get the trailer because you're flying home."

I swallow. That would mean the end. The end of our time together. The end of the gig and the fame and everything we've built so far. I don't want it to be over.

"Either way, I need an answer by Monday," Adam says and then checks his phone. "And I have to go. My Uber is getting impatient and I have a plane to catch back out to Utah."

"Did you fly all the way here just for this?" I ask.

He gives me a small, sad smile. "I wanted to meet you once before it was over. Besides, it's better to do this kind of thing in person."

He reaches out to shake my hand and I open my mouth to thank him but I don't get the words out before Tessa's loud outburst interrupts us.

"I'll do it." She's flushed, eyes wide, chest heaving under her white T-shirt. She's never looked so beautiful. Or so desperate. "I'll do it. I'll marry Brent."

Her eyes flick uncertainly to me and I give her one firm nod — just a very subtle jerk of the head. I'm still holding Adam's hand in a handshake and it suddenly squeezes mine and begins to pump.

"Well, this is great news!" He says, a huge smile spreading across his face. "Really great! Congratulations to both of you! I'm so happy about this that I'm going to fast-track finding you a film crew. Get it all done and send pictures of the paperwork to me ASAP and then we'll adjust your route to start heading in my direction and hitting up the races along the way. I'll see you in a few weeks and we will party. This is perfect."

He lets go of my hand and grabs Tessa's, shaking it with wild vigor and then grabbing her in a hug. She looks stunned, like she still isn't sure what happened, and then he's turning around, chuckling to himself. He leaves, but before the door shuts, he pops his head back in.

"Seriously, you two. You are not going to regret this!"

And then he's gone and it's just the two of us staring at each other with wide eyes.

Tessa's voice is shaky when she speaks, but I'm caught by the sight of her parted, vulnerable lips, of the way her eyes are so wide that she looks like she needs someone to protect her, at how her slight curves are accentuated by her tight white T-shirt and the race suit tied around her hips.

"I'm so sorry," she manages.

"Why?" I ask. My voice is quiet.

I know that marrying someone who doesn't love me is a terrible idea. But I can't help the thrill it gives me knowing that I'm going to be married to *Tessa*. To this woman who is seeping into every inch of me and marking me with her every glance and shiver. I want to hold onto the thrill and try not to think about the fact that she would have married literally any man if it would give her the chance to keep racing. It's not me she loves. It's the opportunity. And that's okay. It is. I won't ask for more from her than this — I just want to be at her side for it all.

"For dragging you into all of this." She bites her lip. And I want to kiss her, I do, but I know I can't. Not now. I would seem like I was making demands that I'll never make, like I have expectations I won't ever have of her. All she has to be is herself.

Instead, I carefully put my arms around her and pull her into a hug, and to my relief, she melts into it and into me and I whisper.

"No one dragged me, sweetheart. I'm racing as fast as I can just trying to keep up with you."

# Chapter Thirty

*TESSA*

IT'S NOT until after the feature that I have time to think about what we're doing — what I'm doing. I don't place in the feature, though I also don't wreck the car or even get very many bad dings, so I guess it's an okay showing even if it's nothing to write home about.

But I'm so stunned by all this that I can hardly think — which I guess explains the driving. When Brent comes over — serious-faced and intense — to help me out of the car and look it over, I finally realize this is really happening. I'm going to marry this man. The one who said no to me.

Why in the world did he agree to it?

I watch him checking over the car. Now that he's starting to recover from his injury, he has these moments where he seems charged with a kind of underlying energy that makes it feel like he's about to spring into action at any moment. His movements are spare, as if he's conserving energy for it, his long fingers precise in how they move over the car. I can't help the way my eyes skim over him, taking in all the lean muscle lengthening and then tightening into intriguing shapes under his T-shirt and jeans.

I've spent so long with him that sometimes I forget how beautiful he is, how his sandy blond hair always looks like he just got out of bed and his face always looks like he forgot to shave that morning. His dimples pop at even the slightest smile and the tiny crinkles around his eyes are a reminder that before all this started he was someone who could laugh with a stranger and kiss her boldly before he knew her name.

If I marry this man, will there be anything to keep me from tumbling head over heels for him? He wrote me a letter telling me not to do it. That should be reason enough to guard my heart.

I don't understand why he suggested this at all. He's not the one who would benefit the most from it, even if he does get well enough to start racing again soon. And it ties him into something he's been very very clear that he doesn't want and can't handle — life with me. More than that, an intimate relationship with me.

Does he ... is it possible that he's softening for me?

"Why did you agree?" I ask him abruptly when we finish loading the car into the trailer. His hands are full of tools to be put away and there's a smear of something on his face but when he looks up at me with that searing look in his eyes it makes me breathless.

He clears his throat. "You're the best new racer I've seen, Tessa. You have the potential to blow us all away. I didn't think we should just throw it all out the window." He shrugs and won't meet my eye. "It doesn't have to be a big deal. It's not like it's real."

"The papers we sign will mean it's real, Brent. They'll make us legally tied together. And you know that our families will enforce that. We can't just get an easy divorce later without breaking a lot of hearts."

His eyes whip back to mine. He looks awkward as he sets the tools down on the workbench.

"We don't have to do this." He clears his throat — again. "Look, I know girls dream about their weddings and the romance and everything. It's not going to be that."

"I'm not that kind of girl," I say wryly. "I generally dream about the night afterward."

His face goes so pink that I suddenly feel better about this whole thing.

"Okay, but they want to be with someone they love. Someone who makes their heart speed up. Someone they want in their bed."

"I thought I was pretty clear that you would fit very nicely in my bed." I arch an eyebrow at him and he goes redder.

"Yes, but you'll be tied to me, okay? You won't be able to bring other men home. Even if this wedding is like ... for professional reasons, I would have to insist on that part."

He's ... so ridiculous it's hilarious. "I know how marriage works, Brent."

"Okay, well I'm just saying that it's okay to back out. To say it's too much for you."

I look him up and down slowly, letting my eyes darken. "Are you scared, Brent Bolt? Scared of what might happen when you sleep in my bed after I have a piece of paper that legally says I have rights to you."

"No," it comes out thick and gruff. "And I don't have any expectations in that regard. I'm not marrying you to fuck you, Tessa."

It's hard not to grin at that but I keep my face straight. "Yes, but you're also not marrying me *not* to fuck me."

His brow furrows. "This isn't going the way I thought it would."

Maybe I should put him out of his misery.

"Look, are you saying that you don't want to marry me?" I

say "Because it makes sense to me that you wouldn't. I'm the one who benefits most from this and I'm not going to hold you to a split-second decision. You can just say the word and I'll back off."

"No," he shakes his head, looking down at the ground.

"Why are you doing this, Brent. And don't tell me that it's because I am a great racer and need this chance. That's why *I'm* doing it. Not why you're doing it."

"It's a good chance for me, too," he blurts out, but his eyes are still studying the ground and the textured rubber floor is not that interesting. "If we lose the show in disgrace, I won't get another and I won't be funded for my racing here in the US. It will be a huge setback for me. I'd have to start all over again. This builds my reputation and gives me a shot at going further."

I almost believe him but something isn't quite right.

"Okay, listen," I say. "I know you aren't telling me everything." His eyes dart up, snag on mine and then go back to their doctoral study of amazing rubber flooring through the ages. "I'm not going to pry it out of you but I'm only going to move forward on this on two conditions, and just so you know, they're both for you."

"You don't have to do anything for me," he says, and his voice is all tense and rough.

"I beg to differ. I'm pretty sure I snuck a peek at a letter that was called '*When I won't admit I need help*' and it said, '*Please give it to me anyway because I'm an idiot*,' so here you go, Brent. These are my conditions. First, we don't tell our families about this until we reach Utah because it's going to be too much already and they'll just make it so much worse."

He's nodding. Good. That's the easy one and it's nice to see we can both live with it. We'll see if he can manage this next one, though. I bite my lip and let my eyes run over him again. He scuffs the rubber floor with the toe of his boot. I guess his doctoral study involves stress testing. His bicep is all flexed where he's leaning up against the workbench and I think he might be getting tired but this is too important to pause until it's all out there.

"Second, we only do this if it's a real marriage."

His eyes shoot up and meet mine and if I wasn't used to reading him by now, I'd think he was angry. They burn at me with something I can't quite put my finger on but I know it's not anger.

"No," he says quietly and his eyes haven't left mine. They do things to me like he has a remote control of my body and is jamming all the buttons from rapid heart rate, to uneven breathing, to sexual attraction and is turning everything up to full volume.

"We don't get married, then," I say easily. "Because I've seen this go down in books and movies and it's always super lame. Two people keeping secrets, miserable, and trying to hide their attraction while they're sharing kitchens, and bathrooms, and beds. It's full-on ridiculous. I don't want to play that game. If we do this, we do it for real. We do it with shared bank accounts, and sex, and family vacations."

He swallows so hard that I see his throat bob. "Sex?"

"Not until you're ready. I'm not into non-consent," I say breezily.

"What if I'm never ready?" he asks in a husky voice.

"Then I guess we'll both be disappointed," I say acidly. But I'm not backing down on this. I'm not agreeing to a marriage with no fun at all — not even to save my career. "I'm not asking you to love me, but I want you to keep the door open for a little fun at least."

He nods in a jerky fashion like this somehow makes it worse.

"Either way, we need to leave the racetrack and get on the road. I'm driving. You look like a tire that needs more air in it. You can tell me what you think in the morning."

He doesn't look at me, just hands me the keys and follows

me as I lock everything down, gather snacks for the road, and buckle up.

"Ready to roll?" I ask him breezily as he clips his seatbelt.

"Hardly." His tone is dry.

"Even so, here we go."

I take a deep breath and start to drive.

# Chapter Thirty-One

*BRENT*

THE PROBLEM IS NOT that I don't like her proposal. The problem is that I do.

I like it far too much and it seems like a terrible idea to put myself in a position where I'll know her inside and out and keep falling and falling in love with her all on my own forever, like a man cut loose in outer space.

It feels like something no one would be stupid enough to do, and yet here's me utterly enchanted with the idea and biting my lip, hoping she doesn't change her mind. As we drive, I search for pretty girls on the street and in the cars we pass. I want to imagine myself with them. I want to show my brain what I'll lose if I agree to this, but while the women of this city are objectively lovely, I can't seem to care. Not a single one sparks anything inside. I try with memories of girls of the past in their place but find I'm only making myself miserable.

Fine. I'm slain. I will never recover. I might as well accept it.

I'm going to marry Tessa Harstone and I'm going to give her my name and all my worldly goods, my body and my heart, and

I'm going to be so entangled with her that when she finally cuts me out of her life, there will be nothing left of me without her. I'm a fucking moron.

And I'm going to do it anyway. Because I feel like the first guy to dig into a pyramid and find treasure. Now that I've found it, I can't just put it back. I can't just walk away. I'm drawn in, completely consumed. Look, it's not healthy. I should call in to a talk radio program or something. And the nice doctor on the line can tell me I'm an idiot and that I should have a fulfilling career, and friends, and hobbies so that one person doesn't eat me up like this. And I wouldn't listen.

I know that it's a bad idea not to call our families. I'm pretty sure that Ian would try to talk me out of doing this, and maybe he'd make more headway than I'm making on my own, but I see her logic. If we're going to do this for real then it's going to be delicate at the beginning and perhaps it's best not to let anything disrupt it as it blossoms into whatever it's going to be.

By the time she finds us a campground in the dark of night, pays the fees, and parks, I'm swaying and barely upright. I've pushed it too far today.

"C'mon big fella," she says with a wry smile. "Let's get you to bed."

And her hands are gentle when she leads me to the trailer and helps me get my boots off. I stumble to the ladder and climb up into the bed and I'm surprised when she doesn't follow me. I try to tell her that she can, that the couch is uncomfortable and she might as well sleep up here — I mean, if I'm going to set my life on fire why not start throwing gasoline around, right? — but it only comes out as a garbled moan.

"Go to sleep. You have an important decision to make in the morning," is all she says and then the lights are out and so am I.

I wake to sunshine and a sense of heaviness. My thoughts keep chasing each other around and around. Sometimes, my better judgment is winning, reminding me this is crazy and I'm going to get hurt and probably so will she by the time it all shakes out, and also that my brain is taxed from recovery and this is not the time to be making big life choices. But other times, it's the other side of me that's winning, and that side just wants to lean in, to stop denying what's happening, and just spend the day kissing her and showing her why this is definitely the right choice.

In the end, I sneak out while she's still sleeping and go for a walk. This campground isn't very far from civilization. A short walk brings me to where I can buy breakfast and coffee from a cute little shop. I should get her some kind of gift, right? To show that I'm on the same page as her. Flowers maybe? Chocolates? I wander into a little tourist shop with my hands still full of coffee and pastries in a bag and I'm so flustered I don't even know what to do with them until a woman in her forties stands up from behind the counter and laughs.

"Well, if those are for me, I'll drag you off to the preacher and marry you right now."

I smile at her, bemused. She's probably twenty years older than me, but pretty despite the grey threading through her hair. My smile might be a bit too frozen because she laughs and it makes me think of Tessa who is never awkward at all but takes absolutely everything into her cheerful stride.

Whatever my expression looks like, she seems to soften. "Easy now, I'm only joking. You can put the coffee and food on the cash counter while you browse. I swear I won't eat it ... or wed you against your will."

I do as she says, cheeks flushing, because her teasing hits far too close to my actual situation.

The little shop is one of those typical tourist shops, filled with so many different varieties of things that you can hardly settle on one before the next strikes your eye. It smells of cedar wood and spices and there are incense sticks on the counter and little pots of lip balm and beeswax candles. When I turn, I see books and clothing in the same area as hand-thrown pottery and local fudges, and I hardly know what I'm looking for until my eyes settle on a case of silver rings and suddenly I know exactly what I need. A ring.

I wander over to the case to look and the shopkeeper follows me.

"They're designed in such a way that you can buy any size and pinch it or pull it to fit," she says, slipping an owl ring off her finger and demonstrating. "The rose ones are always popular. And the orcas."

"What about this one?" I ask, lifting up a tiny silver hummingbird ring.

"I haven't sold one of those in ages, but if it suits the lady then it's best," she says.

"She's fast and I have trouble keeping up with her," I say and she leads me back to the cash register, laughing the whole way.

"Sounds like the best kind of woman. And like the proper person to wear a hummingbird. I hope she likes it."

She wraps it for me in a tiny velvet bag and I leave the shop with my breakfast and a wedding ring and I guess that means I've made up my mind. I'm going to go ahead and set my own life on fire. Why the hell not.

Tessa's still sleeping when I find her in the trailer and when I look down at her, I can barely breathe. She's small and vulnerable when she's sleeping, not like the ball of energy and joy she is when she's awake — always moving, always striving. In this moment, she's soft and alone and the idea that I could make her forever safe and loved, supported as she conquers the world, well, it melts me.

I let my features soften. No one is looking. I don't have to hide. I can just watch her and let my heart want all the things it wants so desperately. Let my body be drawn to her. Let my mind grow still, and breathe, and recognize that some things whirl into your life with an unstoppable force, and when that happens it's better just to let go, and let the wind carry you.

Her eyes flutter open and I carefully pack all of that back and tuck it away where she won't see it. By the time she realizes I'm there, I'm all buttoned up again and I can risk a small smile.

"I brought breakfast," I tell her. "And an answer. Which one do you want first."

"I want both as quickly as possible," she says, laughing and sitting up. "Don't you know me by now?"

She's adorably mussed. It's maybe the sexiest thing I've ever seen. I want to kiss her. I want to bite the corner of her mouth very softly. I want to tangle my fingers in those long strands of chaotic hair and run the tip of my nose across her cheek. I want to feel all her skin next to all of mine and memorize its warmth and what tiny empires on its surface kindle pleasure and how to kindle them. I want all of her. Which is why it shows all my restraint when I say.

"I'll marry you. But I have two conditions, too."

# Chapter Thirty-Two

*TESSA*

I'M ALMOST RELIEVED to hear that he has conditions. After I helped him to bed last night, I was worried that this thing was going to become so awkward that he wouldn't be able to talk to me, and frankly, I would miss him. I've grown used to his slightly cranky, serious ways.

I sat up for a long time last night sitting outside the trailer and looking at the stars while he slept and I thought about my life — about what I want from it.

I was born to go fast. I feel it in my bones when I race. And I was born for hard work and creativity. I start to panic when I think about working a nine-to-five again, about locked-in hours and other people telling me how to be and how to think. It makes my throat close up and my breathing go sharp and quick. It brings tears welling up in my eyes and little shakes in my hands. It feels like prison. A terrible prison of working for the weekends, and the vacation, and the retirement.

And look, I know my parents did that. I know they're so happy now, retired and easily able to live on the money they saved up from working their shifts at jobs governed by other people. My mom loved being a nurse so much that she's still friends with all the "girls" she worked with. She couldn't have been more happy than when she was nursing. And even Ian likes to work for someone else. He's excited that the job with BOOM is a dream job for him, but he found his time in Australia stressful. Having to fund everything on his own ideas and drive was a constant topic of conversation when he called home. He hated the instability of having to take care of his own paycheck. Hated the way all the weight of it was on his shoulders.

But I'm not like them. I was born with a wild streak that won't be tamed. I'd rather sleep on a cot in the garage than work a steady every-day job. Just thinking about doing it again makes me sick to my stomach. I can't. I just can't.

I also know that I wasn't doing very well before this BOOM opportunity, but if I hold onto it and don't mess up, it will set me up with enough connections, enough experience, and enough of a reputation that I'll never have to work for someone else again. I mean, technically BOOM is paying me for the show, but I'm a private contractor. I set my days. I make my choices, and if I want to drop it, and move on to something else, I can. Nothing limits my creativity or drive or choices.

I don't dare lose that.

It's the main reason that I want Brent to agree to this.

But I know that when I tell my family about it, they're going to want more from me. They'll want to know why I've tied myself to someone if I don't love them. Because that's a bit mercenary, isn't it? It's using Brent to get what I want. That's why I insisted that it be real if we do it. He should at least have the benefits of being married to me and I think those include an enthusiasm for bedroom activities and a cheerful bright outlook on life. I can give him that — sex and companionship — and isn't that what most marriages are? The passion fades for most people and becomes that, so is it really so terrible to offer that from the start?

He's worried that I'll want someone else eventually, but I don't think I will. All I want to do is race and build cars, and having a friend along to do it all with sounds amazing. Why would I want more than that? I've never really been swept up by another person and I don't think I will be. I won't be missing a thing.

But maybe he will be.

Maybe he'll regret this.

I went to bed worried about that. Because it's the one thing we're really gambling with here — his happiness.

Which is why I'm thrilled when he greets me with conditions. He's thought this through, and he knows what he wants.

I offer him my brightest, sunniest smile, take the coffee from his hands, and hop out of bed.

"Great! Let's eat this outside by the lake and you can tell me all about your conditions."

We find our way to a picnic table. The campground is quiet — it's not even ten in the morning yet — and there are still flecks of dew on the ground where the sun hasn't burned it off yet. I shiver lightly, my yoga pants and tight crop top are not very warm despite the fact that it's summer.

To my surprise, Brent shrugs off his hoodie and passes it to me and his T-shirt underneath stretches so nicely across his chest, revealing powerful biceps below the short sleeves, that my mouth is momentarily dry. I recover by taking his hoodie and slipping it on.

"Thank you," I say, suddenly feeling shy now that I'm surrounded by Brent's scent. It's cedar and male musk and just a hint of car exhaust. The scent is heady and addictive and I just want to keep drinking it in forever.

We sip our coffee in shared silence for a moment before he

offers me a cherry danish and my mouth is already watering when I tear off the first piece.

"My mom used to play tracks of bird song in the house on a loop," he says after a moment.

I steal a glance at him. He has a fond smile on his face as he looks out over the lake but his smile is wistful. Without thinking about it, I thread my fingers through his. He squeezes my hand gently, eyes still far away. His voice is quiet when he speaks again.

"I'd be happy to have a family again."

"You have Olivia and Ian."

"Yes, but they have to make their own family. They'll be far away. That's what you offered me, isn't it? A real marriage? One that would make us family?"

I've seen Brent angry and exhausted, laughing and turned on. I've never seen him deeply emotionally vulnerable. I want to wrap him up in blankets and tuck him into a chair and make him hot drinks. Instead, I lean my shoulder against his.

"Yes," I whisper.

He sounds a little choked up and his hand squeezes mine before relaxing again, just like his throat squeezes a bit as he says, "I'd like that."

"Tell me what your conditions are." I want to make this real. I want it to be real for both of us.

"I want you to promise never to lie to me. Not to spare my feelings. Not to make us feel more married. I know you want a real marriage and I can give you that. I know you want to keep it from your family until we get settled. Okay, I can do that. But don't pretend with me. I don't like being played. I don't want to have to play guessing games."

I'm actually kind of touched that this is what he's asking for — that we are bare to each other emotionally just as I told him I wanted us to be bare to each other physically.

"I'm going to give you my whole life," he says, still not looking at me. I hunker into his hoodie but I don't let go of his hand. "My family. My money — what there is of it. My days. My prospects. My body. Everything." I shiver when he says that and his grip on my hand tightens like he's anchoring me. "I'm not asking you to feel things that you don't feel for me. But I'm asking you to be honest about what you *do* feel. Can you do that for me, honey?"

And it's the 'honey' that kills me. It makes my breath feathery and my skin tingle all over. It feels like the pleasure of anticipation right before a kiss. It makes warmth wash over me and settle low in my abdomen and I suddenly want to lay him down on this table and straddle him. I want to brush kisses all over his skin right here in the bright light of the summer morning. I want him inside me, sliding into me and bringing that same shiver of pleasure right through my inmost parts. He just broke me open with one word.

"I can do that," I say, the words fluttering on my tongue, barely there, sweet as cotton candy.

And he finally looks at me, the faintest hint of a smile in his expression, and a glowing burn in his eyes that almost looks like desire, and misery, and happiness all swirled around each other.

I hold his gaze as it softens and his smile deepens until his dimple shows.

I can't help it. I lean in so that our faces are so close that our breath is mingling. I give him a moment to pull back if he wants to. And when he doesn't, I move the rest of the way, close my eyes, and bestow the softest of kisses on his lips.

I'm worried about how he'll react but when my eyes flutter open, his smile is pleased. He reaches up tentatively and brushes a strand of hair from my face. His fingers trail down my jaw and then, with the lightest of touches, he tilts my chin up and kisses me back with the same soft, sweet kind of kiss.

Only now, it's too much for me.

I sweep my body around and straddle his knees. One of my hands is still interlaced with his and I catch his other hand with my free one and interlace those fingers, too, and then I lean in and kiss him with just the edge of my sudden appetite for him.

His laugh as he kisses me back is low in his throat and when I move to deepen our kiss further, he leans back and draws our joined hands between us, holding me back.

"I swear, I can't give you an inch, Tessa."

I bite my lip, but I'm laughing even through my blush. "Then give me all eight inches."

"Damn, woman," he groans. "This is what I'm talking about."

"Well, I don't win races by holding back."

"No, you don't." His mouth curves in a way far too decadent for his face. I want to taste it, and taste it, and taste it. "But I think you should wait, honey."

Oh, fuck he's going to kill me. My eyes roll slightly as that name washes over me again. I feel buzzed with it. I think it's how he says it, like he's tasting actual honey every time.

"Don't you want to hear my other condition?" His whisper makes all the hairs on my arms stand up and sets my whole body to attention.

"You can tell me anything you want," I gasp out.

"I want to write you letters," he says, suddenly sober. "Contingency letters like before, but for our marriage. And I want your promise that you'll read them at the right time and not before."

I nod. I don't care what he asks for. If he wants me to change my name to "Honey" or give up chocolate forever, or if he wants to take me right here on this picnic table — whatever it is, he can have it.

"I need to hear it," he whispers, his lips and teeth brushing the shell of my ear.

I gasp and when he chuckles wickedly, I know he knows exactly what he's done to me. And good for him, finally taking a little. Finally teasing me like I tease him.

"Yes," I manage to grit out between waves of excitement. "You can write your letters."

He draws back and I'm suddenly cold. I cling to his hands, but he gently untangles them and then lifts me with his forearms under my butt so he can twist and set me on the picnic table while he stands.

Here we go!

But he shakes his head at me.

"I'm going to spend the afternoon writing those letters, honey." Dammit, he said it again. "And it will give you the afternoon to think. And to change your mind if you want to, because by this time tomorrow, it will be too late."

"Promise?" I manage to make it sound like a challenge rather than pleading, but barely.

"Yes," he agrees, and then he leaves me cold and bereft with only his scent and hoodie to comfort my empty arms as he slides away.

I pout a bit. There's no one to see, so I can do what I want.

But when I look out at the lake, I see the eyes of a man who desperately wants a family and will agree to a raw deal like marriage with me just to get one.

And I think I can give him that much at least.

And it makes me warm inside to think that finally, I have something to give him that he wants.

# Chapter Thirty-Three

*BRENT*

TESSA, to my surprise, makes herself scarce all afternoon. I finish my letters and I nap. By dinner, I'm restless and lonely, watching the windows and worrying. I receive two worried texts from Ian, but I just read them and then stuff the phone back into my pocket. I promised Tessa that I wasn't going to talk to him about this and he must have seen Adam by now. He must know our plans. I don't dare break her requests already.

I go out and sit at the picnic table and I stare at the lake and I think about what Mom would have said if she'd seen this. I think she would have shaken her head at me. But she wouldn't have stopped me.

"Love never worked out for me until I had children," she'd told me once. "Forget romance, Brent. Build a family. That's what counts in the end."

And she had built a family, even if it felt empty and howling without her.

And now here comes the woman about to be my family. I see her from afar, stalking toward me with all the single-mindedness of a hunting dog. But I want more than my mom told me to want. I want the family she's offering, but I want more. I want the romance. I want the love.

I wonder if that means I'm a fool.

When Tessa finally reaches me, her face is flushed lightly and her mouth is already pushing up into a smile.

"I want to take you to dinner," I say before she can speak, and her smile is all I need to know it was the right choice. "Wherever you want to go, we're going there."

We find a local burger place and we eat burgers outdoors under twinkle lights and talk about the traffic going by.

"Is that a Carolina squatted truck?" she asks in outrage, pointing to a bright yellow truck going by. I'm already laughing before she speaks, because I know it's going to be good. "Dude just announces to potential bosses that he drags his butt around before he even gets out of his ride."

I snicker and give her a nod toward a white OBS Ford truck.

She whistled and takes a long pull of her root beer. "I'd drive that."

"I'd lift it four inches first," I agree.

And that's how we pass dinner. Appreciating good vehicles, nodding in mutual enjoyment, and loudly mocking the ones that deserve it. By the time that we're done, I don't think I've ever had so much fun.

"Let's get ice cream," Tessa suggests, pointing down the road to a place that advertises twenty-six flavors. "I want to try at least three of those flavors."

"We just ate!"

But my weak objections mean nothing to her. We get ice cream. Mine is peanut butter. And we settle into sugar-induced delight as we saunter down the sidewalk and comment on the neighborhood. Tessa chats to me cheerfully about what it would be like if we lived here.

"We'd buy flowers there, of course," she points to a flower shop.

"I don't buy flowers."

"You do now." She fixes me with a level stare. "And over there is where we'd get our hardware."

"Sure," I agree, because I realize I'm not required to say more. And by the time we get to the trailer again, she's practically skipping with joy.

"We'd live here," she says, just before we reach the door.

"Sure."

"And when you say, "sure" I'll kiss you and invite you inside."

I bite my lip because I've been waiting, but I don't think I should wait anymore. I've given her time. But I can't hang back forever. That would be its own kind of selfishness.

She deserves to know she's wanted, even if it exposes me. She deserves to be adored. I promised her honestly. It starts now.

I step forward, lean in, and whisper, "Sure," as my hands find her waist.

I feel her melt in my arms and I never want to stop feeling it. I want to soak in it forever, I want all my heartbeats to be echoed by hers. I don't want her just to be my wife legally. I want her heart to be mine, too.

But I have work to do here. I lean in and give her the kind of kiss that's a promise. It's soft and slow with the patience of a man about to marry — a man in no rush. I take my time, drawing out her little inhales and leaning in to kiss her neck when finally she breaks away to catch her breath. I draw her backward so she's leaning on my chest gasping and laughing.

"You love driving, Tessa," I say and when her eyes meet mine they're sparkling.

I can't help how my smile is attuned to hers. How it surfaces every time hers does.

"I love it so much."

"But I want you to let me drive for a little bit."

"In the next race?" She sounds breathless but not reluctant, which is surprising. I didn't realize she was that generous.

"No," I murmur as I lead her into the trailer. "In this relationship. You've been driving the car, and the truck, and the social media, and the decisions. Let me drive this."

"Okay." She laughs lightly, watching me, as if I've amused her and might amuse her again. "What's the shot for tonight then, driver? Are you taking me to bed with you?"

I'm already shaking my head as I lean in and run my hands through her hair and draw her in for a delicate kiss. She's flushed when I finish, meeting my eyes with a challenge in them.

"Not tonight," I say, caressing her cheek with my thumb. "Then, when I see Steve again I can honestly say I gave you every opportunity to change your mind before our wedding."

She smirks. "Are you saying that once I've tasted you I won't be able to let you go?"

"That's exactly what I'm saying," I say, and then I lean in to whisper in her ear and I'm gratified by her little shiver. "You have all night to think. And to reconsider. It's your very last chance. Because in the morning, I'll drive you to the nearest courthouse and we'll make arrangements and get married. And after that, I'm going to make you fall in love with me, Tessa Harstone. You deserve more than a marriage to advance your career. You deserve to be honored. And you deserve to love."

"Brent," she pulls back, confusion on her face. "You don't need to do that. It's too much."

"Try to stop me," I say and maybe I'm not all the way recovered yet but I feel like I did when I was well and I raced. I feel like I'm riding a car with just a bit too much power down an uncertain track and it's only my nerves and my rigid will holding me together.

Tessa smirks in that way I'm starting to think is just for me, and then she leans in and whispers in my ear. And when I take a turn shivering, I know that I'm going to love every minute of this ride. I'm in another kind of race now, and the trophy is so much more seductive than anything I've raced for before.

"I'll let you drive," she whispers. "Mostly because I'm eager to see what that means exactly, but also because Ian told me you were the kind of racer who makes bold moves."

"I do," I say and my voice is husky. "But that's tomorrow. Tonight, I need my sleep and you need to read my first letter."

And I hand her the stack with the top letter facing her. It's titled,

*So you agreed to let me drive …*

And she shakes her head at me, but she scuttles into the little bathroom and when she comes back out she's back in her yoga sleep gear, her hair is up in a messy ponytail, and she's frowning over my letter.

And I can tell. I can feel it in my bones. This is going to work.

# Chapter Thirty-Four

*TESSA*

I wasn't lying to Brent when I told him that I'm not very hung up on what a wedding should be, but when I rise in the morning, I do put on the only dress I have. A little sundress all sprinkled with flowers. I look cute in it, though I'm not sure most brides would be okay with a twenty-dollar cotton dress bought off the sale rack.

I'm not surprised that Brent is gone. Or that the trailer is spotless. I'm starting to discover he's perpetually tidy and that he's not above cleaning my mess, too. He's also an early riser.

I'm definitely surprised, though, when he arrives at the trailer in a pale button-down shirt that looks more like something someone might wear on safari than to the office, carrying a bouquet of flowers. They're Gerber daisies in bright pinks and purples and oranges and I can't help it. I laugh.

"Are these for me?"

They're the least bridal thing I've ever seen. And I love them. They're just so … me.

He looks up shyly through his lashes. He's tidied his sandy

hair — as much as it can be tidied — and he's shaved. He looks so good it squeezes something in my chest and for a moment I'm completely breathless, not sure what to do or say.

"They made me think of how you laugh," he says and his dimple pops out.

"They're perfect."

And I'm not crying, you're crying. My eyes are just smarting from diesel fumes. Or something.

At least, that's what I tell myself as we pull out of the campground — he's driving — and I find he's brought me breakfast again. A frothy coffee drink and a little yogurt parfait with fruit and granola that looks delectable.

He says nothing as he drives and I don't know if he's feeling awkward or if he maybe has second thoughts — but no, when he glances at me, his smile is small, but his eyes are glowing and hungry, like *his* breakfast is glimpses of me and he's going to eat it the whole way to the courthouse.

We're in traffic for a silent, intense hour. Every inhale pierces the air between us. Every exhale clouds it. When his eyes catch mine they hurt with how beautiful they are, like shards of glass burying into my memory and lodging there forever.

I can barely walk straight when we get to the courthouse, I'm so intoxicated by him. And I keep seeing his curling script in that letter last night. It said,

*You made the right choice.*

I feel like he thinks he did, too, if his shy, masculine glances are telling the whole story.

I didn't read the titles of the other letters. Not yet. I was scared they'd freak me out. Instead, I'd texted Kati.

DON'T TELL MY PARENTS WHAT I'M ABOUT TO SAY.

OMG, YOU'RE PREGNANT!

What? No.

Oh. Sorry. The algorithms have caught wind that I'm pregnant and now every ad is for diapers and every YouTube clip is about people who didn't know they were pregnant and OBGYNs analyzing the stories and it just feels like everyone is these days.

You're the only person I know who is pregnant.

Okay, go on.

Correction. You're the only person besides Olivia.

Are you serious? Is she pregnant? Are you going to be a double aunt??

I feel a nice warm glow in my chest at her text. Double aunt. She's calling me the aunt of her unborn baby. I'm blinking back tears at the thought of it.

Maybe??

This is amazing! Don't worry. I won't tell your mom.

I pause, wondering if I should confess this, but in the end, I just do. It's Kati. She won't tell. And I need *someone* to hear this before I do it. To tell me I'm crazy if it's crazy, or calm me down if it isn't.

> No, I mean don't tell her this next part. I'm getting married.

Kati texts me five mind blown emojis.

> You are not.

> I am. BOOM showed up and there's this huge mix-up and long story short, it was this or lose the show. And don't tell me how I should wait for love and how you and Andrew are perfect together because I know all that and I'm marrying Brent anyway.

> Hmm.

> Hmm, what?

> He was okay with that?

> Who wouldn't want to marry me?

> Listen, I forgot to mention this, but when you inflate your tires, you can skip inflating the ego.

She sends a car emoji and a kissy face emoji.

> Ha ha ha. Why is that a hmm?

> Look, I don't know him, okay.

Now I'm nervous. I text back.

Okaaaay.

I can't possibly know what's going on.

You're worrying me.

But why would someone who isn't in love
with you agree to marry you?

Why, indeed. I feel a little rush of shame. Will everyone who hears about this be able to tell right away that I manipulated him into this? Yes. The answer is yes. All the more reason to keep it private as long as possible.

Look, just don't tell my mom, okay?

My text sounds as desperate as I am.

Take selfies for me and it's a deal.

So here we are smiling awkwardly as we speak the traditional vows in front of the judge. A cherubic man closer to eighty than seventy. And in my mind I just keep hearing two things, "You made the right choice" and "why would he agree to marry you if he wasn't in love with you?"

But that's crazy. And I don't need him to be in love with me for this to have been the right choice. So why does the idea enchant me? Why do I wonder if my heart would race even faster if I was giving myself to a man who was head over heels for me?

I try to imagine how Brent would look at me if he were really in love, but I can't imagine a more powerful expression than the one on his face right now. A look that's barely a hair away from tears, the emotion behind it is so intense.

I take his hand, to try to lessen whatever is going on there, but he looks away suddenly and when he looks back at me, the expression is gone and he's simply smiling. I feel like I lost something before I even had it.

When our vows are said, and he puts his ring on my finger — an absolutely adorable hummingbird ring cast in silver — and the judge tells us we can kiss. I try to put how I feel into that kiss. Gratitude for what he's giving me. Friendship for what we have. Hopefulness for what this maybe could be.

And I don't know what he's giving me, but somehow it feels like it's his whole heart and it makes it hard to breathe and definitely hard to speak. So we don't speak.

When it's over, we get in our truck, send photos of the paperwork to BOOM, and we drive to the interstate highway. We ignore our buzzing, ringing phones, and let the sameness of the miles of the road wash over us until we reach a turn-off I didn't expect and when I look over at Brent, questioning, he smiles softly.

"I told you. I'm driving."

"And where are you driving us to?"

"Right now? A bed and breakfast that the owner claims is a secluded cabin draped in honeysuckle."

"Well, don't let me stop you," I say, and when I laugh his smile lights his whole face up and I just want to keep laughing so I can see more of it.

But I don't have to stop, do I? Because we're married, and somehow, this makes him mine. And I have all the time in the world to let him drive.

Chapter Thirty-Five

*BRENT*

I'm nervous even if I'm trying not to show it as we pull in at the rental place.

"Wow," Tessa says, looking through the thick trees. The truck and trailer barely make it around the circle driveway, but I manage it, and our orange monstrosity is parked in front of a small stone building absolutely dripping in flowers.

It's well into the afternoon. I haven't napped. And I don't think I need to. This day is like sixteen cups of coffee. I don't think I could sleep if I wanted to.

"Can I go look at it?" Tessa asks and I nod, warming to her glow.

She hops out of the truck, her short skirt swirling around her smooth thighs and my mouth is already dry as I slide out of my seat and follow her. She twirls around, trying to see everything at once, her eyes bright with excitement, and it's so much. It's too much. I feel like I'm breaking apart and little bits of me are drifting around like ice chunks calved from an iceberg.

"This is perfect, Brent!" She says, glowing. "It's like a mini honeymoon."

My heart skips a beat and I step toward her, licking my lips. "Is that what you want, Tess? A mini honeymoon?"

She tilts her head to one side. "Is it what you want?"

My "yes" comes out rougher than I'd like.

"Then I want it, too."

It feels a bit like a pinch. She doesn't mean to hurt me, but I know that this isn't the same for her as it is for me. But that's what I agreed to when I said my vows. I knew exactly what we were getting.

I step forward and hesitantly take her hand and she gives it to me with a generous smile. She's not stingy with her affection. Just with her actual heart.

"Do you regret this?" I ask, my voice still rough.

"No." She looks directly into my eyes, the same Tessa she always is. Unfettered. Unworried. Just herself all the time. "And I won't either. And neither will you. You want a family and you're going to have that with me."

"Thank you." My words are precise. Not cold, exactly, but careful. Because I do want that, I do. But thanking her for giving me that feels like turning my back on the thing I do want — Tessa's heart.

"Do you ... " I have to pause and take a breath. "... do you want to go inside?"

"Yes." She raises her eyebrows and lowers them in a quick gesture that is at once a promise and a suggestion.

"Then come with me, honey," I growl and I can see that pet name is working for her by how her cheeks go pink.

If I want her, I must convince her. And she's been very clear that there is one thing that she wants. If I give it to her — if I make it special and as perfect as I can, perhaps it will be the first step in winning her over.

I'm nervous about it. I don't want to cross any lines she

isn't ready for — although so far she's been mostly disappointed with how far behind her I've been with this, so it's hard to imagine a scenario where I am not racing to catch up with her.

I draw her into the cabin and it is exactly as it was in the photos. The area around it is thick with trees and their heavy branches make the inside of the cabin cool and shady. There's a tiny kitchenette and a door that I assume leads to a bathroom and then a set of chairs around an open fireplace and a wide bed draped with patchwork quilts.

"You picked the perfect place," Tessa says, kicking off her shoes. She's looking around the room so she doesn't see when I close the door, pull off my own boots, and then lean in to wrap my arms around her from behind and kiss her neck.

She makes a pleased hum and that's all the encouragement that I need.

I spin her around and catch her gasp in my mouth, kissing her with intent. I want to make her head spin. I want to leave her so overwhelmed with pleasure that thought is impossible. I want to literally sweep her off her feet.

I should stop and savor this, I should, but I don't dare. Not when this is my chance to catch her heart.

I slide my hands delicately down her sides until she shivers and then I lean down to catch her under her thighs and lift her up. I'm not supposed to be lifting, but it's only for a few steps.

I carry her to the bed, still kissing her deeply, passionately, with all the skill I possess. She's keeping up. I haven't gone past her desire yet. I'm watching that with care. One hint of hesitation from her and I'll stop. I will.

I'm having trouble concentrating. I know I want to draw every bit of delight out for her, but she's intoxicating and I keep losing myself in the feel and scent, and taste of her. She's like a full banquet dinner all in one. She's like all twenty-six flavors of ice cream in one delightful dish. I want to taste all of them. I want to spend all night doing it, and all morning reliving it. I want it all.

I lay her back on the bed, still kissing her, reveling in how she feels under me — warm and perfect, every curve in just the right place. I navigate them with my hands, speeding up on the straight stretches like a car on a racecourse. Her breathing is uneven, little gasps and puffs, and then, just when I'm thinking about sliding the sleeve of that dress down, her hands bunch in my shirt and she twists, flipping me onto my back and straddling me. I could stop the move but I don't. I let my hands fall away, open, ready to engage again but waiting.

"What is this?" She asks roughly. Her lips are swollen from my intent kisses, her long hair tangled in the most tantalizing way. Her cheeks flush pink and her breath trembles on her red lips and I want her. I want all of her. I can feel where her thighs are pressed along my sides, hot and tempting and where they meet over my abdomen, pressing a wet spot into my shirt. "What are you doing?"

"I'm giving you what you want," I say.

"No, you aren't."

My hands form fists of disappointment. Shit. I've messed this up again. My throat feels dry with defeat.

"I don't want you to ... whatever this is ... to meet my expectations? To try to what? Pay me what I'm owed? It cheapens what could be so right for us."

"I don't want to cheapen anything, honey," I say like it's a vow and it *is,* because I'd never do that. "I just want to make you smile. I just want to show you that you made the right choice."

She pauses. I can see her thinking by the way her gaze turns inward and her expression turns serious.

"I only want what you want to give," she says and for the first time ever looks shy. "I don't want a performance. I want the true you — the real way you feel. I want you to enjoy what we do and I don't want us to do anything you aren't doing just for the enjoyment of it."

"I want to give you everything," I say, my chest twisting painfully. Everything with her is enjoyment. Doesn't she realize that?

She shakes her head. "I only want to be given what we can share."

"Okaaay." My uncertainty draws the word out.

I understand one thing. She will not let me seduce her heart with my body. I'm choking on the disappointment of that. But I promised her honesty. And I promised myself we would do nothing more than what she wants.

This is what she wants. I must make my peace with it.

"So if we both are enjoying the kiss, then we kiss. If we both are enjoying the caress, then we touch. But if one of us is just doing for the other person — well that sounds like something I don't want to do."

"Okay," I agree. "And if I want all of you?"

She pauses, swallowing. And for a moment there's a look of uncertainty in her eyes.

"Like, all, all?"

I'm scared to answer. Scared of frightening her. Scared of lying. It takes all my courage to force the truth out.

"Yes. All."

"Well," she says a little breathlessly. "That's a race of a different class, isn't it?"

"Is it?"

"Yes." She nods, looking suddenly determined. "But I think you've forgotten something."

"I have?"

She laughs and kisses me briefly and then she's off the bed and running to the door. "I'll be right back."

I flop backward, staring at the ceiling, chest heaving. I don't know what's happening here. I feel like I did when I crashed. I know I've fucked up somehow. I know it got away from me. I'm not sure how bad the damages are.

I can still taste her in my mouth, still feel where my ribs are cold because her hot thighs are gone.

And then she's back, closing the door, and in a single motion, she pulls her dress up and over her head and sets it on the bedside table.

I gust out a breath.

She's so beautiful. So ridiculously beautiful. My heart is stuttering just at the sight of her.

"You just keep dropping this on me like a bomb," I say and my voice is strangled even to my own ears. "Right since the first day I met you. And I am still not used to it."

"Do you enjoy it, though?" she asks coyly.

Do I? Is that a joke? Everything below my belt twists and grows uncomfortable.

I bite my lip hard and then carefully spell it out for her. "I enjoy every glimpse of you from the most casual of glances at your smile to these precious looks at things I hope are only for me."

"Things?" she teases as she slips off her bra and I think it's my ragged gasp that makes her bite her lip devilishly and then widen her eyes in mock innocence. "Like these?"

"Yes," I grit out. I slide to the edge of the bed so I can sit with my knees splayed out and give myself a little relief.

"Do you like looking at these?" she asks, teasing me.

"Yes."

"See?" She smirks coyly. "I told you that mutual can be fun."

She steps forward and takes my hand so she can hook my index finger in the band of her floral panties.

"What else do you want to look at?"

I don't pull them down like she's offering. Instead, I spin her around roughly, cup her lovely rear in my palms, fingers splayed out, and kiss the tiny dents in her lower back just above the lacy hem of her underthings.

"Does that feel good?" I gasp when I'm done.

"Now you're catching on," she says, laughing over her shoulder, and then she turns and with exquisite slowness, begins to unbutton my shirt, watching my eyes, bottom lip caught between her teeth, as she slowly strips me of my clothing.

When the shirt is gone, she takes a long, thorough look at me. I lean back on my elbows so she can see as much as she wants. Her eyes catch on the tent in my jeans and she teases her bottom lip a little more, making me swallow. I have to physically force down the desire welling up in me to drag her down and suck that lip between mine.

Instead, I wait, my patience thoroughly tested as she sets her fingertips delicately against my chest and then narrows them to just the index finger and trails it down the seam in the center of my body to the button of my jeans.

"And how would you feel if I opened these?" she asks and now she's almost as breathless as I am, her voice light and fluttery in a way that makes me think of what it might sound like if I can manage to convince her to take this to its conclusion.

"I'd feel anticipation," I admit.

"Good anticipation?" She emphasizes the "good."

"The very best," I assure her.

And when she leans in to open my pants, I let my fingertips meet the skin on either side of her waist, and this time, I enjoy myself, slowly skimming them over her skin, inching across her belly and up her rib cage with painful slowness until they reach the tips of her breasts and my palms angle down to cup what I've touched. I meet her eyes with the slightest of satisfied smiles.

"I'm enjoying that," she says in a husky voice. And then she leans her weight into my palms and catches the edge of my bottom lip between her teeth until I gasp.

She laughs and replaces the nip with a soft, sliding kiss and I am so overwhelmed by the sensation on my lips and the warm weight in my palms that I hardly even notice when she tugs down my jeans, and somehow — I don't even know how — drags them right down to the ground without ever breaking our kiss.

It's only when we break apart, gasping for breath, and her warm hand finds my length, that I realize she's removed every shred of clothing from me. My mouth falls open in a gasp at the sheer pleasure of her touch. Little fireflies of intensity spark from where her delicate fingertips trace along me and pause at the very tip. They rush up into my belly and fan out down my thighs. I think I might wince from far too much feeling.

Her laugh is low and husky and I won't let her get away with being the only one who teases. I lean forward, catching her fingers in between mine, and graze my teeth down her ribs — light and soft — until they snag on the lacy edge of her under-things. I catch the edge in my teeth and drag them down until they fall on their own and join the rest of our clothing on the floor.

"And now?" I ask as I settle on my knees before her. "Are you enjoying yourself now?"

"Yes."

I can barely hear her gusted answer.

"Was that a yes, my wife?" I ask and at her disbelieving groan, I chuckle. "Let's see if you like this, too."

I kiss her belly just under her belly button and look up at her. She's biting her lip and her eyes are wide, hair all around her face like curtains that can't quite hide her anticipation.

And I'm so in love. I'm ruined for anyone else. Ever. Who could hold my attention after Tessa? No one can tease and tempt like she does. No one can spin my heart up in knots and make it squeeze with a terrible mix of pleasure and pain the way she does.

I slide my chin down her belly and I can tell my five o'clock shadow is tickling her because she parts her lips and huffs a light laugh and I place my kiss low — teasingly low — just above where I'll kiss her in a moment and make things really interesting.

But she surprises me when she suddenly finds my hands splayed out on her hips, threads her fingers through mine, and draws me back up again.

"It's not a race, Bolt," she says, smirking at me as she draws me with her onto the bed.

She lays back, pulling my hands up to stretch over her head so that I have no choice but to hover over her.

My breath is sharp and stilted. I'm so massively turned on that I can hardly form words anymore.

"Is there a letter for this?" she asks me, teasing.

"There will be." I say it like a vow. "There will be so many letters."

Now she really laughs.

"Whatever you do, Brent, do not write me letters about this. They absolutely will fall into the wrong hands. There's practically a law of nature to enforce that."

"Then what would you like?" I ask.

And her gaze is locked on mine and it shows me her wide-open heart and I want to pour love into it like hot honey and melt her right through.

"I'm starting to think I'd like to have your heart," she says and I shiver. I open my mouth to confess. To tell her it's already hers but she speaks too soon. "But for now, I think I'll settle for your pleasure. And I think I'd like that right now."

And then she stretches up and nips my cheek lightly and her laugh is so sweet that I catch it with my lips and take it as my own.

Chapter Thirty-Six



I EXPECTED that being with Brent would be fun. And I expected it would be a massively sexy — which, incidentally, might be my new nickname for Brent Bolt now that I've seen him not just naked but naked *with me* if you know what I mean, wink wink.

I mean it's sex, so that feels like it should be a given, but I'm told that's not true for everyone. I'd had no doubts about us, though. I mean it was fun to make him blush and stammer when he was only a friend I kept catching in awkward situations. It was fun to play games with him when he wouldn't touch me. Of course, it's going to be amazing to actually get to touch him all over, right? To watch his breath hitch and his skin respond. To watch his interest grow.

But this — whatever this is — is blowing away all expectations. Brent is making me dizzy, dazzled, whatever the words are that mean your thoughts are thick as syrup and your body wants to take the driver's seat. If there are words to describe it, I can't find the ones to show how this closeness makes everything so much more intense.

I expected the whole marriage thing to make it awkward — and it kind of did — but at the same time, it *does* something to me. It winds me tight and twanging and reaches down into parts of me that tell me I'm more exposed than nakedness, more vulnerable than if I were tied up in this bed. Letting him in like this gives him access to the steering wheel of my heart and he's driving now — not just this relationship but in some way I can't quite describe, it feels like he's driving me.

I like it. So much.

I mean, I love to drive. I love to make the choices, love leaning into the curves, and pushing everything to the limit. But there's something thrilling about letting go completely and allowing someone else to decide for you how you're going to be touched, how your skin is going to thrill, how you're going to get wet and ready just for him.

I've only seen Brent race once with my own eyes and it was a bit of a disaster. But this feels like how he drives the truck with the massive trailer — like he knows precisely where he wants it at all times and maneuvers it there with ease. He's moving me right where I need to be, feathering the gas and the brakes just right, guiding me with light touches and expert hands.

Really expert. Damn.

"Brent," I gasp while he places gently kisses behind my ear and then trails them down my neck.

He wraps his arms around me and delicately rolls so that I'm on top of him, cradled against his chest.

I take a moment to breathe in the scent of him as he whispers, "Yes?" into my hair.

"How long have you been imagining doing this with me?"

He pauses and for a moment I think he's going to say that he hasn't been imagining it, that it's all me, that I've finally pushed him too far.

"I remember something about a car alarm," he says as if he's having trouble remembering, and I laugh into the hard planes of his chest before pushing up so I can look him in the eyes.

His arms release me and slide so that his hands can come up and skim across my cheeks, brushing my hair back, and then catching behind my head to pull me in for a slow, sweet kiss, and then another, and then another, until I feel drunk on his kisses. They deepen so slowly that I hardly realize we've moved from soft and sweet to open and hungry until we're passionately locked together, tongues tangling and soft little sounds escaping both of us.

These are *Brent Bolt's* sounds I'm hearing. Damn, they're good. I want to collect the whole set. I'll put them in a display case with his blushes.

He pauses just long enough to pull back and meet my gaze. "Still enjoying it?"

I nod and for once I have no teasing words. Nothing to say as he tucks a strand of hair behind my ear.

"How far?" I ask, having to pause to swallow and reorganize my thoughts. "Is this too fast for you? Do you need me to stop?"

"No." He punctuates that with a soft kiss on the tip of my nose.

I laugh and lean over the side of the bed to grab my dress and pull a packet from the pocket.

"What's that?"

I hold it up to show him the bright orange package. "BOOM left the trailer fully equipped with branded items." I pause for effect. "Fully. Equipped."

"What, exactly, did he expect us to do on this trip?" His expression is slightly aghast as I rip open the condom packet, but it turns to pleasure as I fit him with the most indiscrete of the products BOOM sent us off with.

I'm laughing — both at the absurdity of bright orange condoms and at Brent who is blushing like a teenager.

"This?" I suggest, and then I lean in again and kiss him slowly, intently, as I settle myself over his body and slip him into me.

I get to taste his moan as he buries himself deep. I get to taste the way his lips soften with pleasure, and his movements slow, how he slides one palm up to cup my cheek while the other hand guides my waist to help me find the exact right pace.

"This is what I dreamed of," he whispers to me. "Exactly this."

"Funny, me too," I tease as I start to increase my pace.

"You, Tessa. *You* are everything I ever dreamed of. You ridiculously talented, wild girl."

It's just because he's in my bed. It's just the pleasure talking. It's just the sex. I know that, and yet I still thrill at his words, utterly delighted by them. They sweep over me, hitting me so hard in the heart that for a moment I feel like I can't breathe, and then pleasure washes over me, uncontrollable and impossible to stop once it's begun. I cling to him, riding the wave of it, gasping when it slowly recedes like an ocean tide.

"Oops," I whisper.

His soft laugh makes me blush and then he spins me so he's on top, his forearms on either side of my face so he can kiss my hairline, my cheekbone, the dip in my collarbone.

"That's my girl, always first to the finish line," he teases but there's genuine affection there. "Let's see if you have a few more laps in you."

The wave I've been riding might have receded, but it's still there on the edge of my senses, still making every sensation heightened and intensified. I lean my cheek into the soft hair of his forearm and let my hands trace from his broad shoulders right down the ridges of his spine as he moves over me. He's magnificent.

His whispers are addictive. "You're amazing, Tess. Absolutely amazing. I can't believe you're my wife. Come for me, honey. Come for me."

And I ride the encouragement of his whispers and shatter again.

I'm not thinking straight. I'm just delight from head to toe. I'm just sheer joy.

Tessa? Who was that girl?

He's strong and powerful over me, I love to trace his muscles with my fingertips, but it's those words — those words with the power to enchant me, to seduce me, to tease every last scrap of delight out of me — it's those that are putting me into a Brent-shaped trance.

I cling to his chest as he bends down to lay soft kisses down my throat and chest until he can catch the tip of my breast between his lips and run his tongue over it. He stops for just long enough to look up at me with a smile so meltingly sweet that it twists my heart.

Then he laughs softly so that I can barely hear it.

"Let me in on the joke," I suggest in a whisper.

"No joke. Just joy. I can't believe you're my wife. I —" I hear the edge of something on his lips but he seems to swallow whatever it is, his cheeks heating to scarlet as he says in a husky voice. "You're going to think it's ridiculous, but I love it. It's ... unbelievable."

"Tell me the truth," I beg him, eyelashes fluttering as he begins his slow dance with me again.

"Anything."

"How do you feel right now?"

He's flippant, his laugh gusting between lips made slack with pleasure. "Oh, this? It feels really good."

I laugh at that and my laughter makes our bodies rock together in a way that makes him groan, defeated, and makes my core clench tight. Really? I've already had two. You'd think it would slake the thirst a little.

"No," I whisper as he leans down so that his cheek can skim mine with every stroke. "How do you feel about me?"

His words come out more hesitant than I'd expect given that his movements don't pause at all. "I feel happy about you."

"About all of it?"

"I'll never not be happy about you, Tessa honey."

His voice tightens on "honey" and then he's rearing back, eyes locking into mine, teeth biting down hard on his lower lip, and I'm shocked to realize that his climax is as thrilling to me as my own were. I'm locked in this moment with him, two separate people feeling one singular thing and I don't want it to stop.

"Please don't stop."

I don't realize I've said it out loud until he collapses carefully half on top of me, his lips pressed to my cheek, and gusts a last breathy laugh.

"Oh Tessa, honey, if I could keep going, I would."

And I think the next few weeks of the two of us together, and racing, and *this* are going to be the best weeks of my life.

# Chapter Thirty-Seven

*BRENT*

I WAKE up so in love I can hardly breathe.

She's sprawled half over me, fully naked, fully glorious, her dark hair tangled around her arms and mine. I can smell her apples and cinnamon. I just breathe her in, counting the freckles on her cheeks, memorizing the lay of each eyelash. Her eyelids are shell pink, her sweet lips curving upward in sleep, her breath gusting across my skin.

I just want this moment to last forever. And suddenly I don't care.

I don't care if she rips my heart out and tosses it away. I don't care if she ruins me for everything else forever. I don't care. I just want these few weeks with her. I just want whatever she'll give me. I'm suddenly grateful that she decided to make it real. Even if it's only really real for me. Even if my stomach is swimming, and my chest burning, and I'm entirely turned on just lying here with her and she doesn't feel any of it, I'm just going to accept this gift she's given me with all my heart.

She wakes up with a sleepy smile. She gives those out so freely. Too freely.

"When I was little," she says sleepily. "My favorite holiday was Easter. Can you guess why?"

I draw her in tight to me until she squeaks and then I laugh into her hair. "You raced around the house looking for eggs, didn't you? No Christmas with guaranteed gifts for you. No begging like a Halloween junkie. You wanted to earn it and you wanted to be first."

"Yes," her laughing breath gusts over me. "And what about you?"

She looks up at me, fun writ large on her face.

"Guess," I say, smirking.

"Christmas." She bites her lip and her expression turns playful. "You like unwrapping your gifts."

"Do I ever," I growl, and then I flip her onto her back in a single motion. She shrieks and I love it.

I blow a kiss into her belly until she's laughing so hard she can't control herself and then when she's limp and spent from laughter, I slide onto my knees between her legs, take her ankles in each hand, and slide them up the sheets to bracket my knees before I skim my hands down her legs from knee to thigh, to where they meet in the middle, where she's already wet and yearning for me.

"You're the one who likes Christmas," she chides as I slip down onto my elbows. "I'm not supposed to be getting gifts."

"Oh, this isn't a gift for you." My voice is husky with desire. "It's for me. And I want to unwrap it."

"Okay."

Her voice is shivery with anticipation and it makes me so hard that just leaning in to reach her and sliding along the sheets is almost too much for me, but I'm here to unwrap my present and I do. With my tongue. Slowly. Concentrating on her every moan and gasp so that I can unwind all her ties and tease out all her pleasure. I'm unraveling her bit by bit and it's my favorite thing ever.

Forget racing. Forget videography. If I can only be good at one thing. I pick this.

When she comes undone, I nearly come with her. My eyes flutter closed with hers. My moan rolls out right on top of her. I'm tasting her body while I taste her emotions and I'm overwhelmed with sensation, with an endless desire that can only be slowed, never fully extinguished.

I want all of me to belong to all of her. I want to unwrap her delight every day. I want …

My eyelids flutter open when I feel her shift under me and before I can open my mouth to ask her what she's doing, her hands are on my shoulders, pushing me up and back so she can straddle me.

I tangle my fist in her long hair and bite my lip. I am being washed away and she is my ocean. I am falling, dizzy and gasping, wanting her so badly that I can hardly breathe.

"Oh, sweet honey," I moan into her forehead, and then she pulls away from me and I feel her fit another condom on me right before she slides me into her.

For a moment, I can't think, can't breathe.

"You gorgeous man," she says, admiringly, running her hand down my chest and belly as she rides me fast and hard like she's racing me to a finish line only she can see. And she must be winning because losing doesn't feel like this.

She shifts so that both her hands are braced on my chest and she can look into my eyes.

"And how do you feel now?" she asks me breathlessly.

Honesty falls from me unintentionally.

"I love you."

"I love this, too," she says with a gusting laugh. "I told you we make an incredible team."

"I left you a letter about that," I manage, and then I'm coming so fast and hard that everything else is washed away in the wake of the two of us, and the crazy love we make together, and the crazy life that reaches for me — tantalizing — just out of reach.

# Chapter Thirty-Eight

*TESSA*

WE HAVE A RACE THAT NIGHT. You'd think it would make us both tense and focused. It does not.

Instead, we laugh together like children, sharing the shower at the bed and breakfast, leisurely finding a cafe, and eating a big breakfast together.

I've never seen Brent so relaxed. His smiles are easy and natural. His jokes roll off his tongue in sly little digs and side comments. He's the most fun. Maybe ever.

And wow, I'd be fanning myself if I were dishing this to Kati because last night was *hot*. *He* was hot. I still get little flutters in my chest when I think about it.

It would not take much to fall for this man I've married. Not much at all. I will need to be careful about that.

He did write me a letter for when we work well as a team, by the way.

It said,

*Of course we do. Because I adore you.*

It's very close to the "I love you" that fell from his lips in the heat of sex, but I'm going to get all girly and make that like a line in the sand that means now he has to be a certain way. I know how things are. He loved having sex with me. That's all he meant.

And I mean ... yeah! I loved that, too. It was amazing. We are going to be doing that once every — scratch that — twice every day until we get to Utah. Maybe more. This morning it was almost more with the way his eyes went all molten honey and jalapenos when he was watching me in the shower. So yes, I get what the heat of the moment is like. I'm right there with him.

And this note is the same. It's sweet. It's caring. It's meant as encouragement and to bind us together and I love him for it. But I'm not going to pretend it's some kind of huge declaration. It's just Brent being Brent.

We fall into a happy routine when we get to the track. The car has been almost shockingly lucky in how little damage it's taken, but I go over it all and end up tuning a few things while he sets up filming equipment. He only takes one nap after lunch. He's getting better every day. I kind of can't wait. Will he race when he's better? Will he ... race against me?

The thought of that makes me so hot that I climb in with him for the end of his nap and if we do more than cuddle, can you blame us? He winds his fingers through mine afterward, and his kisses are like the adrenaline of a race. They make me want more and more and more.

"Drive safe tonight," he says when we get up and he tidies the trailer. He seems to do it without thinking.

"Shouldn't you say, 'win?'" I tease.

"I already know you're going to try to win. I have no doubt about that," he says, picking up my lacy underwear from the ground and spinning it on a finger.

I laugh. "You're really sweet about cleaning."

He looks a little bashful. "My mom had to work so hard for

us when we were growing up. And Olivia was depending on me. I just kind of ... fell into cleaning and cooking. It's what I do."

"So what you're saying is that I married my mother."

His laugh is so shocked he practically spits. "I hope not."

I love teasing him. I hope he never gets used to it.

"And who did you marry?" I snatch my underwear from his hand.

"You," he says firmly before catching me under the ass and hitching me up against him. "I married you."

And then he kisses me like he's going to lose me, like this is our last kiss and it's poignant and sweet and I can't think of a smart response — or really anything at all.

"I guess we should race." I'm so breathless I can barely get the words out.

"We should," he whispers into my hair.

But we don't right away. We pick up where we left off at the end of the nap and we don't get back to racing until we've both crossed the finish line ... again.

"I admire you like crazy," he tells me as I skim into my racing suit.

"You do?" I say with a teasing grin. "You should consider raising your standards."

I look up to see him snapping a picture of me and I smile shyly.

"My standards can't go any higher." His smile is wistful.

It's so ridiculously sweet that I can barely handle it.

I race like a demon that night, so amped up on excitement and wonder that I hardly even feel like I'm driving on dirt. It feels more like driving in the clouds.

I smoke them all.

Obviously.

I win quite handily.

But the car takes a bit of a beating.

"We'll need a new radiator," Brent says between kisses while we look it over. We're terribly distracted.

"We will," I agree.

"And we'll need to beat the dents out."

"I'm sure you have all the right tools for that."

"But it's the clunk when it shifts from second to third that really worries me. I'm not sure we can get a new transmission on the fly."

"I'm not sure I can rebuild one in this trailer, but I could give it a try."

"Tomorrow," he said, biting his lip. "We'll do it all tomorrow. We make a great team."

"I agree entirely," I say, straight-faced. "Let's turn all that amazing teamwork to something else, shall we?"

————

I get a text from Kati the next morning.

Well?

Well, what?

I text back from the nice little warm home I've found in the blankets cuddled up with Brent.

He's the best person to sleep beside. Even in sleep, he's tidy. He doesn't steal covers. He's just warm and comforting with literally the best heartbeat. I swear I could listen to that all night. I mean, I did. Last night. And the night before. If I'd realized marriage was this amazing I might have caved the second Olivia batted her eyelashes at me and told me I could make her the happiest girl in the world by dating her brother.

Boy, is she going to be smug.

Well, are you in love yet?

I glance furtively over my shoulder. Brent seems thoroughly asleep.

Maybe.

How will I know?

She sends me an eye-roll emoji.

I'm too pregnant for this conversation. Also, your mother is worried about you. She called me twice yesterday. You'd better give her a call.

Absolutely not, I agreed with Brent that we wouldn't talk with relatives until we get to Utah.

That's crazy.

No, what's crazy would be letting all of them up inside our relationship. They'll make me regret it. They'll cheapen it. You know how I am when people try to make me conform.

Yes, you race off in the other direction.

See?

Tessa, if you know that, can't you just not do it?

NO!

Wow. Crazy much?

> If I hear them all telling me I've done the right thing and made their dreams come true I'll want to file for divorce. I don't do well when I'm doing what everyone wants.

> You make no sense. Do you know that? None.

And the thing is, she's right. I know she's right. But do you think I can just call my mom? No. I can't. Because I know that the second she squeals into the phone I won't be able to look at Brent the same way again. I'll feel trapped. I'll need to run. And I can't risk that.

> Are you at least winning races?

> So many.

> Good. Be happy you insane woman. And text me more often.

I probably would have said more but at that moment, my phone rings and it's BOOM so I pick it up. Beside me, Brent gasps in a breath, clearly startled into consciousness.

"Tessa? Adam here. How's things?"

"Great!" I try to sound chipper and not like I'm still in bed.

"Excellent! I wanted to call to tell you guys that the crisis is averted. We made a statement on the website regarding your marital status and that, combined with the race suit with "Bolt" on the back has silenced your critics. Have you had a chance to check out the most recent uploads?"

"No, I'm sorry. We've been so busy ..." I let my voice trail off.

"Well, then let me tell you, things have taken *off*. We're so excited here at BOOM and we can't wait to throw that huge party we talked about when you get here. Text me your ETA today, okay? I have some VIPs I want to fly in for that."

"VIPs?" I ask, worried now.

"Oh, and text your brother. If he keeps pacing around here looking worried, then I'm going to be permanently dizzy."

I laugh a bit lamely. I do not want to text Ian back.

"Okay, talk soon and tell Brent to try to give us a bit more commentary and shots of him talking. Our polling shows the audience likes those and they're great for teasers and shorts."

"Okay," I say brightly.

"Great! Talk soon!"

The moment he hangs up I get a text from Ian.

> Either you call me or I'm coming to you, Tessa. Don't you dare ignore me.

Brent's phone dings, too, and I roll my eyes.

"It's like some kind of nineteen-fifties switchboard over here. Did you volunteer us to be operators?"

He chuckles and shows me his phone. It's an identical text to the one Ian sent me, only he's replaced "Tessa" with "Brent."

"I think we should text him back," Brent says, running his eyes longingly over the length of me.

"I can think of better things to do," I say with my most mischievous smile.

"He really will come here," Brent says, lifting a brow.

He's going to cave. I just know it. Time to head that off at the pass. I raise a single brow.

"You made me a promise."

He holds up his hands as if to fend me off. "I know I did."

"Don't you dare break it."

"Never," he whispers, leaning in. "But if I'm keeping all my promises today, then you need to keep yours, too."

I'm already laughing as he reaches for me under the blankets. This trailer is amazing. I want to have sex in it with Brent forever.

Maybe we'll even run out of these ridiculous condoms.

# Chapter Thirty-Nine

*BRENT*

SO WHAT TESSA doesn't know, and what I'm not telling her, is that she's famous now. It's a good thing that I don't need to rest all the time anymore because if I did, she'd be having to fend all of this off herself and I feel like adding that to her long list of tasks would be just too much.

It's easy enough to keep the more wild fans out of her way in the pits. They aren't allowed back there anyway and a few quiet conversations with the organizers make sure there aren't any slip-ups but as we move from track to track, the show just gets more popular and Tessa gets popular with it.

She used to manage our social media, but I've taken to diving in there myself, quickly deleting a lot of the crasser messages and more threatening content and just keeping all the lovely positive ones up where she can read them.

One responsibility I take seriously as her husband is her safety. I will not compromise it.

We're great together, Tessa and me. She keeps me from stressing too much. Most of the time, I'm too busy laughing to worry about anything. We barely squeaked into the last race with a working car, but Tessa laughed the whole time she stripped the transmission apart, telling jokes that probably should have made the paint peel in the garage part of the trailer. I swear, she must never be allowed to be a stand-up comedian. Blue doesn't even begin to describe the kinds of jokes she makes when it's just her and me. I don't know half the time whether I should blush, or scold her, or laugh, and my bluster only makes her laugh harder.

She rebuilt the whole transmission just hours before the race, and while she didn't win that one, she made a great showing, and I took the time to get more of myself on camera the way BOOM asked me to. It's not hard to be on camera when I'm talking about Tessa. It's pretty much all bragging, anyway. My lady is amazing.

And I keep her on track. The thing about Tessa is that it's easy for her to be distracted, to lose things she literally was just holding, to forget to eat or drink or even what she's working on. Everything is exciting or hilarious to her, and I'm pretty sure I've doubled her productivity just by keeping her fed and pointing to where she's set something down so she can find it.

Together, we make the perfect team. And if I miss racing a bit, I don't miss it enough to want to stop this wild ride. I've heard the term "ride or die" but now I know what it means right down to my bones. I want my life with Tessa. Only that. Forever. And I'm not too worried, suddenly, about my solo career because this show we do together is amazing.

At night we cuddle up together in the cramped trailer and it doesn't feel cramped anymore. Not when every tight squeeze means squeezing up against her. Not when I can keep the little bathroom door open to shower and change in the main room because she likes to watch me with admiration dancing in her eyes. Not when her small body fits perfectly with mine in the bed — even if she's a sprawler and thinks literally everything is hers to steal including the covers ... and my breath.

And in the morning, we wake up together, and I get to show her every day that I love her by bringing her sweet pleasure, by making her breakfast, by keeping her things on track, and by laughing at her ridiculous jokes, and fucking her as often as she wants.

Which is all the time.

I swear. This girl is going to kill me.

And I'll die a happy man.

It's when we reach the last race before Utah — at a place called the Aztec Speedway in New Mexico — that she smiles at me as we're lined up to enter the pits and says, "Do you want to race this time, Brent?"

And I do, but I shake my head. "I promised BOOM that you'd do all the racing until the party."

She bites her lip in thought, looking out the windshield. "And after Utah?"

"What do you want after Utah?" I ask carefully.

"I want you to be happy."

"I am happy." And I really am. Incandescent, really.

"And *I* want your career to keep growing beside mine. I think we should alternate races."

And when I glance at her she looks so hopeful that I can't help but smile. "Really?"

"Yes," she says, and she's wearing her serious face, which always looks a bit fake because she's bad at looking serious and not teasing. "I won't take no for an answer. You've been so generous to me, Brent, but you're healed up now and I won't be the reason you lose your career. You've already lost so much for me."

"I've lost nothing." I make my voice firm.

"You know what I mean."

"No." There. I'm making it firmer. "Tessa Bolt, you ridiculously funny, wild girl, I've lost nothing at all. I've given *nothing* compared to all I've received."

And this time, when I look at her, she's blushing and she seems pleased but she steals a little glance toward me. "Then give me this one thing more."

"I'll give you this," I agree. "But not as one thing more. As one thing in a long line of forever things that I plan to give you through a lifetime."

I reach out and take her hand.

"Do you think we'll last that long?" she asks in a small voice.

A stab of fear runs through me. What does she mean?

"Why wouldn't we?" I don't like how my voice feels faint when I ask that.

But she only shakes her head and looks sad and now my heart is pounding, and I want to ask her what's wrong, but it's our turn to check in at the gates and then we're lost in all the careful work of preparation and there's no room for a big talk. I have to fall into the rhythm of things. I have to check tires, and cameras, and batteries. I have to be there for the drivers' meeting, and to film B reel, and to film myself introducing the track and talking about Tess's strategy for tonight.

But I'm dying inside, little spikes of panic shooting through me every time I catch a glimpse of Tessa.

Did I do something wrong? Did I say something wrong?

Or is she just bored of me already? I'm not as exciting as she is. I'm not as funny. I'm not constantly seducing her the way she does me — I mean, seriously, she beats me to the punch every time — and I'm worried now that it's time for a reckoning and I will finally have to pay for all the joy I've had. I'll have to pay in weeks of pain and loss for the hours of happiness I've had and I'm not ready. I'm just not ready.

I help her buckle her belt, and I wish her luck, and I can feel she's watching me as if she can tell something is off and can't puzzle out what it is. But I can also tell that she means it. She doesn't think we'll last. Because she doesn't love me like I love her, and she never will.

# Chapter Forty

*TESSA*

I DON'T KNOW what rattled Brent up, but it's making me nervous, and nervous is not a great starting point for a race.

I see him in the stands when it's my turn to launch onto the track. He's right there as always, ready to film me, ready to catch it all on camera along with his commentary. This time feels different. He's mobbed with fans — mostly young women — and though he's obviously trying to disentangle himself from them, he's not managing it very well.

I remember his hands helping to lovingly clip me in place while his words were distant and hollow as if his mind was on something else. My heart gives a painful squeeze. Is our marriage weighing on him? Is it just too much of a sacrifice to make? Is he feeling the squeeze of being trapped? He should have taken this race. He shouldn't be shoved off to the sidelines, behind the scenes, while I get the spotlight. I'm worried that he'll grow bitter and it will ruin what we have.

Because the thing is, I'm starting to treasure what we have together.

These last weeks have been probably the most exciting of my life, and it isn't all the racing. It's seeing his soft smiles, it's making him laugh, it's the friend who is there for hours on the road, telling me little tidbits about what it was like to travel in Australia, or musing with me about the importance of family and how we feel about the things we hear on the radio. We have the same politics. We like mostly the same music. We just jive. I've never had this with someone else. I've always been kind of the odd girl out. Too headstrong. Too intense. Kati loves me, but we have different perspectives on things. We don't just *agree* like Brent and I do.

But tonight I glance over at the stands and I see a pretty girl lean in to whisper in Brent's ear. He's smiling politely. What if I've trapped him and kept him from what he really wants? What if he'd be happier with someone else? Someone better at being supportive while he was the star? Someone who kept things tidy instead of being a walking spontaneous disaster area?

The thought of it sends a little spike of panic through me. I think I might be falling for him. Unintentionally. I keep thinking of when he told me that he loved me. Even though he didn't mean it like that, I just keep hearing it in my head.

I wake up in the morning and see him sleeping like an angel fallen to earth, all dark gold and hard planes and I think about those words and get little butterflies in my stomach fluttering wildly like they're trapped in a jar. But I don't feel trapped.

I accidentally bump him as we work together on the car and when he looks at me, a bit chagrined, I hear it again and I feel a little stab of longing in my heart.

I wish it were true. I wish he loved me.

And that's crazy, right? It's crazy.

My hands are sweating in my gloves as my car eases up the ramp. It's my turn to hit the track. I shoot one last glimpse at the stands and see Brent laughing with the fan who was chatting with him. He's having a good time. The announcer's voice is blasting over the noise of the track. The crowd roars with excitement and I smell exhaust and dust.

I grip the wheel tightly, sit back hard in my seat, and launch onto the track, joining the cars before me, about to be joined by the cars following me.

Here we go.

The car feels good beneath me. I think that transmission is holding up alright and it sure had better. I need this race. I need this win.

I hit the accelerator and I try to push everything else out of my mind as I whip around the track, and when the green flag drops, I'm ready. I race hard, fast on the straight stretches, tight in the curves. I edge past the car in front of me on the first corner and the car after that on the next corner.

But something doesn't feel quite right. I don't know what it is. It might be the car or it might be me. Something just feels … jittery.

And then — suddenly — before I can so much as gasp, I'm flying up and over the tail of the car in front of me, and then the world spins, and spins again, and I don't know what is up or down until I come down hard. Upside down.

I'm so rattled that I can't remember what to do. My heart is racing. I just freeze for a moment. I can't … I can't remember the last few seconds. I know I've crashed. I know I'm upside down.

I swallow and try to pull myself together. Something hurts in my arm.

I hear a voice calling my name and I realize it's the radio in my helmet.

"I'm … I'm fine …" I stutter. I'm not sure if it's true but I'm also not sure it isn't true.

I hear the announcer and the track officials speaking into my headset and it's all too much to process and then someone I don't know is looking in through my driver's window.

"Do you think you can squeeze through here?" he asks.

The roll cage is intact. I think. It looks fine.

"I think so," I gasp and I don't know if he hears me or not but he's telling me he's going to unbuckle me and I'm going to drop but he's going to try to brace me so I don't just fall on my head. I'm supposed to catch myself with my arms. Can I do it?

"I think so," I say again, even though my arm hurts a lot. It's probably fine, right? It will just have to be.

And then there's another voice, and another, and they're arguing about something outside the window.

"Okay, I'm going to release your harness. Ready?"

The voice says as he helps to brace me. A second set of arms reaches in to support me and then the catch releases and I fall.

I think maybe I screamed. The jar to my arm is nothing but ragged, sharp-edged pain. For a moment, it blocks out every other sensation, every other thought. I'm nothing but darkness and pain.

When my thoughts slowly untangle I'm being carried in someone's arms.

"She needs to be on a stretcher," someone is arguing. "If her back is hurt —"

But they're cut off by a voice I know. A voice I love.

"I've got her."

Brent. The arms around me are Brent. My eyes flutter open and I see his face, twisted with what looks like fear and some other emotion that makes his lower lip tremble and the lines of his face stand out. His bright eyes burn as he hustles me across the track to where an ambulance is waiting. The planes of his face are stark under the fluorescent lights and the black of the night sky.

I want to tell him that I'm fine. That I'll be okay. But pain cuts through my thoughts and instead I bite my lip and fight to muffle a whimper.

I can feel the huff of his breathing against me and the vibration of his feet pounding on the ground as he runs with me in his arms. I can't hear him. It's too loud out here with the announcer on the speakers and the roars of vehicles and voices.

I might not hear him, but I can see his lips moving. I can read "Tessa, honey" on them and it makes my heart squeeze.

And then we're at the back of the ambulance bus and he's passing me off to a paramedic. I don't mean to cry out but when the paramedic touches my arm I can't help it.

"I think her arm's broken." I can just hear Brent over the noise.

They take me from him, more careful of the arm this time, and settle me onto a stretcher. One man is in his twenties. He's checking my heart rate while a woman in her forties closes the ambulance door.

"Brent," I gasp. "I need Brent."

"You need the hospital, honey," the woman is saying but then I hear Brent's voice calling over her.

"I'm riding with her."

"Family only," the paramedic says baldly.

"I'm her husband!"

And like they're magic words he's suddenly on the bus with us and they're slamming the other door.

"Sit here," the female paramedic barks at Brent while the male paramedic holds a finger over my face.

"Follow my finger."

I reach my good hand out and Brent takes it.

"Brent," I gasp.

And I think he's about to say something, but then he drops my hand, suddenly and slumps to the side, hitting the cot he was sitting on hard, his head knocking against the wall.

"Shit," the paramedic looking at me barks. "Don't move."

He rushes to the other cot as the ambulance lurches forward. His hands are checking Brent.

"Sir, can you hear me? Sir?"

"He had a blood patch," I say. "For a spine injury."

"How long ago? Where?"

I rattle off the details.

"He's not supposed to lift!" the paramedic says, cursing again.

As if I don't know that. As if I wouldn't have prevented it if I had been tracking properly.

I can't see Brent with the paramedic between us. I can only see his camera dangling over the side of the bed, hanging from the strap around his body.

I blink back tears.

What does this mean? Has he re-injured himself? Will he ... he won't die, will he?

I feel like I can't breathe. I feel like I'm being buried alive. My vision is blurry and my thoughts are sluggish because dammit, it will break my heart to lose him.

Images run through my brain of what these past weeks would have been like without him. Of me alone. And I hate them.

I didn't realize.

I can hear my heart pounding in my chest. I try to sit up but the paramedic pushes me back down.

"Stay put, please." His voice is tense.

I try to obey him but it feels wrong. My eyes sting. I just want to see him. I just want to make sure he's okay. But the hand pressed to my chest is keeping me in place and I can't get up.

When we reach the hospital, they wheel him out first, a flurry of orders and information exchanged back and forth between them. I try to tell them I'm his wife and I need to stay with him, but no one is listening to me. They just keep pressing me back and telling me to please remain calm, that they have everything under control.

But I'm not under control.

Because I've realized something.

I love Brent.

And even though I've been married to him for just a couple of weeks, I've just realized that I can't live without him.

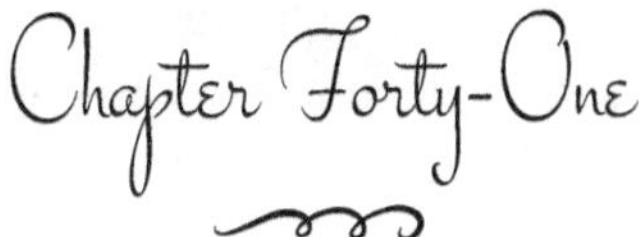

# Chapter Forty-One

BRENT

I'M PANICKED when I wake up.

Tessa.

She was hurt. And then I lost track of her.

"You're going to be fine, sir, just lie still."

I black out again and when I come to, they're whispering over me.

Time is hard to wade through. I don't know how much has passed or what's happening. I have a few false starts and when I finally wake up properly, it all comes out.

It was a big mistake to lift Tessa. It re-triggered the leak in my back. That must have been that dripping feeling I felt when I handed her off to the paramedics.

I'm lucky because they say it isn't a bad leak. Just a little one.

"You need rest," they tell me. "You need to stay lying down. You can travel, but you shouldn't travel very far very quickly."

I'm starting to panic and I'm asking them where Tessa is and if she's okay when I realize someone's holding my hand.

"Hey," she says gently. "I'm right here. I'm okay. I've got you."

I turn to look at her and my whole face feels numb with the movement, but she's there. She's okay.

She has a cast on her arm right up to the shoulder and she's pale and there are dark circles under her eyes but she's okay.

My throat suddenly feels thick and tight. My eyes are swimming with tears I'm determined not to shed.

"BOOM paid a guy from the track to move our trailer to a campground," she says. Her voice is rough. I'm worried about why. "They're sending Ian out tomorrow to help us. I'll get a ride-share to take us back to the trailer."

I'm nodding. I already feel tired again. I can't seem to find my voice or how to tell her that just seeing her is like taking a breath of oxygen. She's okay. That means I'll be okay, too.

The flurry of activity involved in getting me up and dressed and out the door leaves me reeling and exhausted.

I think I fall asleep on Tessa's good shoulder on the ride-share. She has to wake me up to get me out.

"Are you two going to be okay?" the middle-aged woman who drove us asks.

I'm not sure what to say to that. I feel like my thoughts are far away.

"Absolutely!" Tessa's trying to be positive, but her voice sounds thread-thin.

"Let me help you, hun," she tells Tessa and I'm grateful, even if I can't express it. Tessa needs help. And I'm no use right now. "I have three grown children and sometimes they need my help, too. Here we go, up you get, sunshine."

She helps Tessa haul me to my feet and between the two of them, they get me into the trailer and up into the bed. My head is reeling. The nausea rolls in threatening waves over me.

I'm grateful to collapse in the blankets, but I'm worried

about Tessa and I can't even find the energy to ask her if she's okay.

She almost died today. I saw the car. It was nothing but a crumpled wreck around that roll cage. Damn, that was close. My chin starts to tremble every time I think about it because I can't lose her. I just can't. I don't want to live in a world she isn't in.

I want to tell her that my love for her is real. That I'm so grateful she's alive that I could cry. That she's my everything.

But the words won't come, and the black waves wash over me and sweep me away.

# Chapter Forty-Two

*TESSA*

I pass a terrible night in pain from my arm — a compound fracture (ouch!) and a dislocated shoulder are no joke even after the shoulder has been put back in place.

The pain is ridiculous, barely manageable with the painkillers I scooped up at the pharmacy next to the hospital. I check on Brent multiple times through the night in between water and more painkillers. He's passed out so hard that I'm worried he's dead every time I wake up to the stillness in the trailer. My heart is in my throat when I check, but each time when I put my palm in front of his open mouth I feel that gust of breath and know he's okay. Or at least he will be.

"It was the stupidest thing he could have done," the doctor had said when he went over it all with me, the morning after the accident when my arm was finally patched up. "For an injury like his — it's set him back practically to where he started."

"Does he need another surgical procedure?" I'd asked, twisting my hair between my fingers. My whole body felt like one big knot and my arm was in agony.

"Hopefully, not. Hopefully, with rest and staying on his back, he'll recover on his own, but there are no guarantees. This kind of injury is rare and research on it is still being developed. Your husband shouldn't have played hero back there. When he comes to, tell him to let the professionals help. No matter how in love he is with you, he can't carry you any better than anyone else."

And then he'd left me to Brent's care and I kept thinking about those words. "No matter how in love he is."

They weren't true. But I knew now that they were true of me. Because as hurt as I was, and in all the pain I was in, all I cared about was seeing him again and making sure he was okay.

And I still feel that way when I wake up on the couch of the trailer. I don't think I can crawl into the bed with him — not with my arm like this. The smallest jostle and it flares in pain. I could maybe drive, but only with my good hand and only for a short time. Any more than that and I'll get hot and sweaty and too flushed to keep going.

It's noon when a knock sounds on the trailer door. Brent doesn't so much as grunt. He hasn't woken up yet from yesterday.

I ease myself to my feet and check myself over. I struggled into one of Brent's button-down shirts and a pair of loose shorts last night — all I could handle with this huge cast. My hair is tangled, but I can't even put it up with just one hand. I look like I just climbed out of a dumpster.

I open the door blearily.

Ian pushes in and past me so fast that he knocks me backward, jostling my cast and making me hiss in pain.

"Don't be a drama queen," he says, marching past me, looking over Brent, and then spinning back to me.

"What the fuck, Tessa?"

His face is red. His hands are on his hips. I glance out the door and see he's driven a BOOM truck here.

"Don't fucking look out the door, look at me."

I close the door carefully, blinking back tears.

I don't know what I expected, but it wasn't this. Sympathy, maybe? A little kindness? Someone to take some of the responsibility off my shoulders? I did not expect hostility and a mouth that could use a good soap-washing.

"What have you done?"

"I wrecked the car," I say in a small voice. "It was an accident."

Tears spring up in my eyes but I refuse to shed them in front of someone who speaks to me like this. I blink them away.

What is Ian's problem? He's been nothing but a jerk to me since he came back here from Australia. I already wish BOOM had sent anyone else. Even that Tanner guy.

"Is Olivia with you?"

"No." His tone is curt and he crosses his arms over his chest, a wince flashing over his face. "You crashed the car and then what?"

"I broke my arm and Brent hurt himself lifting me."

He looks over at Brent's sleeping form in the bed. "How bad is he?"

"They don't know. They think if he rests enough he'll heal on his own but they aren't sure. They might have to do the procedure all over again."

My voice is small and I have to fight through the tears threatening to fall. I don't want to cry in front of Ian. Not when he's being like this.

"Fuck, Tessa. Could you have screwed up worse? Huh?"

He goes to grab my arm — the broken one that's hidden in the big sleeve of Brent's button-down — but when he feels the cast through the sleeve he flinches back.

"What's this?"

"I broke my arm. I told you."

He makes a sound that conveys all his frustration and anger

and then the hand that had reached for me runs over his face, and when he's composed himself his voice turns cold.

"I should never have trusted you with this, Tessa. You're so fucking unreliable. So fucking prone to just spontaneously act without any thought. You married him. You fucking *married* him. Do you realize how that's screwed up his life? He's twenty-five. He has everything ahead of him. He shouldn't be tied up and shackled to you."

"I thought you wanted us together." My voice is tight. It's so hard to hold back tears. It's been just so much in just a few hours and I can't think straight to defend myself. "I thought Olivia wanted us to have babies together and go on vacations."

"Don't talk to me about Olivia."

"Why not? Isn't she your wife?"

He leans in and he's shaking and I realize I've never seen him like this before. He's furious and sorrowful and he looks like he wants to kill me. It's such a ridiculous overreaction to me marrying his friend — no matter how young we are — that a shocked laugh escapes me.

"You're gonna laugh?" His voice is shivering with fury. "You're going to laugh when my wife lost her baby over the stress of hearing her brother got married and didn't tell her?"

"No." I feel the blood rush from my face. He has to be lying.

"Yes, Tessa. And I can just about guess whose brainy idea that was."

"I ..."

"No. Don't even try to defend it. I know it was you who made that choice. Just like it's you who drove the car way past where Brent was well enough to drive it again. Don't you think I've seen him in the footage? Don't you think I know that he's well enough to drive now and it could be him with mobs of fans at races instead of you? It could be him with fan clubs, and funding, and sponsors approaching BOOM every five minutes, but no, it's all you. You took that from him, and he let you because he's a nice guy. Just like you married him to keep it, and he let you — again, because he's a nice guy. And he's vulnerable, and injured, and reliant on you, and you fucking used him, Tessa, to get what you wanted just like you use everyone."

"Wait. What?" My head is too thick for this. I know he's wrong. I know it wasn't like that, but I can't even find the words to fight him.

"You used Mom and Dad the exact same way when you sold everything and moved back into their house. Don't you think they would have liked to spend their retirement without a kid at home? But no, you didn't think of that."

"I'm not a kid."

I take up my bottle of pills with shaking hands. Maybe a painkiller will clear my mind enough to think.

He snatches the bottle away. "No. You're gonna listen to me."

He starts opening cupboards and when he finds the one with my duffel bag in it, he pulls it out and starts opening draw-ers, throwing my clothes and things into the duffel.

"I'm going to take Brent to a specialist," he says grimly. "And *again* I'm going to get him taken care of."

"He's my husband. I stay with him." I make my voice firm.

"No, you don't. You just keep ruining his life and it stops right now. I'm not watching my wife lose another baby all because of me setting my unmanageable sister in her brother's life. It's my fault and I'm fixing it. I'm going to get him sorted out and find him a place in Utah, and we'll figure out a job for him with BOOM somewhere that *he* will shine instead of being exploited before it's too late and the career he's carefully built for himself is gone forever. You'll take the truck I drove here and go straight back to Canada."

"And do what?"

"I don't fucking care what, as long as it doesn't involve my wife and her family. I swear to God, Tessa, you fucked this up so bad and it's all on me now. Everyone is looking at me because they know you're my fault. And I'm not you. I clean up my damn messes. And that starts right now."

He grabs the pill bottle and throws it on top of the bag and tosses the whole bag out the door of the trailer.

"Come on." His words are sharp.

I hesitate, looking at Brent. He's slept through all of this. And I don't want to go. I want to stay here with him and make sure he's okay. I want to be with him while he recovers.

Ian's tone changes to something softer when I take a step toward Brent. "Don't you think you've done enough damage, Tessa? Can't you just let him rest now?"

If he'd yelled again, I think I could have ignored him but it's the soft voice. It breaks down my defenses the way the yelling and cursing can't. Is he right? Did I take advantage of Brent? I was the one who needed the marriage. I was the one who insisted it be real and that we not tell our families. My throat feels thick.

Did he only do this because he's a nice guy?

Did I really ruin his life?

I want to kiss him goodbye. I don't want to just leave him without speaking first.

But if I do, I'm not sure I'll be able to hide from him that I've fallen in love with him. And if that happens, I know he wouldn't let me leave. He'd feel responsible for me like he does for Ian and Olivia and then he'd be stuck with me and what if what Ian says is true? What if I've ruined his whole life and career and made his sister lose a little niece or nephew? What if all of that is on me?

My lip trembles and the tears I've been holding off start to fall, and then my brother puts an arm around my shoulders, careful this time not to hurt my arm.

"I know you aren't a bad person underneath it all, Tessa. You wouldn't be cruel if you knew what you were doing."

And I don't know why his words make me so angry and so

hurt all at once, but I also don't have a defense because, from one perspective, I did use him, didn't I? From one perspective, I've been selfish and mean. It's just not *my* perspective where I've fallen wildly in love with this man.

But my mind isn't working well, and I can't find the words, and when Ian guides me out of the trailer my vision is too blurry to even catch a last glimpse of Brent's dear face. All I can do is snatch up the last of his letters from the counter and stuff them in my purse and then Ian is leading me outside and helping me into his truck. It's a huge lifted BOOM truck — not orange, thank goodness — with their customizations all over it.

"It's a giveaway truck for next month, but they don't mind lending it to you. Just drive it straight home," he says before walking around the side of the truck to grab my duffel and throw it into the passenger side of the truck.

But that's the problem. Because home for me is in that trailer. Home for me is in the arms of the man who broke himself trying to take care of me. Home for me is in the heart that never cared that he was giving me everything.

And if I have to go on without him, then I don't want to go on at all.

"You know it has to be this way, Tessa. Don't be stubborn about it," Ian says from the passenger door. "Drive safe this time."

And then he slams the door and walks back to the trailer, and he doesn't look back, and I can hardly breathe.

# Chapter Forty-Three

*BRENT*

HAVE you ever had one of those dreams where terrible things are happening around you but you can't seem to move or even speak?

Yeah, that's real life for me right now.

# Chapter Forty-Four

*TESSA*

I DRIVE NORTH and make it just over the Colorado border before I break down sobbing and can't go anymore. My arm feels like it's on fire. I ran out of tissues an hour ago and I can't deal anymore. I find the nearest Airbnb with an open room — a ridiculously expensive tree house that looks gorgeous in the photos. I book it and then drive there, stopping only to grab a little food, a lot of painkillers, and a fuzzy sweater big enough to wear over my cast, from a truck stop along the way. High fashion and good nutrition it is not, but frankly, I'm not in the mood for either.

I park the truck, leave my cell phone in it, climb up into the high-class treehouse, and cry myself to sleep.

When I wake up, I have no idea what time it is. Bright sunlight pours in through the wide windows. This place is so charming that it would suit a second honeymoon. Just the thought of that sets me crying again, and I cry myself to sleep a second time.

I wake to night. I try to eat but I feel like throwing up and I can't even stomach a single bite. I'm a terrible person. I've hurt everyone I love. I hate myself.

And I'm completely brokenhearted. I miss Brent. I miss him so much. I want him here even though Ian was super clear that I do nothing but ruin his life.

I want to cry more, but I think I used all my tears up and now my eyes just burn the same way my broken arm does.

In the end, I go to the truck and find my laptop. I don't even look at my phone. I don't want to know who's been calling. I don't want to know what they have to say to me. None of it will be good and I don't care. I just want to see Brent again.

I set the laptop up in the living area, connect to the Airbnb wifi with the password they gave me, and log in to BOOM Motorsports, and I turn on our show to watch while I start to make a fire with one arm.

It's charming. The footage that Brent took, the way it's all stitched together — we look like we're having so much fun together. We're laughing and racing and building. I keep catching glimpses of my own smile and thinking it's like watching someone from a faraway country. A country I once lived in and can never return to. The old Tessa is so happy, so free. The new Tessa is just an aching broken mess.

But it's the little glimpses of Ian that break my heart. I love watching any glimpse of him. He walks past a camera and my heart tugs to follow him. He turns the camera on himself to introduce the race and the track, and I just want to reach out and draw him to me. And I never can again. For the rest of my life, I'm just going to see him in little glimpses like this with a camera and an internet connection and a thousand miles between us.

I go and throw up in the bathroom.

It's started to rain outside — actually storm is a better way to say it. It's so dark that the fire and the laptop are all the light there is. The trees outside the treehouse sway in the wind and lashes of rain beat against the windows.

The weather suits my mood perfectly.

Bring it on, sky. It's you and me both. Just know you'll run out eventually like me and then it will burn which kind of sucks.

When I come back, the video is of me talking about how great Brent is. All true, by the way, though old Tessa is a big fat idiot who didn't fully know what she had until it was gone.

In the background of the shot is one of his letters and it reminds me I brought some with me.

I dig them out of my pocket and spread them out. Two are from before and they don't really apply.

"When your mom calls" is one and another one is "When Olivia pressures you."

They don't seem relevant and it doesn't seem fair to read them without permission, so I add them to the fire. I let them burn up with my heart. But it's the third one that I can't quite let go of. It's one he wrote after we got married. The only one I have left.

It says, "When you see my interview about you on BOOM."

That condition hasn't been met yet. But it's about to be. So I open up the letter and I read it.

*Tessa, Honey,*
*It's all true. It's always been true.*

I bite my lip and look up just as he comes on screen clearing his throat awkwardly. He talks about his history racing in Australia and meeting my brother and then he starts talking about me and that old look is in his eyes. The one I crave. The one I want to treasure. I can't hear or see anything but that. This whole cabin could burn down and I wouldn't realize it until it was too late because I'm mesmerized by what I'm watching.

*"She's the wildest, most laughing, most positive person,"* he says, looking contemplative. *"Sure, she's ridiculously competent. You've all seen how she can build, how fast her mind is at solving mechanical problems, how she drives like some kind of a whirlwind. But I think it's her spirit I like best. She doesn't let anyone bring her down. She's bright laughter, and melting butter, and sunshine on a summer day. She's the best person I've ever met."*

He looks up at the camera and I want to cry again. I feel my lower lip trembling.

*"What can I say? Everyone who meets her falls in love with her."*

I gasp.

It's right there in his eyes. He's not speaking just for other people. He's speaking for himself. He looks *exactly* like he did when he told me he loved me when he was in bed with me. And it stuns me.

Because I remember when BOOM asked us to do this. It was way before anyone talked about marriage. It was way before there was any story to keep straight.

I look down at the letter — the one he wrote the day we got married. And I look up at the screen, at the soft, slightly pained look in his eyes. And I thought I was out of tears, but it turns out that I'm not.

And when I hear the banging on the door I jump, dropping the laptop so hard that I think it might be broken.

The door is right behind me and it's mostly made of windows, and when I turn to look there's someone silhouetted against them, the lightning flashing behind them, revealing nothing of the face of whoever is here.

And I don't know what to do. I should open the door. It's not even locked. But also, I probably should have locked it, because this is like a total horror movie scene.

The door opens and the firelight spills across the soaking-wet figure in the doorway. His light-colored button-down is plastered to his skin — which is maybe the hottest thing ever — and his jeans are leaving a puddle on the doorstep, and his tousled hair looks twice as long when it's plastered around his face in the rain and he's looking at me with that same half soft, half sorrowful look on his face and when I let out an agonized gasp he makes the exact same sound.

"You wrote me a letter," I say, and I sound strangled. The rain is still beating down on him. He hasn't come in the door.

"I wrote you a lot of letters. Sent some texts, too, which you haven't answered."

I hold the letter up to show him. And my voice is raw and trembling.

"This one says you love me."

He pauses to swallow, his hand flexing as if by instinct. "So do the rest of them."

*Untitled*

## Chapter Forty- Five

*BRENT*

Whoa. Whoa. Whoa. Back up.

We'll get to the good part in a moment.

First, I should tell you — I punched Ian. It took me a few hours to get to the point where I could because I couldn't quite rouse myself to full consciousness. The minute that I did, I stumbled out of my bed, half fell down to the lower part of the living area of the trailer and landed a very poorly aimed punch on his ear. It was meant to be his jaw. And it was meant to be about ten times harder. As it was, he looked up from his cell phone more annoyed than actually hurt.

"What the hell, Brent?" he said, shaking me off as I attempted a follow-up blow.

"I heard it all. I couldn't get up. I couldn't stop you. But I heard it all." I sounded breathless, like I'd run a marathon rather than botched a beating. In my defense, I was so nauseated I was lucky I hadn't already puked.

"Heard what?" He leaned back into the couch cushions enough to avoid a third attempt at a blow. "Dude. You can't fight me right now so can you please cool it with the lame attempts?"

"You sent my *wife* away. And I don't give a damn that she's your sister. She's hurt and she's heartbroken and you sent her away from her husband and her home and made her think it's all her fault. I'm going to fucking kill you and bury your body." I manage to get it all out before swaying on my feet. "Right after my next nap."

"Wait," Ian said, doing that annoying Ian thing where he's sure he's right even when evidence to the contrary is presented to him. He's as hard-headed as his sister and not nearly so charming. "You're confused because you're sick, but that's not what's happening at all. I'm here to rescue you from a disaster that I created by sending you out into the world with my harebrained sister."

"I'm not confused. I'm furious. Give me your keys."

I could go through the rest of the conversation, but talking to really sick people is like talking to drunks — not all that entertaining — so suffice it to say, I had to sleep another day before I managed to sound sober enough to get keys from Ian. By then, I was sensible enough not to try to punch him. It's not that I didn't want to. But I understood by then that I needed to conserve my energy if I was going to go find Tessa.

"The BOOM truck she took has a GPS in it," Ian admitted, holding his hands up. "Don't look at me like that. I didn't install it. They put them in all of them for safety reasons."

I looked at the app he showed me. Tessa didn't go far. If I started driving right away, I'd probably make it before my energy gave out. I downed a cup of coffee, took the keys, and drove.

We arrive in the pouring rain. The app on his phone shows the truck is up a narrow driveway, but between the rain and the trees, neither of us can see anything. I hop out of the truck and throw the keys at Ian. I don't care where he goes or what he does. I'm still furious with him.

"I can't even tell if that's a driveway." He looks worried.

"You lost the right to worry about me when you sabotaged my marriage."

We've hardly spoken since the first argument. I listened when he told me about my sister and I gave her a call. This isn't her fault. And she deserves all the love and support right now. That bastard Ian should be with her instead of here ruining things for me.

"I'm not sure we're still friends, man," I'd said after I got off the phone with Olivia. "We're family, so I'll do right by you. But I'm not sure we're still friends. When I get to the spot where she's stopped, you'll take the truck back to my sister. Right away. I don't want you around when I try to patch this up."

He'd tried to protest then that I wasn't up to this, just like he's protesting now. He's not wrong, but that's the thing: I don't care.

I have only one thing I want right now and it's not my health. It's not his friendship. Other than making sure that my sister is okay, I have had only one thing on my mind and heart since my former best friend stormed into my home and ejected my wife.

I need to get her back.

I need to find some way to show her that she's loved and wanted and I'll do anything to keep her as mine. I need to finally confess what I've been trying to hint at — that I don't want a future without her. That I don't want a life without her. That she's made a home inside my heart like we did in that trailer, and without her in it, everything is empty.

I just want her in my arms forever. I just want her to be okay.

The rain lashes at me, pushing me around on the path. I didn't bother to bring a duffel. Whatever. I can't manage to carry one right now anyway. It's just gonna be me and my soaking wet clothes, and my heart in my hands, and if she sends me away, then I won't need that stuff anyway. I'll be too broken to care.

Which is how I arrive on her porch, and I knock at her door, and I let myself in with a storm whirling around me and lightning lacing through the sky.

She looks like she hasn't slept properly since she saw me last. Her eyes are deep holes in her face. Her cheeks are sunken. She certainly hasn't eaten.

I swallow. My throat is thick and I can't quite breathe as my heart squeezes tightly and painfully. Just the sight of her sweeps my breath away.

"You wrote me a letter," she says and the look in her eyes stabs right through my chest. I want to cross the room and take her in my arms. I want to heal her heart. I'm paralyzed with fear of ruining everything.

"I wrote you a lot of letters. Sent some texts, too, which you haven't answered."

I've been texting her all day.

Her pretty lips tremble.

"This one says you love me."

I can hardly speak, but she has to know.

"So do the rest of them."

I feel like I'm falling as I wait to see what she'll do.

She's staring at me, her lips parted, eyes blazing with something. And then she closes her mouth and swallows and a single tear slips loose and I feel my breath gust out at the same moment that she gives me one of her bold Tessa looks, strides across the room, and takes my breath away when she wraps her arms around me and knocks me backward.

I let my arms wrap around her, my breath caught in my throat. She's not mad. She's not shaken up by my confession. Does that mean...is it possible that she...

Her words cut through any defense I had left.

"I love you Brent Bolt."

I have to swallow down a lump in my throat before I can speak. I didn't know your heart could feel like it was breaking when you were happy.

"I love you, too," I whisper in her ear. "You have to know. I've loved you from the beginning."

"But I hold you back," she says in a small voice — so different from her usual confidence.

This time, it's my turn to laugh. "You don't. You're like gasoline in my engine. You make me powerful."

"I took your chances." She sounds like she's begging me to contradict her.

"Honey, you never took a thing I didn't willingly give you. Your brother filled you up full of lies."

Her voice is clouded and muffled from where her face is buried in my chest. "Then what's the truth?"

"The truth?" I pull back so I can look into her eyes and smooth the hair and tears from her cheeks. "You're my Tessa. And I love you. And I don't want to live another minute without you." I pause to swallow. What I'm feeling is too big. I'm choking on it. "Please say you'll take my heart."

And her soft, wondering laugh is exactly what I hoped for. I draw her back into the house and close the door behind us. She has a fire blazing in the fireplace but I lead her past it to the bedroom.

"Are you in a lot of pain?" I ask her, biting my lip. "I was so worried about you. I was so worried that the accident had really hurt you and I couldn't help you."

"I'm okay." She laughs softly again. "That doesn't seem like a big enough word. I'm golden, Brent. Completely golden. I can't believe you're here."

She is *exactly* golden. Like the sun. I can barely stand to look at her.

I look away, only to look back immediately, both unable to look and unable to stop looking.

"I don't ever want to leave you." My voice is rough.

"Sleep in my bed tonight?" She bites her lower lip.

"I'm soaking wet," I laugh looking down.

"Then put your clothes by the fire and sleep in your skin." Her eyes dance playfully.

"Deal," I agree, leaning in to place a soft kiss on her forehead. "But only if you sleep in yours, too."

In the end, she sleeps in what she's wearing. She is in pain, even though she pretends she isn't, so she can convince me to nestle in naked against her. I drape my clothing out in front of the fire, stoke it well, and then climb into the bed with her.

With her broken arm, we don't make love, but there are other ways to feel close. I cup her cheek with one hand and lay my other hand across her ribs, careful to avoid her arm, and I whisper to her all the things I love about her — about us. All the things I've been dreaming about since the first moment that I realized it. And when her tears slip out, I kiss them. And when she tells me the things she loves about me, I kiss her again. There's a tenderness between us that I've never known before. It goes beyond sex. It goes beyond attraction. It sinks into shadowy parts of me and warms them up and makes me feel full.

But we're both worn down to nothing, and before I even know it, we've drifted off to sleep together, wrapped in warm quilts and more love than I thought was possible.

# Chapter Forty-Five

*TESSA*

I WAKE to a pounding on the door.

Brent is still fast asleep — and I know it's exhaustion not just regular sleep gluing him to the pillow. He probably pushed himself way too hard chasing after me, and now he'll have to pay for it.

There's another urgent knock and I pull myself to my feet, wincing at my arm — yeah, it still hurts — and stumbling out to the main room. I make a grab for Brent's clothes strewn all over the floor in front of the fire. They're dry now. I toss them behind me into the bedroom, in case he wakes up and needs to hurriedly dress, and then I run to the door. There are windows set in it, but whoever is here is standing to one side and I can't see them.

I open the door carefully.

"Tessa! There you are!" Adam Boomhower — Big Daddy BOOM — says in his huge voice as if he's mislaid me and been looking for me. "Thank goodness. The party is tonight and Gracie is going to be disappointed if you aren't there."

"Party?" I gasp.

"The one I promised you when you got to Utah. Trust me. You don't want to disappoint Gracie."

"You really don't," the man behind him says. I gape when I realize it's Tanner. He's looking over the exterior of the tree-house with the air of someone annoyed that he wasn't consulted before construction began. Behind him, it's only our truck in the driveway.

"How did you get here?" I ask, still trying to process what's happening.

"Oh, I landed the chopper back there, closer to the main road," Adam says gesturing over his shoulder. "Too many trees close to the house."

How do you argue with that?

"Yes. Umm. Come in?" I say, backing up into the tree house and gesturing for them to come inside.

"No time for hospitality," Adam says and as if that is code for something, Tanner turns and bustles over to the BOOM truck, opening up the doors.

"Should I get dressed?" I ask, confused, but I've already lost that thought when my mouth forms an "o."

Tanner has opened all the truck doors and with the efficiency of a highly paid professional assistant, he is tearing through the contents of the truck, stacking my things to one side, and shoving travel garbage into a small plastic bag. He's almost done and I'm still staring.

"Oh," Adam says like it just occurred to him. "Tanner will drive your truck home. There's no time for driving if we're gonna get you back to my place and prettied up for your wedding reception, so we'll fly you in the chopper."

"Oh," I say stupidly.

"It was all in the texts I sent you."

"Boss." We both look at Tanner and he holds up my cell phone from the pile on the ground.

"Ohhhh!" BOOM says and his grin gets huge and boyish as

he takes in the phone, and then at me in my pajama shorts and fuzzy sweater, and then past me to the lump in my bed that is clearly Brent. "Well."

He leans in close like he's going to tell me a secret.

"I try so hard not to set people up, but it never works. This is like the third time it's happened to me."

"He's not trying at all," Tanner complains from the truck.

"The third time?" I say, still stunned.

Look. Just twelve hours ago I thought my happiness was ruined forever. Now, I've been told my husband loves me, I've spent a night cuddled up with him, and was awoken — suddenly — by a bearded, slightly sweaty, creatine-soaked fairy godmother who I'm pretty sure flew a blaze orange helicopter here. It's a lot.

"Oh yeah," Adam says. "I'm almost at the point where I'm going to have to ask people to sign indemnity waivers." He laughs like it's an amazing joke. "Anyways, go get Brent for me. We need to leave in twenty if we're going to keep on schedule."

"Sure," I agree because this is crazy and what else do you say.

I hurry back into the house, closing the door carefully on the chaos behind us, sneak into our room, and find him there, blinking awake, pushed up on his elbows. He's beautiful when he offers me that sleepy smile.

"Sunshine," he sighs when I come through the door.

"Hi," I say nervously.

"I heard it all." He's cute when he yawns. "Are you okay with this, Tess? He didn't really ask."

"Am I okay with a billionaire throwing me a wedding reception?" I ask with a smirk.

"Yes." He's deadly serious and I love it. I love that he'd say no to BOOM for me. That he'd say no to everyone else just for me.

A bit misty-eyed, I kiss his forehead. "I'm not sure if I can handle seeing Ian right now. But otherwise, I'm okay with a party."

His hands creep up to either side of my waist and he leans into my kiss greedily.

"Forget Ian," he whispers. "Your brother doesn't get a say in this marriage. It's between you and me only."

I nod and he stretches up to kiss me again.

"I guess we'll have a wedding reception then," I say softly when he's done.

"I guess we will. Do you need help dressing?"

I do need help. Really the only thing that fits around my cast is the tiny sundress I wore for our wedding. Brent helps me on with it and I swear it's almost sexier to be dressed by him than to be undressed. His hands are gentle and hesitant. And he gifts me with small, shy smiles as he helps me strip out of what I'm wearing into what I'm putting on.

I'm terribly distracted as he does it. Between the brush of his fingers, his heated looks full of promise, and the fact that he's still stark naked, I feel very turned on. He huffs a laugh once I'm dressed and pulls on his crumpled clothing. They smell like woodsmoke, and I've never been so in love with the smell of a fire before.

By the time we make it out of the cabin with my stuffed duffel bag, Tanner and the truck are already gone, and Adam has everything from the truck in a shopping bag which he hands to Brent.

"Take that, would you, son? We're gonna have to hustle to keep up with Gracie's schedule. Can you walk to the end of the driveway? Ian sounded a bit frantic about your capabilities when he called me last night, but the boy's a drama queen about his sister, so I mostly ignored him about that. Now that I'm here, though, I can see it's dragging at you."

"I'll be fine," Brent says with a confidence that I'm pretty sure is feigned. But he won't let me carry the bag or even the duffle. He just slips me my phone before hefting the whole thing onto his shoulder. His finger slides across the home button as he hands it to me and it lights up for me.

His text is on the top. And he wasn't lying.

It reads:

I love you, Tess. Always.

And my heart feels so full that I can't even properly appreciate the blaze orange helicopter when we get there. Or the fact that Adam has had BOOM wrapped onto it in huge black lettering that looks like it was carved from a rock. Or that *he's* our pilot.

One of his other employees is in the co-pilot seat and he gives us a thumbs up and a big grin but doesn't say anything more. BOOM is talking on our headsets so steadily that the other man couldn't get a word in edgewise anyway.

I should be concentrating on how cool my first-ever helicopter ride is, but I keep stealing little glances at Brent, trying to gauge how he feels, if he's feeling what I'm feeling, if he's really as happy as I am.

I am buoyant. I'm the kind of happy that really can only come once because it settles in your bones and deepens minute upon minute, day upon day. I'm that kind of happy.

Brent reaches out and takes my hand to give it a soft squeeze and then he just holds onto it for the rest of the short helicopter ride to Big Daddy BOOM's huge ranch-style mansion in the hills of Utah.

"We're having your wedding reception at my place," Adam says happily. "I love parties. So does Linda — my second wife. When I told her she could throw one with Gracie's help — well, let's say you're doing me the favor here instead of the other way around."

And that's the thing about Adam. He makes you feel so at home and welcome that you forget sometimes that he's both the crazy billionaire funding your dreams and also the crazy billionaire who kinda, sorta manipulated you into marrying the love of your life.

We land at his insanely huge and gorgeous home. Honestly, he could probably rent it out for weddings full-time if he wanted to. He's greeted by a squealing woman in her fifties — Linda, I presume — and I'm greeted by a squealing Olivia.

"I knew it. I just knew you two would be perfect together," she screams in my ear.

"I'm so sorry about your baby," I whisper in her ear. "I wanted badly to be an auntie."

When she pulls back she's blinking away tears. "Me, too. But your mom is taking me home with her after this, which is exactly what I need." She sucks in a long, steadying inhale. "For now, we are hosting a wedding. And that means I get to dress you, Brent."

I'm still blinking from all of this when she rips Brent's hand out of mine and hauls him away. He looks over his shoulder at me and winces dramatically, but he lets her pull him along while I'm thrust into the arms of my mother.

"Mom?" I say, shocked.

"Diane has been amazing!" Linda trills from beside Adam. "Such great taste! So many ideas!"

And if I were maybe a better girl I could tell you all the details of what happens next, but I'm really not, and as I find myself pulled from person to person and room to room, I can only really grasp the bare details.

My mom is here. Somehow, she and Olivia and Linda and Gracie — Adam's daughter — have produced an extravagant wedding reception that is going to be photographed for BOOM social media and partially filmed.

A dapper-looking man in a vest gives me a wave as we pass. Apparently, he's Gracie's husband and one of the people who will be photographing all of this. He's barely older than me, and so is Gracie who comes bustling out of a back room with a garment bag over one arm and a tissue box under the other.

She shoves the tissues at my mom who needs them already, the garment bag at Linda, mouths "I'm sorry" to me, and then is gone again and you know, good for her, because I wish I was gone, too.

Or at least, I do until I get a hug from Dad who is magically there with a beer in his hand.

"I'm so happy for you, honey, and you've made your mother very proud."

And then he's whisked away and I'm thrown into the arms of Kati who is also magically here and kissing my cheek.

"I helped your mom pick the dress!" she says and while I'm still thanking her, Linda and my mom shuffle me into a magical bathroom with an honest-to-goodness waterfall set in the granite wall and they clean me, and flat iron my hair, and put things on my face that I never asked for, and then, ignoring my modesty and loud protests, they strip me down to my panties, slap a white strapless bra on me, and step me into a sleeveless wedding dress that looks filmy and whimsical next to the black cast I'm rocking on my other arm. I look like a skater punk rocker from a previous generation.

I stare at myself in the mirror in semi-horror — look, it's not the dress. They picked a gorgeous dress. It's drop-waisted and full-skirted and slightly blush-colored, and pretty much perfect.

It's the whole picture that's the problem. I'm not even a little bit bridal. I'm...me. Half tom-boy, half disaster. It's partially hidden by tulle and blush satin, but the black cast is a dead giveaway.

When Brent sees me he's gonna steal that helicopter to make his getaway. I just know it.

But there's no time for more than a token protest before they have me out the door again and now they're hustling into their finery — my mom looks amazing in a plum-colored dress

— and I've been brought out to the desert in the back where Gracie's husband has my wrecked car pulled out of the back of the trailer. I guess Ian brought it home.

Jasper directs me to pose around it and I'm so shell-shocked at this point that I'll do anything just to get it over with so I do. And if I look like I don't know how the hell I got there, well, that seems very fair right now.

"You can relax, you know," he says as he takes a few more shots. "Adam has everything covered. He always does."

That's when I catch a glimpse of Ian striding toward us and I feel sick when I see him. I bet there's a photo of the exact moment I see him and I bet the photographer is snapping so many now because he's scared I'm going to puke on this dress and it will be game over.

But I don't.

Thank goodness.

"Can I have a minute?" Ian asks.

I think they might be buddies because they fist-bump. Awesome. Even the photographer is on Team Ian.

I watch him silently. Not sulkily. Silently. There's a difference and seriously, would you have words for this? Because I don't. He tried to rip us apart. He succeeded in ripping my heart to shreds.

"Brent told me I was selfish right around the point where he tried to punch me," Ian says quietly, as he comes to lean against my wrecked car with me.

"How about that." Yeah, I'm not feeling super gracious. But then I bend. "I'm sorry about the baby."

"It's not your fault."

I scoff and he runs a hand over his face.

"I think I've ruined things," he says.

I just stay silent. It's my gift to him, when sarcasm would be so much easier.

"I shouldn't have blamed the death of my child on you."

If he'd said anything else, I'm not sure I would have listened. Forgiveness had felt like a far-off planet. But this is like a gut punch, so I grab him with my good arm, and I tug him into a hug, and to hell with it hurting my arm. To hell with all the anger I feel toward my harsh, meddling brother. People who are hurting sometimes hurt others. He hurt me a lot. But he's hurting too.

And when he's done soaking my shoulder, I pat him on his and say, "I think Mom has a whole box of tissues."

"I guess crying on your shoulder doesn't really make up for treating you like you are less than the rest of us." His voice is small.

"No."

"Does it help if you know I've realized it now?"

I nod.

"When Mom and Dad go home I'm going with them — with Olivia. Not for long. BOOM can only hold my job for so long. But for long enough that she can have a break. I think I've put her through too many changes. I think she just needs a minute to catch her breath."

"I like that," I say. "There's a cot in the garage if you need it."

He snorts.

"After Olivia heard about my drive down to see you ... well, yeah, I might need it." He looks around awkwardly and when no one appears to be eavesdropping he runs a hand over his face. "It turns out she considers you a sister now."

"Duh. I am her sister now." I roll my eyes. "Twice over, if you're keeping score."

He shoves his hands in his pockets. "*She* is. And she has opinions about how sisters should be treated."

"Good," I say gently, taking his arm. "Because maybe your kids will have sisters someday and you'd want them to have a mom who makes sure that everyone is loved."

"Yeah." He looks a bit misty when he says. "I would like that."

And then Linda is there out of nowhere, and tissues materialize, and I'm being handed off again to Kati and then Mom who tells me she's thrilled that big family vacations with lots of babies are back on the table, and then Dad who kisses my cheek again, and then straight into the huge party where Adam is at the front about to make a speech, and I still haven't seen Brent yet, and my heart is in my throat. I can hardly take it. It's like some kind of nightmare where you're at your own wedding and you can't figure out who the groom is supposed to be.

Adam is waxing eloquent about the beauty of love and how he always seems to find himself in the middle of it, and then just when I think I'm literally never going to see Brent, Linda hustles me over to a wedding arch made entirely of flowering cactus — don't even ask me how she came up with this — and she jams a bouquet of lilies in my hands, which — hey, at least they aren't more cacti. I'm taking that as a win.

And then the crowd parts, and I see him.

He's being hustled over here, too. Apparently, Adam is going to make an announcement and everyone is going to look at us before the party can start.

And boy will they have a lot to look at because the second I lay eyes on Brent, I can't see anything else. He ducks his head slightly, like he's embarrassed by all the attention. Of course he is. But when he looks at me from underneath those long lashes and bites his lip nervously, he steals the last scraps of my breath away. And when he meets me under the spiky arch, he takes away my lily bouquet so that he can hold my hand.

I think we're supposed to say something. I don't know what it is. I don't really care.

The look in my husband's eyes is like a man who found a treasure.

And I can't help it. I push up on my tiptoes, and I let go of his hand so I can pull his head down and kiss him properly.

There's the sound of a hundred indrawn breaths, and then a cheer, and when someone whistles, I catch Brent throwing my bouquet right in their face. It's a perfect throw. And he didn't even open his eyes to do it. And then both of his arms are around me, and I'm fine if everyone here wants to have a party for our sake, but I don't care about them. Because the only person I care about is right here with his arms around me and his husky whisper in my ear.

"Let's get out of here," he breathes. "I don't like sharing you."

And I nod my agreement because I don't like sharing either.

# Chapter Forty-Six

*BRENT*

WE DON'T GET to leave right away like I was hoping we could. Actually, it's hours before the guests finally start to wear out and go home and there's even a hope that we can escape. I've met more BOOM employees than I can possibly remember. They're just a blur of faces and names and congratulations. I haven't let go of Tessa's hand and I won't.

An hour ago, Olivia suggested a nap for me. And I need one. I really do. Exhaustion dogs my heels. But my heart is still raw and nervous. I can't quite believe that I have her back with me and I don't want to let go. When I'm forced to let go of her hand so she can eat or drink, I pinch a bit of her filmy skirt. Call me crazy, I don't care. Call me anything you like. My heart is so tuned to her that it wants to touch her constantly. And I can't say no to it anymore.

Jasper takes what feels like a thousand pictures of us. I'm wearing his three-piece suit.

"A gift from BOOM," he'd told me wryly when he shoved it at me after Olivia deposited me with him. "Adam keeps sending a personal stylist to me which is pretty rich coming from a man who doesn't wear sleeves unless it's snowing. "Oh — and I don't want it back. My closet is already too full of things I'll never wear."

When — finally! — the party starts to quiet, Adam pulls us aside. I'm worn to a frazzle, but I owe this man everything. Tessa's career, mine, our marriage, and this extravagant wedding party — all of it.

"Thank you for all of this, Adam." I mean it.

His huge grin is like a little kid's when he replies, "Come on! There's one more thing!"

He wraps an arm around my shoulders and draws us both around his shop to where the original BOOM truck and trailer that we started with are parked. Only now, the side is wrapped with a huge Tessa in a race suit that says "BOLT" on the back. She looks over her shoulder and winks at the viewer and my wife — my crazy, hilarious wife — starts to laugh. And what's worse is that Adam joins her, his laugh booming out over the desert.

"Amazing, right? I love it, too! Linda, honey, the rest!"

Linda is shaking her head when she presses an envelope into my hands and a map. "We told the guests cash and gift cards only because you two are on the road. But the map is from me. Adam — that dear fool — thought you'd be happy to spend the night in our yard, but I knew better. Here's a map to our property just down the road. Totally private. You can stay there until you hit the road again. As long as you want. My gift to you."

I kiss her cheek as thanks and my throat is tight. I can't seem to find the proper words of gratitude, but she seems happy enough with the kiss. She blushes, pats me on the shoulder, and then she's gone and Adam's gone, and I've barely had a chance to thank them, though Tessa did a much better job of it.

Then it's just family. And if I hug Diane and Olivia a little tighter than maybe I should, I don't think they mind. And if things are still a bit tense between me and Ian — well, some things take time, and rebuilding trust is one of those things.

And then — finally — it's just the two of us about to hop into a vehicle again.

"I'll drive," Tessa says, hitching up her frothy skirts. "That way you can nap."

But before she can get in, I spin her around and gently pin her against the vehicle.

"Did you want to drive?" she asks a little breathlessly, laughing.

"Honey," I growl. "I'm happy to let you do all the driving. So long as I get to kiss you."

And I lean in and do just that — as thoroughly as I know how. I've missed these lips. I've been thinking about them all day.

I pull back, feeling a little smug, but this time it's her who reaches out and gently pulls my face down and kisses me with such savage enthusiasm that when she finally releases me, I have to gasp in a breath.

"I can't afford to give you an inch." I gust a laugh and she winks at me before pulling my head low but this time she just whispers in my ear.

"Just one inch, Brent? When I get you to where we can park this terrible monstrosity, I plan to take all eight inches of you."

"That joke is getting old," I tell her, but it's not. I could go ahead and hear that joke about a hundred more times if it's coming from her.

This time when she pulls back, I'm the one who is breathless and a bit flushed, and she's laughing when she sees what she's done to me and how these stupid suit pants are not going to be roomy enough to deal with the result.

"You'd better slow down," I warn. "We still have to get out of here."

"Haven't you heard, Brent," she teases. "I don't ever slow down. I'm actually getting a bit famous for it."

We're both laughing as we get into the truck that's as familiar to me now as my own skin. And I think I might be the luckiest man in the world now because I'm married to the woman who makes me laugh no matter what the circumstances and no matter how rich Adam Boomhower thinks he is with his mansions and helicopters and online empires, I'm so much richer because I have Tessa, and Tessa is like the shining sun.

# Chapter Forty-Seven

*TESSA*

I DON'T DO what anyone expects. I don't drive to the convenient property close by — even though it was really kind of Linda to offer it. I don't answer all the texts on my phone. I don't even wake Brent who is snoring adorably against the door jam.

Instead, I drive clear through Utah, Nevada, and California until I hit the beach somewhere north of San Francisco just as morning is starting to peak into noon and Brent's eyes are fluttering open.

He smiles at me sleepily as I park the trailer in the spot I've rented for us, and then we both slide out of the truck and into the warm afternoon sun.

There's something hilarious about being dressed in a filmy wedding dress and walking barefoot through the sand. You should have seen me at the gas stations. Someone hooted at me like I was in the rodeo. I strip my shoes off immediately and start dancing in the sand, letting the long skirt of my wedding dress swirl around me until laughter bubbles up and I seek out Brent's eyes.

When I find his gaze, it's on me, of course. That's the thing about Brent. He always sees me.

He's stripped his own shoes and jacket off and is standing in bare feet with his trousers rolled up, his fancy vest rumpled, and matching laughter in his eyes. And his smile is warmer than the California sun, his eyes brighter than the waves.

I run to him, still laughing, and steal a kiss. Well, I say steal, but I'm pretty sure he gives it to me. Just like he is going to give me all his kisses forever.

"Swim with me in the ocean like this?" I ask him. "How amazing would that be?"

"It will ruin what's left of Jasper's suit." His words might be reluctant, but I don't think he is. That's adoration in his eyes. And he's shining it all on me.

"I don't think he'll miss it."

"You have to protect that cast," he reminds me.

Which is why when we take our sexy, dramatic dip in the ocean together — me in my romantic strapless A-line dress and him in his borrowed three-piece suit — minus the jacket — my left arm is wrapped up in a black trash bag he found in the trailer. The cast is safe. My heart is not. He's stealing it all over again.

We're making a very "us" memory. It's sweet and deadly romantic, unique, and maybe just a little bit ridiculous. And I love it.

And when we stand in the water with the waves swirling the skirt of my wedding dress around my knees and tugging me forward and then back, and we look up at each other and kiss, I know this is my forever.

"Do you have a letter for what I should do if I find I'm in a soaking wet wedding dress?" I tease.

"I do," he says a little huskily. "It's back in the trailer."

Which is how he convinces me to come and look for it with him.

"I'm writing this one as we go," he whispers when we get there. "It starts with stripping off these sandy clothes so we don't make a mess of the trailer."

"Very sensible." I agree, though my feet are so sandy that it's probably a lost cause.

"And it ends with us in other clothes walking over to that taco stand I saw down the beach."

"Mmmm tacos. Reminds me of the first time I kissed you."

"Exactly."

"And what comes in between?" I ask when we make it through the door and I start to unbutton his vest.

"That's the best part," he whispers in my ear, reaching behind me to unfasten the hook at the top of my dress and then slide the zipper down. "But I can't tell you about it. I have to show you."

And he does show me.

He shows me how to strip out of my lacy dress and let it fall wet and sandy to the ground. He shows me how he likes me to unbutton his vest and shirt, and while he doesn't show me how to sharply inhale at his shirtless majesty, he certainly does preen a bit.

He shows me how it feels to have his warm hands unclip my strapless bra and then how it feels when he explores each of my breasts with intent devotion, tracing their swell with fingertips and then crowning each with reverent kisses.

He shows me how he likes his pants undone and then shows me how very enchanted he is by me when they spring the rest of the way open all on their own.

He shows me how good it feels to be totally naked together and how much better it feels the closer we are to one another, and the closer, and the closer, to where he can suck on the skin of my shoulder while his hands tangle in my hair. To where I can kiss the roughness of his throat and run idle fingers down the ridges of his spine until he shivers and his full bottom lip falls open, and I draw it into my mouth until I hear him moan.

And then he shows me what it's like to be pressed against a soft mattress in a little cave of light shining through white blinds, completely blissed out as he joins me. And I want to show him something, too. I want to show him how I can make his heart race and his thoughts shatter, but when I shift to take charge he lays a single finger on my lips and whispers.

"Wait. I'm the one writing this letter."

"Then what's the next line?"

"It's something about how it feels to be inside you."

"Then write it," I dare him.

And he does. And him inside of me is exactly what I need right now. Maybe it's all I'll ever need. I don't know. I'm not the one writing this letter. But I'm very happy with what it's showing me.

"Tell me more," I whisper and he quickens his pace. "Tell me everything."

"I will. But it's going to take time."

"How much time?" I tease, but it comes out as a gasp.

"All the time. And I'm going to have to tell it to you in this exact way, but with small variations, again and again, over years and years."

"Good thing I'm not in a hurry," I say, but my voice is tight with pleasure and his laugh is low and triumphant and when he shows me how I can come for him, well I lose track of where I am in the letter, so I guess he'll have to tell me again just like he promised.

And again.

And again.

# Epilogue

BRENT

I WAS this excited on my wedding day. And I was this excited when Tessa told me that she loved me, too.

But other than those two times, I've never been this excited before.

"Hurry, Tess!" I say, as if she isn't already leaning into the corners and taking the straight stretches way too quickly.

My ego isn't so swollen that I can't admit she's a better racer than I am. Why do you think I threw her the key when I pulled it out from under the mat where her dad left it for us. Our plane was delayed five hours and every extra minute feels like a year.

"Sunshine, if you think you can drive faster, you are welcome to try," Tessa says, but there's no ire behind her words. Just concentration as she squeezes a few kilometers an hour more out of her dad's truck and I cross my fingers and hope there aren't any cops on the route to her parent's house.

We're almost there. Almost there.

The second she throws the truck into park, I'm out the door and sprinting — I can do that now. I'm completely, totally healed which feels like a miracle all its own. I've even started racing again in the events that Tessa doesn't need to run. Why not? It makes for great social media posts for our channel, which is still the most successful BOOM channel other than the main one, by the way. Who says America isn't ready for really talented female dirt track racers?

I throw open the door of the house and I can already smell that we're at Tessa's house. It smells like cookies, and roast something, and apples, and love.

Tessa slams the door behind me, as excited as I am for once, and then Steve is there, hustling in from the kitchen with a finger over his lips and an urgent grimace.

"Shhh!" he says at the same moment that I hear Ian's laugh.

"We're in here," he calls to us — but it's a quiet call. The kind of call you use around puppies, or newly hatched chicks, or

...

... babies.

Like the newborn Ian is leaning over, and my sister Olivia is cradling. And when she looks up at me, my heart almost breaks in half. She looks just like Mom. And mom used to look at me just like that.

I have to pause in the doorway and swallow and blink back a few tears. And I guess it takes me too long because Tessa pushes past to hug her brother — they've made up now — and kiss Olivia's forehead, and tell them both they've done such a good job, and then adamantly refuse to hold the baby. Which is so Tessa.

She's already making faces at our little niece, and goofy noises, and saying she's the sweetest thing ever, and I love Tessa for being a baby person for someone else, even though she isn't one usually.

And I love her for the bright grin she shoots back at me that helps me pull myself together.

And I love her because I know that indulgent look in her

eyes right now. It's a look that says what she told me on the plane
— that she'll do this for me if I want her to, even though she
isn't a baby kind of person, because she loves me just that much.

And right now, in this moment, my heart is full.


THE END

# Haven't had enough of Brent and Tessa?

You'll want this exclusive bonus scene available only to my subscribers.

Visit www.alicedukeauthor.com for extra bonus scenes.

## Dear Reader

You don't need to be an adrenaline junkie or obsessed with swoonable romance, but it will help!

Join us in cheering on these adorable couples. We're smitten with them and we're certain you'll love their spark and sizzle just like we do!

Each of Alice Duke's books is a stand-alone romantic comedy ready for you to savor, but they all share one thing in common: unforgettable characters, falling in love like only they can.

So, come join us to thrill at the sizzle and swoon at the heat!

## PLAY STUPID GAMES, WIN STUPID PRIZES

Gracie's always been her daddy's girl and when your daddy is Big Daddy Boom, popular vlogger in the hopped up world of off-road wheeling, that comes with a lot of visibility. Gracies' dad has high expectations, even now when she's twenty-two, freshly graduated and running his biggest marketing campaign ever.

But when Gracie'sdad tells the world in a live video that she's single and he's going to pick her next boyfriend ... and hopefully the heir to his profitable online empire, all hell breaks loose, all of rural America shows up at their door, and Gracie is starting to think that not only will this be the end of her family, it might be the end of her freedom forever.

Jasper has been secretly in love with Gracie since they were kids. But with Gracie in the crosshairs of every redneck, gearhead, and rebel in the lower forty-eight, the job of winning her heart becomes a lot more difficult. Especially when Gracie comes to him with a proposal: pretend to be her husband to drive her suitors away and she'll set him up with his own online empire to rival her father's.

Jasper doesn't care about the fame and fortune. He's not here to play stupid games. But he does want the ultimate prize -- Gracie's heart -- and he'll do anything to get it.

## TWO RIVALS. ONE PROJECT. THREE DAYS TO BLOW UP THEIR LIVES.

When Ada's tiny vlogger channel, "Pin Up Stichin" finally takes off, she hopes it will mean success for her hotrod upholstery company. What she doesn't expect is that enigmatic billionaire Big Daddy Boom will hire both her and her professional nemesis to work on a super-secret project.

But Ada can't pass up this opportunity when it means finally "making it" and finally being able to pay down her Pop's ongoing debts. Not even when she realizes the person she'll be working with is her most vocal critic.

Nicola has been in the business of vehicle restoration for a long time and between his obsession with perfecting his craft and his family issues, he hasn't had much time for anything else. When he's offered the chance to get ahead in business and also work with a woman whose work he admires -- even if he expresses that through online critique -- he's in.

Until one huge mix-up leaves them stranded in the woods together with the project on the line and two huge personalities in the way. Ada sparks all kinds of emotions in Nicola -- including some he's never felt before.

Suddenly, this project -- and maybe even the state of California -- don't seem big enough for the both of them, and what seemed like explosive online content might just be explosive. Period.

Alice Duke

SWOON & SIZZLE

Alice Duke is someone who is always falling in love: with fresh ideas, with mouthwatering foods, with beguiling books — and now with vivid characters and their romances on the page. Come fall in love along with her, again and again.

www.alicedukeauthor.com

9 781990 516436